Goosebumps

COLLECTION 11

COLLECTION 11

Revenge of the Garden Gnomes
A Shocker on Shock Street
The Haunted Mask II

R.L. Stine

Hippo

Scholastic Children's Books,
Commonwealth House, 1–19 New Oxford Street, London WC1A 1NU, UK
a division of Scholastic Ltd
London ~ New York ~ Toronto ~ Sydney ~ Auckland

First published in this edition by Scholastic Ltd, 1998

Revenge of the Garden Gnomes
A Shocker on Shock Street
First published in the USA by Scholastic Inc., 1995
First published in the UK by Scholastic Ltd, 1996
The Haunted Mask II
First published in the USA by Scholastic Inc., 1995
First published in the UK by Scholastic Ltd, 1997

ISBN 0 590 11338 0

Typeset by Rowland Phototypesetting Ltd, Bury St Edmunds, Suffolk
Printed by Cox & Wyman Ltd, Reading, Berks.

10 9 8 7 6 5 4 3 2 1

CONTENTS

Revenge of the
Garden Gnomes

Clack, Clack, Clack.

The table tennis ball clattered over the basement floor. "Yes!" I cried as I watched Mindy chase after it.

It was a hot, sticky June afternoon. The first Monday of the summer holiday. And Joe Burton had just made another excellent shot.

That's me. Joe Burton. I'm twelve. And there is nothing I love better than slamming the ball in my older sister's face and making her chase after it.

I'm not a bad sport. I just like to show Mindy that she's not as great as she thinks she is.

You might have guessed that Mindy and I do not always agree on things. The fact is, I'm really not like anyone else in my family.

Mindy, Mum and Dad are all blond, skinny and tall. I have brown hair. And I'm quite pudgy and short. Mum says I haven't had my growth spurt yet.

So I'm a shrimp. And it's hard for me to see over the table tennis net. But I can still beat Mindy with one hand tied behind my back.

As much as I love to win, Mindy hates to lose. And she doesn't play fair at all. Every time I make a great move, she says it doesn't count.

"Joe, *kicking* the ball over the net is not legal," she whined as she scooped out the ball from under the couch.

"Give me a break!" I cried. "All the table tennis champions do it. They call it the Soccer Slam."

Mindy rolled her huge green eyes. "Oh, puh-lease!" she muttered. "My serve."

Mindy is weird. She's probably the weirdest fourteen-year-old in town.

Why? I'll tell you why.

Take her room. Mindy arranges all her books in alphabetical order — by author. Do you believe it?

And she fills out a card for each one. She files them in the top drawer of her desk. Her own private card catalogue.

If she could, she'd probably cut the tops off the books so they'd be all the same size.

She is *so* organized. Her wardrobe is organized by colour. All the reds come first. Then the oranges. Then the yellows. Then come the greens, blues and purples. She hangs her clothes in the same order as the rainbow.

And at dinner, she eats around her plate clockwise. Really! I've watched her. First her mashed potatoes. Then all her peas. And then her meat loaf. If she finds one pea in her mashed potatoes, she totally loses it!

Weird. Really weird.

Me? I'm not organized. I'm cool. I'm not serious like my sister. I can be pretty funny. My friends think I'm a riot. Everyone does. Except Mindy.

"Come on, serve already," I called out. "Before the end of the century."

Mindy stood on her side of the table, carefully lining up her shot. She stands in exactly the same place every time. With her feet exactly the same space apart. Her footprints are worn into the carpet.

"Ten—eight and serving," Mindy finally called out. She always calls out the score before she serves. Then she swung her arm back.

I held the bat up to my mouth like a microphone. "She pulls her arm back," I announced. "The crowd is hushed. It's a tense moment."

"Joe, stop acting like a jerk," she snapped. "I have to concentrate."

I love pretending I'm a sports announcer. It drives Mindy nuts.

Mindy pulled her arm back again. She tossed the table tennis ball up into the air. And . . .

"A spider!" I screamed. "On your shoulder!"

5

"Yaaaiiii!" Mindy dropped the bat and began slapping her shoulder furiously. The ball clattered on to the table.

"Gotcha!" I cried. "My point."

"No way!" Mindy shouted angrily. "You're just a cheat, Joe." She smoothed the shoulders of her pink T-shirt carefully. She picked up the ball and swatted it over the net.

"At least I'm a *funny* cheat!" I replied. I twirled around in a complete circle and belted the ball. It bounced once on my side before sailing over the net.

"Foul," Mindy announced. "You're always fouling."

I waved my bat at her. "Get a life," I said. "It's a game. It's supposed to be fun."

"I'm beating you," Mindy replied "That's fun."

I shrugged. "Who cares? Winning isn't everything."

"Where did you read that?" she asked. "In a comic?" Then she rolled her eyes again. I think someday her eyes are going to roll right out of her head!

I rolled my eyes, too — back into my head until only the whites showed. "Neat trick, huh?"

"Cute, Joe," Mindy muttered. "Really cute. You'd better watch out. One day your eyes might not come back down. Which would be an improvement!"

"Lame joke," I replied. "Very lame."

Mindy lined up her feet carefully again.

"She's in her serve position," I spoke into my bat. "She's nervous. She's . . ."

"Joe!" Mindy whined. "Quit it!"

She tossed the table tennis ball into the air. She swung the bat, and —

"Gross!" I shouted. "What's the big green blob hanging out of your nose?"

Mindy ignored me this time. She tapped the ball over the net.

I dived forward and whacked it with the tip of my bat. It spun high over the net and landed in the corner of the basement. Between the washing machine and the dryer.

Mindy jogged after the ball on her long, thin legs. "Hey, where's Buster?" she called out. "Wasn't he sleeping next to the dryer?"

Buster is our dog. A giant black Rottweiler with a head the size of a basketball. He loves snoozing on the old sleeping bag we keep in the corner of the basement. Especially when we're down here playing table tennis.

Everyone is afraid of Buster. For about three seconds. Then he starts licking them with his long, wet tongue. Or rolls on to his back and begs to have his belly scratched.

"Where is he, Joe?" Mindy bit her lip.

"He's around here somewhere," I replied. "Why are you always worrying about Buster?

He weighs over seven stone. He can take care of himself."

Mindy frowned. "Not if Mr McCall catches him. Remember what he said the last time Buster chomped on his tomato plants?"

Mr McCall is our next-door neighbour. Buster loves the McCalls' garden. He likes to nap under their huge, shady elm tree.

And dig little holes all over their lawn. And sometimes big holes.

And snack in their vegetable garden.

Last year, Buster dug up every head of Mr McCall's lettuce. And ate his biggest courgette for dessert.

I suppose that's why Mr McCall hates Buster. He said the next time he catches him in his garden, he's going to turn him into fertilizer.

My dad and Mr McCall are the two best gardeners in town. They're nuts about gardening. Totally nuts.

I think working in a garden is quite fun, too. But I don't let that get around. My friends think gardening is for nerds.

Dad and Mr McCall are always battling it out at the annual garden show. Mr McCall usually gets first prize. But last year, Dad and I won the blue ribbon for our tomatoes.

That drove Mr McCall crazy. When Dad's name was announced, Mr McCall's face turned as red as our tomatoes.

So Mr McCall is desperate to win this year. He started stocking up on plant food and insecticides months ago.

And he planted something that nobody else in North Bay grows. Strange orange-green melons called casabas.

Dad says that Mr McCall has made a big mistake. He says the casabas will never grow any bigger than tennis balls. The growing season in Minnesota is too short.

"McCall's garden loses," I declared. "Our tomatoes are definitely going to win again this year. And thanks to my special soil, they'll grow as big as beach balls!"

"So will your head," Mindy shot back.

I stuck out my tongue and crossed my eyes. It seemed like a good reply.

"Whose serve is it?" I asked. Mindy was taking so long, I'd lost track.

"It's still my serve," she replied, carefully placing her feet.

We were interrupted by footsteps. Heavy, booming footsteps on the stairs behind Mindy.

"Who is that?" Mindy cried.

And then he appeared behind her. And my eyes nearly bulged right out of my head.

"Oh, no!" I screamed. "It's . . . McCall!"

"Joe!" he roared. The floor shook as he stomped towards Mindy.

All the colour drained from Mindy's face. Her hand grasped her bat so tightly that her knuckles turned white. She tried to swing around to look behind her, but she couldn't. Her feet were frozen in her table-tennis-ball footprints.

McCall's hands balled into two huge fists, and he looked really, really angry.

"I'm going to get you. And this time I'm going to win. Throw me a bat."

"You jerk!" Mindy spluttered. "I-I knew it wasn't *Mr* McCall. I knew it was Moose."

Moose is Mr McCall's son and my best friend. His real name is Michael, but everyone calls him Moose. Even his parents.

Moose is the biggest kid in the whole sixth grade. And the strongest. His legs are as thick as tree trunks. And so is his neck. And he's very, very loud. Just like his dad.

Mindy can't stand Moose. She says he's a gross slob.

I think he's cool.

"Yo, Joe!" Moose bellowed. "Where's my bat?" His big arm muscles bulged as he reached out to grab mine.

I pulled my hand back. But his beefy hand slapped my shoulder so hard that my head nearly rolled off.

"Whoaaa!" I yelped.

Moose let out a deep laugh that shook the basement walls. And then he ended it with a burp.

"Moose, you're disgusting," Mindy groaned.

Moose scratched his dark brown crew cut. "Gee, thanks, Mindy."

"Thanks for what?" she demanded.

"For this." He reached out and snatched the bat right out of her hand.

Moose swung Mindy's bat around wildly in the air. He missed a hanging lamp by an inch. "Ready for a real game, Joe?"

He threw the table-tennis ball into the air and drew his powerful arm back. *Wham!* The ball rocketed across the room. It bounced off two walls and flew back over the net towards me.

"Foul!" Mindy cried. "That's not allowed."

"Cool!" I exclaimed. I dived for the ball and missed. Moose has an amazing serve.

11

Moose slammed the ball again. It shot over the net and whacked me in the chest.

Thwock!

"Hey!" I cried. I rubbed the stinging spot.

"Good shot, huh?" He grinned.

"Yeah. But you're supposed to hit the table," I told him.

Moose pumped his fat fists into the air. "Super Moose!" he bellowed. "Strong as a superhero!"

My friend Moose is a pretty wild guy. Mindy says he's a total animal. I think he's just got a lot of enthusiasm.

I served while he was still throwing his arms around.

"Hey! Not fair!" he declared. Moose charged the table and clobbered the ball. And flattened it into a tiny white pancake.

I groaned. "That's ball number fifteen for this month," I announced.

I grabbed the little pancake and tossed it into a blue plastic milk crate on the floor. The crate was piled high with dozens of flattened table-tennis balls.

"Hey! I think you broke your record!" I declared.

"All right!" Moose exclaimed. He leaped on top of the table-tennis table and began jumping up and down. "Super Moose!" he yelled.

"Stop it, you jerk!" Mindy screamed. "You're going to break the table." She covered her face with her hands.

"Super Moose! Super Moose!" he chanted.

The table-tennis table swayed. Then it sagged under his weight. He was even starting to get on my nerves now. "Moose, get off! Get off!" I wailed.

"Who's going to make me?" he demanded.

Then we all heard a loud, sharp *craaaaack*.

"You're breaking it!" Mindy shrieked. "Get off!"

Moose scrambled off the table. He lurched towards me, holding his hands straight out like the zombie monster we'd seen in *Killer Zombie from Planet Zero* on TV. "Now I'm going to destroy you!"

Then he hurled himself at me.

As he smashed into me, I staggered back and fell on to the dusty cement floor.

Moose jumped on to my stomach and pinned me down. "Say 'Moose's tomatoes are the best!'" he ordered. He bounced up and down on my chest.

"Moo . . . Moose's," I wheezed. "Tomat . . . I can't . . . breathe . . . really . . . help."

"Say it!" Moose insisted. He placed his powerful hands around my neck. And squeezed.

"Ugggggh," I gagged. I couldn't breathe. I couldn't move.

My head rolled to the side.

"Moose!" I heard Mindy shriek. "Let him go! Let him go! What have you done to him?"

13

"M-Miiindy," I moaned.

Moose pulled his hands from my throat and lifted his powerful body off my chest.

"What did you do to him—you big monster?" Mindy shrieked. She knelt down by my side and bent over me. She brushed my hair from my eyes.

"Y-you're a . . . a . . ." I stopped and coughed weakly.

"What, Joe? What is it?" Mindy demanded softly.

"You're a SUCKER!" I exclaimed. And burst out laughing.

Mindy jerked her head back. "You little weasel!"

"Tricked you! Tricked you!" I cheered.

"Way to go, dude!" Moose grinned.

I scrambled to my feet and slapped Moose a high five. "Suc-ker! Suc-ker!" we chanted over and over.

Mindy folded her skinny arms in front of her and glared at us. "Not funny," she snapped. "I'm never going to believe another word you say! Never!"

"Oh, I'm sooooo scared!" I said. I knocked my knees together. "See? My knees are trembling."

"I'm shaking, too," Moose joined in, wiggling his whole body.

"You guys are totally juvenile," she announced. "I'm out of here."

She slid her hands into the pockets of her white shorts and stomped away. But then she suddenly stopped a few feet from the stairs.

In front of the high basement window.

The window that looked out on to Mr McCall's front garden.

She stared up through the window's sheer white curtain for a second. She squinted her eyes. Then she cried out, "No! Oh, no!"

"Nice try," I replied, flicking a dust ball from the carpet in her direction. "There's nothing out there. I'm not falling for your lame trick!"

"No! It's Buster!" Mindy cried. "He's next door again!"

"Huh?" I sprinted to the window. And jumped on to a chair. I yanked the filmy curtain aside.

Yes. There sat Buster. In the middle of the vegetable patch that covered Mr McCall's front garden. "Oh, wow. He's in the garden again," I murmured.

"My garden! He'd better not be!" Moose declared, stomping up behind me. He shoved me off the chair to take a look. "If my dad catches Buster in his vegetables, he'll turn that big mutt into mulch!"

"Come on! Hurry!" Mindy pleaded, tugging on my arm. "We have to get Buster out of there. Straight away. Before Moose's dad catches him!"

Moose, Mindy and I raced upstairs and out the front door. We charged across our front lawn, towards the McCalls' house.

At the edge of our lawn, we leaped across the line of yellow and white petunias that Dad had planted. It separates our garden from the McCalls' garden.

Mindy squeezed her fingernails deep into my arm. "Buster's digging!" she cried. "He's going to destroy—the melons!"

Buster's powerful front paws worked hard. He scraped at the dirt and green plants. Mud and leaves flew everywhere.

"Stop that, Buster!" Mindy pleaded. "Stop that—now!"

Buster kept digging.

Moose glanced at his plastic wristwatch. "You'd better get that dog out of there fast," he warned. "It's almost six o'clock. My dad comes out to water the garden at six sharp."

I'm terrified of Mr McCall. I admit it. He's so

big, he makes Moose look like a shrimp! And he's mean.

"Buster, get over here!" I begged. Mindy and I both shouted to the dog.

But Buster ignored our cries.

"Don't just stand there. Why don't you *pull* that dumb mutt out of there?" Moose demanded.

I shook my head. "We can't! He's too big. And stubborn. He won't budge."

I reached under my T-shirt and searched for the shiny metal dog whistle I wear on a cord around my neck. I wear it day and night. Even under my pyjamas. It's the only thing Buster will obey.

"It's two minutes to six," Moose warned, checking his watch. "Dad will be out here any second!"

"Blow the whistle, Joe!" Mindy cried.

I brought the whistle up to my mouth. And gave a long, hard blow.

Moose sniggered. "That whistle's broken," he said. "It didn't make a sound."

"It's a dog whistle," Mindy replied in a superior tone. "It makes a really high-pitched sound. Dogs can hear them, but people can't. See?"

She pointed to Buster. He had lifted his nose out of the dirt and pricked up his ears.

I blew the whistle again. Buster shook the dirt from his fur.

"Thirty seconds and counting," Moose told us.

I blew the silent dog whistle one more time. Yes!

Buster came trotting slowly towards us, wagging his stumpy tail.

"Hurry, Buster!" I pleaded. "Hurry!" I held my arms open wide.

"Buster—run—don't trot!" Mindy begged.

Too late.

We heard a loud slam.

Moose's front door flew open.

And Mr McCall stepped out.

"Joe! Come over here. Now!" Moose's dad barked at me.

He lumbered towards his vegetable patch, his big belly bouncing in front of him under his blue T-shirt. "Get over here, boy—on the double!"

Mr McCall is retired from the army. He's used to barking out orders. And having them obeyed.

I obeyed. Buster trotted by my side.

"Was that dog in my vegetable patch again?" Mr McCall demanded, eyeing me coldly. His cold stare could make your blood freeze.

"No, s-sir!" I stammered. Buster settled down beside me with a loud yawn.

I usually don't tell lies. Except to Mindy. But Buster's life was on the line. I had to save Buster. Didn't I?

Mr McCall bounced up to his vegetable patch. He circled his tomatoes, his corn, his courgettes, his casaba melons. He examined each stalk and leaf carefully.

Oh, wow, I thought. We're in major trouble now.

Finally, he gazed up at us. His eyes narrowed. "If that mutt wasn't in here, why is the dirt all pawed up?"

"Maybe it was the wind?" I replied softly. It was worth a try. Maybe he'd believe it.

Moose stood silently next to me. The only time he's quiet is when his dad is around.

"Um, Mr McCall," Mindy began. "We'll make sure Buster stays out of your garden. We promise!" Then she smiled her sweetest smile.

Mr McCall scowled. "All right. But if I catch him even sniffing at my melons, I'm calling the police and having that dog hauled off to the pound. And I mean it."

I gulped. I knew he meant it. Mr McCall doesn't kid around.

"Moose!" Mr McCall snapped. "Bring the hose out here and water these casabas! I told you they need to be watered at least five times a day."

"See you later," Moose muttered. He ducked his head and ran towards the back of his house for the hose.

Mr McCall shot one more dark glance at us. Then he lumbered up his front steps and slammed the door.

"'Maybe it was the wind?'" Mindy rolled her eyes again. "Wow, that was fast thinking, Joe!" She laughed.

"Oh, yeah? Well, at least I had an answer," I replied. "And remember, it was my whistle that saved Buster. All you did was smile that phony smile."

Mindy and I headed towards our house, arguing all the way. But we stopped when we heard a low moan. A frightening sound. Buster cocked his ears.

"Who's that?" I whispered.

A second later, we found out. Dad lurched around the side of the house, carrying a big watering can.

He was wearing his favourite gardening outfit—trainers with holes in both toes, baggy checked shorts, and a red T-shirt that said "I'm All Thumbs in the Garden".

And he was moaning and groaning. Which was really weird. Because Dad is always in an excellent mood when he's gardening. Whistling. Smiling. Cracking lame jokes.

But not today.

Today something was wrong. Really wrong.

"Kids . . . kids," he moaned, staggering towards us. "I've been looking for you."

"Dad—what is it? What's wrong?" Mindy demanded.

Dad clutched his head and swayed from side to side. He took a deep breath. "I-I have something *terrible* to tell you."

"What, Dad?" I cried. "Tell us."

Dad spoke in a hoarse whisper. "I found a
. . . a fruit fly on our tomatoes! On our biggest
tomato. The Red Queen!"

He wiped his sweaty forehead. "How could
this happen? I misted. I sprayed. I pruned.
Twice this week alone."

Dad shook his head in sorrow. "My poor tomatoes. If that fruit fly ruins my Red Queen, I-I'll
have to pull out of the garden show!"

Mindy and I glanced at each other. I knew
we were thinking the same thing. The adults
around here were getting a little weird.

"Dad, it's only one fruit fly," I pointed out.

"It only takes one, Joe. Just one fruit fly. And
our chances for a blue ribbon—destroyed. We
have to do something. Straight away."

"What about that new bug spray?" I reminded
him. "The stuff that came last week from the
Green Thumb catalogue."

Dad's eyes lit up. He ran a hand through his flat, rumpled hair. "The *Bug Be Gone!*" he exclaimed.

He jogged up the driveway to the garage. "Come on, kids!" he sang out. "Let's give it a try!" Dad was cheering up.

Mindy and I raced after him.

Dad pulled out three spray cans from a carton in the back of the garage. The words "Wave Bye-Bye to Bugs with *Bug Be Gone!*" were printed on the labels. A drawing showed a tearful bug carrying a suitcase. Waving bye-bye.

Dad handed one can to Mindy and one to me. "Let's get that fruit fly!" he cried, as we headed back to our garden.

We ripped the caps off the cans of *Bug Be Gone.* "One, two, three . . . spray!" Dad commanded.

Dad and I showered the two dozen tomato plants tied to wooden stakes in the middle of the garden.

Mindy hadn't started yet. She was probably reading the ingredients on the can.

"What's all the fuss about?" my mother called, stepping out the back door.

Mum was wearing one of her around-the-house outfits. A pair of Dad's old baggy check shorts. And an old blue T-shirt he'd given her when he came back from a business trip a few years ago. The T-shirt said "I Mist You!" One of Dad's lame garden jokes.

23

"Hi, honey," Dad called. "We're about to destroy a fruit fly. Want to watch?"

Mum laughed, crinkling up the corners of her green eyes. "Pretty tempting. But I have to finish a greeting card design."

Mum is a graphic artist. She has an office on the first floor of our house. She can draw the most incredible pictures on her computer. Amazing sunsets, mountains and flowers.

"Dinner at seven-thirty, everybody. Okay?"

"Sounds good," Dad called as Mum disappeared into the house. "Okay, kids. Let's finish spraying!"

Dad and I showered the tomato plants one more time. We even sprayed the yellow squash plants nearby. Mindy squinted. Aimed the nozzle of her can directly at the Red Queen. And let out a single neat drizzle.

One tiny fruit fly flapped its wings weakly and fell to the ground. Mindy smiled in satisfaction.

"Good work!" Dad exclaimed.

He clapped us both on the back. "I think this calls for a celebration!" he declared. "I have the perfect idea! A quick visit to Lawn Lovely!"

"Oh, nooooo," Mindy and I groaned together.

Lawn Lovely is a shop two blocks from our house. It's the place where Dad buys his garden ornaments. A lot of garden ornaments.

Dad is as nuts about garden ornaments as he is about gardening. We have so many garden ornaments in our front garden, it's impossible to mow the lawn!

What a crowd scene! We have two pink plastic flamingos. A cement angel with huge white wings. A chrome ball on a silver platform. A whole family of plaster skunks. A fountain with two kissing swans. A seal that balances a beach ball on its nose. And a chipped plaster deer.

Weird, huh?

But Dad really loves them. He thinks they're art or something.

And do you know what he does? He dresses them up on holidays. Pilgrim hats for the skunks on Thanksgiving. Pirate costumes for the flamingos on Hallowe'en. Stove-pipe hats and little black beards for the swans on Lincoln's birthday.

Of course, neat and tidy Mindy can't stand the garden ornaments. Neither can Mum. Every time Dad brings a new one home, Mum threatens to throw it in the rubbish bin.

"Dad, these garden ornaments are really embarrassing!" Mindy complained. "People gawp from their cars and take pictures of our front garden. We're a tourist attraction!"

"Oh, please," Dad groaned. "One person took a picture."

That was last Christmas. When Dad dressed all the ornaments as Santa's helpers.

"Yeah. And that picture ended up in the

newspaper!" Mindy moaned. "It was soooo embarrassing."

"Well, I think the ornaments are cool," I replied. Someone had to defend poor Dad.

Mindy just wrinkled her nose in disgust.

I know what really bugs Mindy about the ornaments. It's the way Dad sticks them in the garden. Without any order. If Mindy had her way, they would be lined up like her shoes. In nice neat rows.

"Come on, guys," Dad urged, starting down the driveway. "Let's go and see if a new shipment of ornaments has come in."

We had no choice.

Mindy and I trudged down the pavement after Dad. As we followed him, we thought—no big deal. It's almost dinnertime. We'll just glance over the ornaments at the shop. Then we'll go home.

We had no idea we were about to start the most horrifying adventure of our lives.

"Can't we drive, Dad?" Mindy complained as the three of us hiked up the steep Summit Avenue hill towards Lawn Lovely. "It's too hot to walk."

"Oh, come on, Mindy. It's only a couple of blocks. And it's good exercise," Dad replied, taking long, brisk strides.

"But it's sooooo hot," Mindy whined. She brushed her fringe away from her face and blotted her forehead with her hand.

Mindy was right. It was hot. But get serious. It was only a two-block walk.

"I'm hotter than you are," I teased. Then I leaned into Mindy and shook my sweaty head at her. "See?"

A few small beads of sweat flew on to Mindy's T-shirt.

"You are so gross!" she shrieked, drawing back. "Dad! Tell him to stop being so disgusting."

"We're almost there," Dad replied. His voice

27

sounded as if he were a million miles away. He was probably dreaming about buying his next garden ornament.

Just up the block, I spotted the tall, pointy roof of Lawn Lovely. It jutted into the sky, towering over all the houses around it.

What a weird place, I thought. Lawn Lovely is in an old, raggedy three-storey house, set back from the street. The whole building is painted pink. Bright pink. The windows are covered with brightly-coloured shutters. But none of the colours match.

I think that's another reason why Mindy hates this place.

The old house is not in good shape. The wooden floorboards on the front porch are all sagging. And there is a hole in the porch where Mr McCall fell through last summer.

As we marched past the flagpole in the front yard, I spotted Mrs Anderson in the driveway. She owns Lawn Lovely. She lives there, too. On the first and second floors.

Mrs Anderson kneeled over a flock of pink plastic flamingos. She was ripping off their plastic wrap and setting them in crooked rows on her lawn.

Mrs Anderson reminds me of a flamingo. She's really skinny and wears pink all the time. Even her hair is sort of pink. Like candy floss.

Garden ornaments are the only things Mrs

Anderson sells. Plaster squirrels. Kissing angels. Pink rabbits with wire whiskers. Long green worms wearing little black hats. A whole flock of white geese. She has hundreds of ornaments. Scattered all over her garden. Up the front steps to the porch. And right through the door into the entire ground floor of the house.

Mrs Anderson carefully unwrapped another flamingo and set it down next to a deer. She studied this arrangement, then moved the deer about an inch to the left.

"Hello, Lilah!" my dad called out.

Mrs Anderson didn't answer. She's a little hard of hearing.

"Hello, Lilah!" Dad repeated, cupping his hands around his mouth like a megaphone.

Mrs Anderson raised her head from the flamingos. And beamed at my dad. "Jeffrey!" she cried. "How nice to see you."

Mrs Anderson is always friendly to Dad. Mum says he's her best customer.

Maybe her *only* customer!

"It's nice to see you, too," Dad replied. He rubbed his hands together eagerly and gazed around the lawn.

Mrs Anderson stuck one last flamingo into the ground. She made her way over to us, wiping her hands on her pink T-shirt.

"Do you have something special in mind today?" she asked my father.

"Our deer is a little lonesome," he explained, shouting so that she could hear him. "I think it needs company."

"Really, Dad. We don't need any more garden ornaments," Mindy begged. "Mum will be furious."

Mrs Anderson smiled. "Oh, a Lawn Lovely lawn always has room for one more! Right, Jeffrey?"

"Right!" Dad declared.

Mindy pressed her lips together tightly. She rolled her eyes for the hundredth time that day.

Dad hurried over to a herd of wide-eyed plaster deer, standing in the corner of the garden. We followed him.

The deer stood about four feet tall. White spots dotted their reddish-brown bodies.

Very lifelike. Very boring.

He studied the deer for a few seconds. Then something caught his eye.

Two squat gnomes standing in the middle of the lawn.

"Well, well, what have we here?" Dad murmured, smiling. I could see his eyes light up. He bent down to examine the gnomes.

Mrs Anderson clapped her hands together. "Jeffrey, you have a wonderful eye for garden ornaments!" she exclaimed. "I knew you'd appreciate the gnomes! They were carved in Europe. Very fine work."

I stared at the gnomes. They looked like little

old men. They were about three feet tall and very chubby. With piercing red eyes and large pointy ears.

Their mouths curved up in wide, silly grins. And coarse brown hair sprouted from their heads.

Each gnome wore a bright green short-sleeved shirt, brown leggings and a tall, pointy orange hat. Both wore black belts tied tightly around their chubby waists.

"They're terrific!" Dad gushed. "Oh, kids. Aren't they wonderful?"

"They're okay, Dad," I said.

"*Okay?*" Mindy shouted. "They're *horrible*! They're so gross! They look so . . . so evil. I *hate* them!"

"Hey, you're right, Mindy," I said. "They are pretty gross. They look just like you!"

"Joe, you are the biggest—" Mindy started. But Dad interrupted her.

"We'll take them!" he cried.

"Dad—no!" Mindy howled. "They're hideous! Buy a deer. Buy another flamingo. But not these ugly old gnomes. Look at the awful colours. Look at those evil grins. They're too creepy!"

"Oh, Mindy. Don't be silly. They're perfect!" Dad exclaimed. "We'll have so much fun with them. We'll dress them as ghosts for Hallowe'en. In Santa suits at Christmas. They look just like Santa's elves."

Dad pulled out his credit card. He and Mrs Anderson started towards the pink house to complete the sale. "I'll be back in a minute," he called.

"These are the ugliest yet," Mindy groaned, turning to me. "They're completely embarrassing. I'll never be able to bring any of my friends over again."

Then she stomped off towards the pavement.

I couldn't take my eyes away from the gnomes. They were kind of ugly. And even though they were smiling, there was something unfriendly about their smiles. Something cold about their glassy red eyes.

"Whoa! Mindy! Look!" I cried. "One of the gnomes just moved!"

Mindy slowly turned to face me.

My wrist was held tightly in the chubby hand. I twisted and squirmed. Tried to tug free.

"Let go!" I squealed. "Let go of me! Mindy — hurry!"

"I — I'm coming!" she cried.

Mindy came racing across the garden.

She leaped over the flamingoes and sprinted around the deer.

"Hurry!' I moaned, stretching my left arm out towards her. "He's *hurting* me!"

But as my sister came near, her face twisted in fright, I couldn't keep a straight face any longer. I burst out laughing.

"Gotcha! Gotcha!" I shrieked. I danced away from the plaster gnome.

Mindy swung around to slug me. Swung and missed.

"Did you really believe that gnome grabbed me?" I cried. "Are you totally losing it?"

She didn't have time to reply. Dad came jogging down the pink porch steps. "Time to bring our little guys home," he announced, grinning.

He stopped and stared down happily at the ugly gnomes. "But let's name them first." Dad names all of our garden ornaments.

Mindy let out a groan. Dad ignored her.

He patted one of the gnomes on the head. "Let's call this one Hap. Because he looks so happy! I'll carry Hap. You kids take . . ."

He stopped and squinted at the other gnome. There was a small chip on the gnome's front tooth. "Chip. Yep, we'll call this one Chip."

Dad hoisted Hap into his arms. "Whoaaa. He's an armful!" He made his way towards the driveway, staggering under the gnome's weight.

Mindy studied Chip. "You take the feet, I'll grab the top," she ordered. "Come on. One, two, three . . . lift!"

I stooped down and grabbed the gnome by its legs. Its heavy red boot scraped my arm. I let out a cry.

"Quit complaining," Mindy ordered. "At least you don't have this stupid pointy hat sticking in your face."

We struggled down the hill, following Dad.

Mindy and I inched forward, struggling side by side. "Everyone in the neighbourhood is gawking at us," Mindy moaned.

They were. Two girls from Mindy's school, wheeling their bikes up the hill, stopped and stared. Then they burst out laughing.

Mindy's pale face grew as red as one of Dad's tomatoes. "I'll never live this down," she grumbled. "Come on, Joe. Walk faster."

I jiggled Chip's legs to make Mindy lose her

grip. But the only thing she lost was her temper. "Quit it, Joe," she snapped. "And hold your end up higher."

As we neared our house, Mr McCall spotted us trudging up the block. He stopped pruning his shrubs to admire our little parade.

"More garden ornaments, Jeffrey?" he called out to Dad. I could hear him chuckling.

Mr McCall is mean to Mindy and me. But he and Dad get along fine. They're always kidding each other about their gardens.

Mrs McCall poked her head out the front door. "Cute!" she called out, smiling at us from under her white baseball cap. "Come on in, Bill. Your brother is on the phone."

Mr McCall set his pruning shears down and went inside.

We lugged Chip past the McCall driveway and followed Dad into our front garden.

"Over here!" Dad instructed as he set Hap down in the far corner of the garden. Next to Deer-lilah. Deer-lilah is the deer. Dad named her after Lilah from Lawn Lovely.

With our last bit of strength, we dragged Chip over to Dad. These gnomes were heavy. They weighed a lot more than our other ornaments.

Mindy and I plopped the gnome down on the grass and collapsed in the dirt next to him.

Whistling happily, Dad set Chip on one side of the deer. And Hap on the other.

He stepped back to study them. "What cheerful little guys!" he declared. "I've got to show your mum. She won't be able to resist them! They're too cute to hate!"

He hurried across the lawn and into the house.

"Yo!" I heard a familiar cry from next door. Moose jogged across his driveway. "I hear you have some ugly new lawn things."

He charged up to the gnomes and stared. "Way ugly," he boomed.

Moose leaned down and stuck his tongue out at Hap. "You want to fight, shrimp?" he asked the little statue. "Take that!" He pretended to punch Hap in his chubby chest.

"Wreck the runt!" I cried.

Moose grabbed the gnome around his waist and gave him a dozen quick punches.

I scrambled to my feet. "I'll wipe that ugly grin off your face!" I yelled at Chip. I closed my hands around the gnome's neck and pretended to choke him.

"Watch this!" Moose shot out a thick leg and karate-kicked Hap in his small pointy hat. The squat figure wobbled.

"Careful! Stop messing around!" Mindy warned. "You're going to break them."

"Okay," I said. "Let's tickle them!"

"Tickle, tickle!" Moose squeaked as he tickled Hap under the armpits.

"You're a riot, Moose," Mindy declared. "A real—"

Moose and I waited for Mindy to finish insulting us. But instead, she pointed to the McCalls' garden and screamed. "Oh, no! Buster!"

Moose and I spun around and spied Buster. In the middle of Mr McCall's vegetable patch, pawing away at the green stalks.

"Buster! No!" I screamed.

I grabbed the dog whistle and raised it to my mouth. But before I could blow, Mr McCall exploded out of his front door!

"That stupid mutt again!" he shouted, waving his arms wildly. "Get out of here! Shoo!"

Buster whimpered, turned, and trotted back to our garden, head down, stumpy tail between his legs.

Uh-oh, I thought, studying Mr McCall's angry face. We're in trouble now.

But before Mr McCall could start lecturing us, Dad pushed the front door open. "Kids, your mother says that dinner is almost ready."

"Jeffrey, are you deliberately sending that mutt over to ruin my melons?" Mr McCall called.

Dad grinned. "Buster can't help it," he replied. "He keeps mistaking your melons for golf balls!"

"Are those tomatoes you're growing?" Moose's dad shot back. "Or are they olives?"

"Didn't you see the tomato I rolled into the house yesterday?" Dad replied. "I had to use a wheelbarrow!"

Buster danced around the garden. I think somehow he knew he had escaped big trouble.

We started for the house. But I stopped when I heard a heavy thud.

I whirled around to discover Hap lying face down in the grass.

Buster busily licked his face.

"Bad dog," Dad scolded. I don't think Dad likes Buster any more than Mr McCall does. "Did you knock that gnome over? Get away from there!"

"Buster—come here, boy!" I called. But he ignored me and licked at the face more furiously than ever.

I brought my dog whistle to my lips and gave one quick short blow. Buster raised his head, alert to the sound. He forgot about the plaster gnome and trotted over to me.

"Joe, pick Hap up, will you?" Dad demanded, annoyed.

Mindy held on to Buster. I grabbed the gnome by his shoulders and slowly heaved him to his feet. Then I checked for damage.

Legs. Arms. Neck. Everything seemed okay.

I raised my eyes to Hap's face.

And jumped back in surprise.

I blinked a few times. And stared at the gnome again.

"I —I don't believe it!" I murmured.

The gnome's smile had vanished.

Its mouth stood open wide, as if trying to scream.

"Hey—!" I choked out.

"What's wrong?" Dad called. "Is it broken?"

"Its smile!" I cried. "Its smile is gone! It looks scared or something!"

Dad jumped down the steps and ran over. Moose and Mr McCall joined him.

Mindy walked slowly in my direction, with a suspicious scowl on her face. She probably thought I was playing another joke.

"See?" I cried as everyone gathered around me. "It's unbelievable!"

"Ha-ha! Good one, Joe!" Moose burst out. He punched me in the shoulder. "Pretty funny."

"Huh?" I lowered my eyes to the little figure.

Hap's lips were curved up in a grin. The same silly grin he always wore. The terrified expression had disappeared.

Dad let out a hearty laugh. "Good acting job, Joe," he said. "You really fooled us all."

"Maybe your son should be an actor," Mr McCall said, scratching his head.

"He didn't fool me," Mindy bragged. "That one was lame. Really lame."

What had happened? Had I imagined that open mouth?

Mr McCall turned to Buster. "Listen, Jeffrey," he started. "I'm serious about that dog of yours. If he comes into my garden again . . ."

"If Buster goes over there again, I promise we'll tie him up," Dad replied.

"Aw, Dad," I said. "You know Buster hates to be tied up. He hates it!"

"Sorry, kids," Dad said, turning to go inside. "That's it. Buster gets one more chance."

I bent down to pet Buster's head. "Only one more chance, boy," I whispered in his ear. "Did you hear that? You only get one more chance."

I woke up the next morning and squinted at the clock radio on my night table. Eight a.m. Tuesday. The second day of the summer holidays. Excellent!

I threw on my purple-and-white Vikings jersey and my gym shorts and ran downstairs. Time to mow the lawn.

Dad and I had an agreement. If I mowed the

41

lawn once a week all summer, Dad would buy me a new bike.

I knew exactly which model I wanted, too. Twenty-one gears and really fat tyres. The coolest mountain bike ever. I'd be able to fly over boulders!

I let myself out the front door and raised my face to the warm morning sun. It felt pretty good. The grass shimmered, still covered with dew.

"Joe!" I heard a loud bellow.

Mr McCall's bellow. "Get over here!"

Mr McCall leaned over his vegetable patch. An angry red vein throbbed in his forehead.

Oh, no, I thought as I edged towards him. What now?

"I've had it," he roared. "If you don't tie that dog up, I'm calling the police! I mean it!"

Mr McCall pointed to the ground. One of his casaba melons lay in the dirt, broken into jagged pieces. Melon seeds were scattered everywhere. And most of the orange fruit had been eaten away.

I opened my mouth, but no sound came out. I didn't know what to say. Lucky for me, Dad showed up just in time. He was on his way to work.

"Is my son giving you some gardening advice, Bill?" he asked.

"No jokes today!" Mr McCall snapped. He

scooped up the broken pieces of melon and shoved them in my dad's face. "See what your wild dog has done! Now I have only four melons left!"

Dad turned to me. His expression grew stern. "I warned you, Joe! I told you to keep the dog in our garden."

"But Buster didn't do this," I protested. "He doesn't even like melons!"

Buster skulked around behind the flamingos. His ears drooped flat against his head. His tail hung low between his legs. He looked really guilty.

"Well, who else could have done it?" Mr McCall demanded.

Dad shook his head. "Joe, I want you to tie Buster up in the back. Now!"

I saw that I had no choice. No way I could argue.

"Okay, Dad," I mumbled. I shuffled across the lawn and grabbed Buster's collar. I hauled him to the corner of the back garden and sat him next to his red cedar kennel. "Stay!" I commanded.

I rummaged through the garage until I found a long piece of rope. Then I tied Buster to the tall oak tree next to his kennel.

Buster whimpered. He really hates being tied up.

"I'm sorry, boy," I whispered. "I know you didn't eat that melon."

Buster pricked up his ears as Dad came around back to make sure I had tied the dog up. "It's just as well that Buster is tied up today," he said. "The painters are starting on the house this afternoon. Buster would only be in their way."

"Painters?" I asked in surprise. Nobody told me that painters were coming. I hate the smell of paint!

Dad nodded. "They're going to paint over that faded yellow," he said, pointing to the house. "We're having the house painted white with black trim."

"Dad, about Buster . . ." I started.

Dad held up a hand to silence me. "I have to get to work. Keep him tied up. We'll talk later." I watched him make his way to the garage.

This is all Mr McCall's fault, I thought. All of it! After Dad had driven away, I stamped angrily into the garage and grabbed the lawn mower. I pushed the mower around the side of the house and into the front garden. Mindy sat on the front steps, reading. I rammed the mower forward.

"I hate Mr McCall!" I exclaimed. I shoved the mower around a flamingo. I felt like slicing off its skinny legs. "He is such a jerk. I'd like to smash the other four stupid melons!" I cried. "I'd love to wreck them all so Mr McCall will leave us alone!"

"Joe, get a grip," Mindy called, peering up from her book.

After I finished mowing, I ran into the house and grabbed a large plastic bag for the grass clippings. When I came back out, Moose was sprawled on our lawn. Several brightly coloured plastic rings lay scattered on the grass around him.

"Think fast!" he cried. He hurled a blue plastic ring at me. I dropped the bag and leaped for it.

"Nice catch!" he said, scrambling to his feet. "How about a game of Hoopla? We'll use the gnomes' pointy hats."

"How about using Mindy's pointy head?" I replied.

"You are so immature," Mindy said. She stood and walked to the door. "I'm going to find somewhere quiet to read."

Moose handed me a few rings. He flung a purple one towards Hap. The ring slid neatly around the gnome's hat.

"What a throw!" he exclaimed.

I took a ring and spun around like a discus thrower. I tossed two yellow rings at Chip. They slapped against the gnome's fat face and slipped to the grass.

Moose chuckled. "You throw like Mindy. Watch me!" He leaned forward and hurled two rings. They settled neatly around Chip's pointy hat.

"Yes!" Moose cried. He flexed his bulging muscles. "Super Moose rules again!"

We tossed the rest of the rings. Moose beat me. But only by two points—ten to eight.

"Rematch!" I cried. "Let's play again!"

I dashed over to the gnomes and gathered up the rings. As I pulled a handful from Chip's hat, I stared into his face.

And gasped.

What *was* that?

A seed.

An orange seed about half an inch long.

Stuck between the gnome's fat lips.

"Is that a melon seed?" I asked, my voice trembling.

"A what?" Moose stomped up behind me.

"A melon seed," I repeated.

Moose shook his head. He clapped a big hand against my shoulder. "You're seeing things," he declared. "Come on, let's play!"

I pointed to Chip's mouth. "I'm not seeing things. There! Right there! Don't you see it?"

Moose's gaze followed my finger. "Yeah. I see a seed. So what?"

"It's a casaba melon seed, Moose. Like the ones scattered on the ground."

How could a casaba seed find its way into Chip's mouth?

There had to be an explanation. A simple explanation.

I thought hard. I couldn't think of one.

I brushed the seed from the gnome's lips and watched it flutter to the grass.

Then I stared at the gnome's grinning face. Into those cold, flat eyes.

And the gnome stared back at me. I shivered in the heat.

How did that seed get there? I wondered. How?

I dreamed about melons that night. I dreamed that a casaba melon grew in our front garden. Grew and grew and grew. Bigger than our house.

Something startled me out of my melon dream. I fumbled for my alarm clock. One a.m.

Then I heard a howl. A low, mournful howl. Outside the house.

I jumped out of bed and hurried to the window. I peered into the shadowy front garden. The lawn ornaments stood in silence.

I heard the howl again. Louder. Longer.

It was Buster. My poor dog. Tied up in the back garden.

I crept out of my room and down the dark hall. The house was quiet. I started down the carpeted stairs.

A step squeaked under my foot. I jumped, startled.

A second later, I heard another creak.

My legs were shaking.

Cool it, Joe, I told myself. It's only the steps.

I tiptoed through the darkened living room

and into the kitchen. I heard a low, rustling sound behind me. My heart started to pound.

I whirled around.

Nothing there.

You're hearing things, I told myself.

I stumbled forward in the dark. Closed my hand around the doorknob.

And two powerful hands grabbed me from behind!

"Where do you think you're going?"

Mindy!

I breathed a sigh of relief. And yanked myself away from her grasp.

"I'm going for a midnight snack," I whispered, rubbing my neck. "I'm going to eat the rest of Mr McCall's stupid melons."

I pretended to cram my mouth full and chew. "Yum! Casabas. I need more casabas!"

"Joe! You'd better not!" Mindy whispered in alarm.

"Hey, I'm kidding," I said. "Buster is howling like crazy. I'm going out to calm him down."

Mindy yawned. "If Mum and Dad catch you sneaking out in the middle of the night . . ."

"It'll just take a few minutes." I stepped outside. The damp night air sent a small chill down my back. I gazed up at the starless night sky.

Buster's pitiful howls rose from the back.

"I'm coming," I called in a loud whisper. "It's okay, boy."

Buster's howls dropped to quiet whimpers.

I took a step forward. Something rustled through the grass. I froze in place. And squinted into the darkness. Two small figures scampered by the side of the house. They scraped across the garden and disappeared into the night.

Probably raccoons.

Raccoons?

That's the answer! The raccoons must have eaten Mr McCall's melon. I wanted to wake up Dad and tell him. But I decided to wait till morning.

I felt much better. That meant that Buster could be set free. I made my way over to Buster and sat next to him on the dew-wet grass.

"Buster," I whispered. "I'm here."

His big brown eyes drooped sadly. I threw my arms around his furry neck. "You won't be tied up for long, Buster," I promised. "You'll see. I'll tell Dad about the raccoons first thing in the morning."

Buster licked my hand gratefully. "And tomorrow I'll take you for a long walk," I whispered. "How's that, boy? Now go to sleep."

I slipped back inside the house and jumped into bed. I felt good. I had solved the mystery of the melon. Our troubles with Mr McCall were over, I thought.

But I thought wrong.

Our troubles were just beginning.

"I don't believe it! I don't believe it!" Mr McCall's cries cut through the quiet morning, waking me from my heavy sleep.

I rubbed my eyes and glanced at the clock radio. Six-thirty a.m.

What's all the screaming about?

I hopped out of bed and hurried downstairs, yawning and stretching. Mum, Dad and Mindy were at the front door, still in pyjamas and robes.

"What's happening?" I asked.

"It's Bill!" Dad cried. "Come on!"

We piled outside and stared into our neighbours' garden.

Mr McCall hung over his vegetable patch in a tattered blue-and-white-checked robe. He grabbed frantically at his casaba melons, screaming.

Moose and his mother stood behind Mr McCall in their robes, wide-eyed and silent. Instead of her usual friendly smile, Moose's mum wore a grim frown.

Mr McCall lifted his head from the garden. "Ruined!" he roared. "They're totally ruined!"

"Oh, boy," Dad muttered. "We'd better get over there, Marion." He started across our front lawn. Mum, Mindy and I followed.

"Take it easy, Bill," my dad said calmly as he stepped into the McCalls' front garden. "Nothing is worth getting so upset about."

"Easy? Take it easy?" Mr McCall shrieked. The vein in his forehead throbbed.

The raccoons, I thought. They attacked the casabas again. I've got to tell Dad. Now. Before Buster gets blamed for this, too.

Mr McCall cradled his four casaba melons in his hands. They were still attached to the vine.

"I came out to water my casabas and I found this . . . this . . ." He was too upset to finish. He held the melons out to us.

"Whoa!" I cried in amazement.

No raccoon could have done this.

No way.

Someone had taken a black marker and drawn big, sloppy smily faces on each melon!

My sister shoved me aside to get a good look.

"Joe!" she shrieked. "That's horrible. How *could* you!"

"What are you talking about?" Mr McCall demanded.

"Yes, Mindy, what *are* you talking about?" Mum asked.

"I caught Joe sneaking outside last night," Mindy replied. "In the middle of the night. He told me he wanted to wreck the rest of the melons."

Everyone turned to stare at me in horror. Even Moose, my best friend. Mr McCall's face was as red as a tomato again. I saw him clenching and unclenching his fists.

Everyone stared at me in shocked silence. The smily faces on the melons stared at me, too.

"But—but—but—" I sputtered.

Before I could explain, Dad exploded. "Joe, I think you owe us an explanation. What were you doing outside in the middle of the night?"

I felt my face grow red-hot with anger. "I went out to calm Buster down," I insisted. "He was howling. I didn't touch the melons. I would never do anything like that. I was only joking when I told Mindy I wanted to wreck them!"

"Well, this is no joke!" Dad exclaimed angrily. "You are grounded for the week!"

"But, Dad—!" I pleaded. "I didn't draw on those melons!"

"Make that two weeks!" he snapped. "And I think you should mow Mr McCall's grass and water his garden all month. As an apology."

"Whoa, Jeffrey," Mr McCall interrupted. "I don't want your son—or your dog—in my garden again. Ever."

He rubbed the casaba melons with his huge fingers, trying to erase the ugly black stains. "I hope this comes off," he muttered. "Because if it doesn't, Jeffrey, I'll sue. Believe me, I will!"

Two hours after the melon disaster, I sprawled on the floor of my room. Grounded. With nothing to do.

I couldn't play with Buster in the garden. Because the painters were outside.

So I stayed in my room and reread all of my *Super Gamma Man* comic books.

I ordered a glob of rubber vomit from the *Joker's Wild* catalogue for five dollars. That's most of my weekly allowance. Then I sneaked into Mindy's room and mixed up all the clothes in her wardrobe. No more colours in rainbow order.

When I had finished, it still wasn't even noon.

What a totally boring day, I thought, as I wandered downstairs.

"Hand me the yellow, please," Mindy's voice rang out from the den.

I crept towards the door and peeked in. Mindy and her best friend, Heidi, sat cross-legged on the floor. They were decorating T-shirts with fabric paint.

Heidi is almost as annoying as Mindy. Something is always bothering her. She's too cold. Or too hot. Or her stomach hurts. Or her shoelaces are too tight.

I watched silently as the two girls worked. Heidi drew a silver collar on a large purple cat.

Mindy hunched over in concentration and slowly outlined a large yellow flower.

I leaped into the den. "Boo!" I screamed.

"Yaii!" Heidi shrieked.

Mindy jumped up, smearing a big yellow blotch on her red shorts. "You jerk!" she cried. "See what you made me do!"

She scraped at the paint with her fingernails. "Beat it, Joe," she ordered. "We're busy."

"Well, I'm not," I replied. 'Thanks to you, Miss Snitch."

"It was *your* bright idea to draw faces on those melons," she snarled. "Not mine."

"But I didn't do it!" I insisted.

Mindy counted off the evidence on her fingers. "You were up in the middle of the night. You went out in the garden. And you told me you wanted to wreck the rest of the melons."

"I was joking!" I exclaimed. "Don't you know what a joke is? You should try making one sometime."

Heidi stretched out her arms. "I'm hot," she said. "Why don't we go to the pool? We can finish our shirts later."

Mindy fixed her eyes on me. "Joe, do you want to go with us?" she asked in a sweet voice. "Whoops. I forgot. You're grounded." Then she burst out laughing.

I turned and left the two girls in the den. I have to get out of this house, I thought.

I headed for the kitchen. Mum and the painter huddled together at the counter, checking paint swatches.

"We want the onyx black for the trim. Not the pitch black," she instructed, tapping the swatches. "I think you brought the wrong paint."

I tugged on her sleeve. "Mum. Buster's really bored. Can I take him for a walk?"

"Of course not," she replied quickly. "You're grounded."

"Please," I begged. "Buster needs a walk. And that paint smell is making me sick." I held my stomach and made gagging sounds.

The painter shifted impatiently from foot to foot. "Okay, okay," Mum said. "Take the dog."

"Excellent! Thanks, Mum!" I cried. I darted through the kitchen and into the back garden. "Good news, Buster," I exclaimed. "We're free!"

Buster wagged his stumpy tail. I untied the long rope and clipped a short lead to his collar.

We walked about two miles. All the way down to Buttermilk Pond. That's our favourite stick-chasing spot.

I tossed a fat stick into the water. Buster plunged into the cold pond and fetched it. We did that over and over until it was three o'clock. Time to go home.

On the way back to the house, we stopped at the Creamy Cow. They have the best ice-cream in town.

I used the last bit of my allowance to treat us both to double-dip chocolate-chip cookie dough cones. Buster liked the cookie dough, but he left all the chocolate chips on the ground.

After we had finished our ice-cream, we continued home. Buster pulled at his lead excitedly as we strolled up the driveway. He seemed really happy to be back.

He dragged me into the front garden and sniffed everything. The evergreen bushes. The flamingos. The deer. The gnomes.

The gnomes.

Was something different about the gnomes?

I dropped Buster's leash and bent down for a closer look.

I studied their fat little hands. What were those dark smudges on their fingertips. Dirt?

I rubbed their chubby fingers. But the smudges remained.

No. Not dirt.

I leaned in closer.

Paint. Black paint.

Black paint. The same colour as the smily faces on Mr McCall's casabas!

I swallowed hard. What's going on here? I wondered. How could the gnomes' hands be covered in paint?

I've got to show someone, I decided.

Mum! She's in the house. She'll help me figure this out.

As I reached our front door, I heard a scraping sound coming from the McCalls' garden.

"Buster! No!" I shouted.

Buster circled Mr McCall's vegetable patch, his lead dragging behind him.

I quickly shoved my hand under my T-shirt and yanked out my dog whistle. I blew it hard.

Buster trotted right back to me.

"Good boy!" I cried in relief. I shook my finger in his face. I tried to be stern. "Buster, if you don't want to be tied up, you have to stay out of that garden!"

Buster licked my finger with his long, sticky tongue. Then he turned to lick the gnomes.

I watched Buster slobber all over them.

"Oh, no!" I cried. "Not again!"

Chip's and Hap's mouths gaped wide open. In the same terrified expressions I had seen before. As if they were trying to scream.

I slammed my eyes shut. I opened one slowly.

The terrified expressions remained.

What was going on here? Were the gnomes afraid of Buster? Was I going crazy?

My hands trembled as I quickly tied Buster to the tree. Then I ran into the house to search for Mum.

"Mum! Mum!" I panted breathlessly. I found her upstairs, working in her office. "You've got to come outside! Now!"

Mum whirled around from her computer. "What's wrong?" she demanded.

"It's the gnomes!" I cried. "There's black paint on their hands. And they're not grinning any more. Come out. You'll see!"

Mum slowly shoved her chair away from the computer. "Joe, if this is another joke . . ."

"Please, Mum. It will just take a second. It's not a joke. Really!"

Mum led the way downstairs. She gazed at the gnomes from the front door.

"See?" I cried, standing behind her. "I told

you! Look at their faces. They look like they're screaming!"

Mum narrowed her eyes. "Joe, give me a break. Why did you get me away from my work? They have the same dumb grins they always have."

"What?" I gasped. I ran outside. I stared at the gnomes.

They stared back at me. Grinning.

"Joe, I really wish you'd stop the dumb gnome jokes," Mum said sharply. "They're not funny. Not funny at all."

"But look at the paint on their fingers!"

"That's just dirt," she said impatiently. "Please, go and read a book. Or clean your room. Find something to do. You're driving me crazy!"

I sat down on the grass. Alone. To think.

I thought about the casaba seed on one of the gnome's lips. I remembered the first time their mouths had twisted in horror. That was the first time Buster had licked them.

And now they had paint on their fingers.

It all added up.

The gnomes are alive, I decided.

And they're doing horrible things in the McCalls' garden.

The gnomes? Doing horrible things? I must be losing my mind!

Suddenly, I didn't feel too well. Nothing made any sense.

I stood up to go inside.
And heard whispers.
Gruff whispers. Down at my feet.
"Not funny, Joe," Hap whispered.
"Not funny at all," Chip rasped.

Should I tell Mum and Dad what I'd heard? I wondered as we ate dinner that night.

"How was everyone's day?" Dad asked cheerfully. He spooned some peas on to his dinner plate.

They'll never believe me.

"Heidi and I rode our bikes to the pool," Mindy piped up. She arranged a mound of tuna casserole on her plate into a neat square. Then she flicked a stray pea away. "But she got a cramp in her leg, so we mostly sunbathed."

I have to tell.

"I heard something really weird this afternoon," I burst out. "Really, really weird."

"You interrupted me!" Mindy said sharply. She blotted her mouth carefully with her napkin.

"But this is important!" I exclaimed. I started shredding my napkin nervously. "I was in the front garden. All alone. And I heard whispers."

I made my voice low and gruff. "The voices said, 'Not funny, Joe. Not funny.' I don't know who it was. Nobody was there. I . . . uh . . . think it was the gnomes."

Mum banged her glass of lemonade down on the table. "Enough with these gnome jokes!" she declared. "No one thinks they're funny, Joe."

"But it's true!" I cried, crushing my shredded napkin into a ball. "I heard the voices!"

Mindy uttered a scornful laugh. "You are so lame," she said. "Please pass the bread, Dad."

"Sure, honey," Dad replied, handing her the wooden tray of dinner rolls.

And that was the end of that.

After dinner, Dad suggested that we water the tomatoes.

"Okay," I replied with a shrug. Anything to get out of the house.

"Want me to get the *Bug Be Gone*?" I asked as we stepped outside.

"No! No!" he gasped. His face turned ghostly pale.

"What's wrong, Dad? What is it?"

He pointed silently at the tomato patch.

"Ohhh," I moaned. "Oh, no!"

Our beautiful red tomatoes had been crushed, mangled, and maimed — seeds and pulpy red tomato flesh everywhere.

Dad stared open-mouthed, his hands clenched

into fists. "Who would do such a terrible thing?" he sighed.

My heart began to throb. My pulse raced.

I knew the truth. And now everyone would have to believe me.

"The gnomes did it, Dad!" I grabbed the sleeve of his shirt and began tugging him to the front garden. "You'll see. I'll prove it!"

"Joe, let go of me. This is no time for jokes. Don't you realize that we're out of the garden show? We've lost our chance for a blue ribbon! Or any ribbon, for that matter."

"You have to believe me, Dad. Come on." I held tightly on to Dad's sleeve. And I wouldn't let go.

As I dragged him out the front, I wondered what we would find.

Blood-red tomato juice smeared all over their ugly faces?

Squishy pulp hanging from their tiny fat fingers?

Hundreds of seeds stuck to their creepy little feet?

We approached the gnomes.

My eyes narrowed on the hideous creatures.

And finally we stood right before them.

And I couldn't believe what we found.

Nothing.

No juice.

No pulp.

Not a single seed. Not one.

I searched their bodies. Frantically. From their ugly, grinning faces to their creepy, stubby toes.

No clues. Nothing.

How could I have been wrong? My stomach lurched as I turned to face my dad.

"Dad . . ." I started in a shaky voice.

Dad cut me off with an angry wave of his hand. "There's nothing to see here, Joe," he muttered. "I don't want to hear another word about the gnomes. Understand? Not one!"

His brown eyes flashed with fury. "I know who's responsible for this!" he said bitterly. "And he's not going to get away with it!"

He whirled around and trotted into the back

garden. He scooped up a handful of smashed tomato. The juice oozed between his fingers as he circled the house and charged next door.

I watched Dad march up the McCalls' steps and jab at the doorbell. He began howling before anyone answered the ring. "Bill! Come out here. Now!"

I crouched behind Dad. I'd never seen him this angry before.

I heard the lock turn. The door swung open. And there stood Mr McCall. In a white jogging outfit. Holding a half-eaten pork chop in one hand.

"Jeffrey, what are you yelling about? It's difficult to digest with all this noise." He chuckled.

"Well, digest this!" Dad screamed. Then he brought his hand up and hurled the smashed tomatoes.

They splattered against Mr McCall's white T-shirt and dribbled down his white track suit trousers. Some of the mushy pulp landed on his clean white trainers.

Mr McCall stared down at his clothes in total disbelief. "Are you nuts?" he bellowed.

"No. You are!" my father shrieked. "How could you do this? For a stupid blue ribbon!"

"What are you talking about?" Mr McCall shouted.

"Oh, I see. Now you're going to play innocent. You're going to pretend you don't know anything. Well, you're not going to get away with this."

Mr McCall stomped down the steps and planted himself about an inch away from my dad. He puffed out his broad chest and hung over my father menacingly.

"I didn't touch your lousy tomatoes!" he roared. "You wimp! You probably *bought* your blue-ribbon tomatoes last year."

Dad shook an angry fist in Mr McCall's glaring face. "My tomatoes were the best at the show! Yours looked like raisins next to mine! And whoever heard of growing casabas in Minnesota, anyway? You're going to be the joke of the garden show!"

My whole body shuddered. They're going to get into a fist fight, I realized. And Mr McCall will *squash* my dad.

"Joke?" Mr McCall growled. "You're the joke. You and your sour tomatoes. And those stupid garden ornaments! Now leave before I really lose control!"

Mr McCall stomped up to his front door. Then he spun around and said, "I don't want my son hanging around with Joe any more! Your son probably wrecked your tomatoes. Just as he wrecked my melons!"

He disappeared into the house, slamming the door so hard, the porch shook.

*

That night I tossed and turned in bed for hours. Faces painted on melons. Crushed tomatoes. Whispering garden gnomes. I couldn't think of anything else.

It was way after midnight, but I couldn't sleep. The gnomes with their leering smiles danced before my closed eyes.

Those grinning faces. Laughing. Laughing at me.

Suddenly the room felt hot and stuffy. I kicked off the thin sheet that covered my legs. Still too hot.

I jumped out of bed and headed for my window. I threw it wide open. Warm, wet air rushed in.

I rested my arms on the window-sill and peered out into the darkness. It was a foggy night. A thick grey mist swirled over the front garden. Despite the heat, I felt a chill down my back. I had never seen it this foggy before.

The fog shifted slightly. The angel slowly came into view as the fog moved away. Then the seal. The skunks. The swans. A flash of pink — the flamingos.

And there stood the deer.

Alone.

All alone.

The gnomes were gone.

15

"Mum! Dad!" I cried, racing to their bedroom. "Wake up! Wake up! The gnomes are gone!"

Mum bolted straight up. "What? What's wrong?"

Dad didn't budge.

"It's the gnomes!" I shouted, shaking Dad's shoulder. "Wake up!"

My father opened one eye and squinted up at me. "What time is it?" he mumbled.

"Get up, Dad!" I pleaded.

Mum groaned as she snapped on the light next to her bed. "Joe. It's so late. Why did you wake us up?"

"They're—they're gone!" I stammered. "They disappeared. I'm not kidding. I'm really not."

My parents glanced at each other. Then they glared at me. "Enough!" Mum cried. "We're tired of your jokes. And it's the middle of the night! Get to bed!"

"Right now!" Dad added sternly. "We've had just about enough of this nonsense. We're going to have a serious talk about this. In the morning."

"But—but—but—" I stammered.

"Go!" Dad shouted.

I backed out of the room slowly, stumbling over someone's slipper.

I should have realized that they wouldn't believe me. But someone had to believe me. Someone had to.

I raced down the dark hall to Mindy's room. As I neared her bed, I could hear the whistling sounds she always makes when she lies on her back. She was fast asleep.

I stared down at her for a moment. Should I wake her? Would *she* believe me?

I patted her on the cheek. "Mindy. Wake up," I whispered.

Nothing.

I called her name again. A little louder.

Her eyes fluttered open. "Joe?" she asked drowsily.

"Get up. Quick!" I whispered. "You have to see this!"

"Have to see what?" she groaned.

"The gnomes. The gnomes have disappeared!" I exclaimed. "I think they ran away! Please, get up. Please."

"The gnomes?" she mumbled.

"Come on, Mindy. Get up," I pleaded. "It's an emergency!"

Mindy's eyes shot wide open. "Emergency? What? What emergency?"

"It's the gnomes. They've really disappeared. You have to come outside with me."

"*That's* the emergency?" she screeched. "Are you crazy? I'm not going anywhere with you. You've totally lost it, Joe. Totally."

"But, Mindy—"

"Stop annoying me. I'm going back to sleep."

Then she closed her eyes and pulled the sheet over her head.

I stood in her dark, silent room.

No one would believe me. No one would come with me. What should I do now? What?

I imagined the gnomes ripping up every last vegetable in our garden. Yanking out the yams and smashing the squash. And for dessert, chomping on the rest of Mr McCall's casabas!

I knew I had to do something. Fast!

I ran from Mindy's room and raced down the stairs. I jerked the front door open and sprinted outside.

Outside into the murky fog.

Swallowed up inside the thick blanket of mist.

So dark and foggy. I could barely see. I felt as if I were moving through a dark dream. A nightmare of greys and blacks. All shadows. Nothing but shadows.

I inched forward slowly, moving as if I were underwater. The grass felt so wet against my bare feet. But I couldn't even see my own feet through the thick carpet of fog.

Like a dream. Like a heavy, dark dream. So many shifting shadows. So silent. Eerily silent.

I pushed on into the haze. I had lost all sense of direction. Was I heading towards the street?

"Ohhh!" I cried out when something grabbed my ankle.

Frantically, I shook my leg. Tried to break free.

But it held on.

And pulled me down.

Down into the whirling darkness.

A snake.

No. Not a snake. The garden hose. The garden hose that I had forgotten to roll up after watering the lawn that night.

Get a grip, Joe, I told myself. You have to calm down.

I pulled myself up and staggered forward. Squinting hard. Trying to see my way. Shadowy figures seemed to reach for me, bend towards me.

I wanted to turn back. And go inside. And climb into my nice, dry bed.

Yes. That's what I should do, I decided.

I turned slowly.

And heard a shuffling sound. The soft thud of footsteps. Nearby.

I listened closely.

And heard the sounds again. Footsteps as light as the mist.

I was breathing hard now. My heart pounding. My bare feet chilled and wet. The dampness creeping up my legs. My entire body shuddered.

I heard a raspy cackle. A gnome?

I tried to turn. Tried to see it in the billowing blackness.

But it grabbed me from behind. Hard around the waist.

And with a dry, evil laugh, it threw me to the ground!

As I hit the ground, I heard the low, evil laugh again.

And recognized it.

"Moose?"

"Scared you big time!" he muttered. He helped me to my feet. Even in the fog, I could see the big grin on his face.

"Moose—what are you *doing* out here?" I managed to cry.

"I couldn't sleep. I kept hearing weird sounds. I was staring out into the fog—and I saw you. What are you doing out here, Joe? Causing more trouble?"

I wiped wet blades of grass from my hands. "I haven't been causing the trouble," I told him. "You've got to believe me. Look—the two garden gnomes—they're gone."

I pointed to the deer. Moose could see that the gnomes weren't standing in their spots.

He stared for a long time. "This is a trick—right?"

"No. It's for real. I've got to find them."

Moose frowned at me. "What did you do, hide the ugly little creeps? Where are they? Come on, tell me!"

"I didn't hide them," I insisted.

"Tell me," he repeated, leaning over me, bringing his face an inch from mine. "Or suffer the Ten Tortures!"

Moose shoved his huge hands hard against my chest. I fell back and landed in the wet grass again. He thumped down on my stomach and pinned my arms to the ground.

"Tell me!" Moose insisted. "Tell me where they are!" Then he bounced up and down on top of me.

"Stop!" I gasped. "Stop!"

He stopped because lights flashed on in both of our houses.

"Oh, wow," I whispered. "We're in major trouble now."

I heard my front door bang open. A second later, Moose's door opened too.

We froze. "Keep quiet," I whispered. "Maybe they won't see us."

"Who's out there?" my father called.

"What's going on, Jeffrey?" I heard Mr McCall shout. "What's all the noise out here?"

"I don't know," my dad replied. "I thought maybe Joe . . ." His voice trailed off.

We're safe, I thought. We're hidden by the fog.

Then I heard a low click. The long, thin beam of a torch swept across the garden. It settled on Moose and me.

"Joe!" Dad screamed. "What are you doing out there? Why didn't you answer me?"

"Moose!" Mr McCall shouted in a deep, angry voice. "Get in here. Move it!"

Moose climbed up and raced into his house.

I hoisted myself up from the grass for the second time that night and slowly made my way inside.

Dad crossed his arms tightly across his chest. "You woke us up twice tonight! And you're outside in the middle of the night again! What's wrong with you?"

"Listen, Dad, I only went outside because the gnomes are missing! Check," I begged. "You'll see!"

My father glared at me with narrowed eyes. "These gnome stories are getting out of hand!" he snapped. "I've had it! Now go upstairs. Before I ground you for the entire summer!"

"Dad, I'm begging you. I've never been so serious in my life. Please look," I pleaded. "Please. Please. Please!" And then I added, "I'll never ask you for anything else again."

I guess that's what convinced him.

"Okay," he said, sighing wearily. "But if this is another joke . . ."

My father stepped over to the living room

window and peered out into the swirling fog.

"Please let the gnomes still be gone!" I prayed silently. *"Please let Dad see that I'm telling the truth. Please . . . "*

"Joe, you're right!" my father declared. "The gnomes *aren't* out there."

He believed me! Finally! I jumped up and shot a fist into the air. "Yes!" I cheered.

Dad wiped at the moist glass pane with his pyjama sleeve and squinted out the window again.

"See, Dad! See!" I cried happily. "I was telling the truth. I wasn't joking."

"Hmmm. Deer-lilah's not there, either," he said softly.

"What?" I gasped, feeling my stomach churn. "No. The deer is there! I saw it!"

"Hold on a minute," Dad murmured. "Ahhh. There she is. She was hidden in the fog. And the gnomes! There they are! They're right there, too. They were hidden in the fog. See?"

I stared out the window. Two pointy hats broke through the mist. The two gnomes stood dark and still, in their places beside the deer.

"Noooooo!" I moaned. "I know they weren't there. I'm not playing tricks, Dad, I'm not!"

"Fog can do funny things," Dad said. "One time I was driving through a real pea soup of a fog. I spotted something strange through the windscreen. It was shiny and round and it sort of hovered in the air. *Oh, boy*, I thought. *A UFO!* A flying saucer! I couldn't believe it!"

Dad patted me on the back. "Well, my UFO turned out to be a silver balloon tied to a parking meter. Now, Joe. Back to this gnome problem." Dad's face turned stern. "I don't want to hear any more crazy stories. They're only lawn ornaments. Nothing more. Okay? Not another word. Promise?"

What choice did I have? "Promise," I muttered.

Then I dragged myself up the stairs to bed.

What a horrible day—and night. My father thinks I'm a liar. Our tomatoes are ruined. And Moose isn't allowed to hang out with me any more.

What *else* could possibly go wrong?

I woke up the following morning with a heavy feeling in my stomach. As if I had swallowed a bowl of cement.

All I could think about were the gnomes.

Those horrible gnomes. They were destroying

my summer. They were destroying my life!

Forget about them, Joe, I told myself. Just forget about them.

Anyway, today had to be better than yesterday. It sure couldn't be worse.

I peered out my bedroom window. All traces of the fog had been burned away by a bright yellow sun. Buster slept peacefully in the grass, his long white rope snaking through the garden.

I glanced over at the McCalls' house. Maybe Moose is outside helping his dad in the garden, I thought.

I leaned further out the window to get a better look.

"Oh, noooo!" I moaned. "No!"

Globs of white paint splattered over Mr McCall's red Jeep!

The roof. The bonnet. The windows. The whole Jeep covered in paint.

This meant major trouble, I knew.

I pulled on a pair of jeans and yesterday's T-shirt and hurried outside. I found Moose in his driveway, his jaw clenched, shaking his head as he circled the Jeep.

"Unbelievable, huh?" he said, turning to me. "When my dad saw this, he had a fit!"

"Why didn't he park in the garage?" I asked. Mr McCall always parks the Jeep in their two-car garage.

Moose shrugged. "Mum's been cleaning out the basement and attic for a garage sale. She stuck about a million boxes of junk in the garage. So Dad had to park in the driveway last night."

Moose patted the roof of the Jeep. "The paint is still sticky. Touch it."

I touched it. Sticky.

"My dad is steaming!" Moose declared. "At first he thought your dad did it. You know. Because of the tomatoes. But Mum told him that that was ridiculous. So he called the police. He said he won't rest until whoever did it is thrown in jail!"

"He said *that*?" I asked. My mouth suddenly felt as dry as cotton. "Moose, once the police start to check things out, they're going to blame you and me!"

"Blame us? Are you nuts? Why should they blame us?" he demanded.

"Because we were both outside last night!" I said. "And everybody knows it."

Moose's dark brown eyes flickered with fear. "You're right," he said. "What are we going to do?"

"I don't know," I replied sadly. I paced back and forth in the McCalls' driveway, thinking hard. The asphalt felt warm and sticky on my bare feet.

I moved to the grass. And noticed a line of small white paint spots.

"Hey, what's this?" I cried.

I followed the paint trail across the grass.

Over the petunias.

To the corner of my garden.

The paint drips ended where the gnomes stood, grinning at me.

"I knew it! I knew it!" I cried out. "Moose,

84

come and look at this trail. The gnomes splashed your car! And did all the other bad things around here."

"Garden gnomes?" Moose sputtered. "Joe, give up. No one will believe that. Why don't you give it a rest?"

"Check out the evidence!" I demanded. "The melon seed on the gnome's lips. This trail of white paint. I even found black paint on their fingers. Right after your dad found the smily faces on his casabas!"

"Weird," Moose muttered. "Very weird. But garden gnomes are garden gnomes, Joe. They don't run around doing mischief."

"What if we prove they're guilty?" I suggested.

"Excuse me? How would we do that?"

"Catch them in the act," I replied.

"Huh? This is nuts, Joe."

"Come on, Moose. We'll do it tonight. We'll sneak out, hide around the side of the house, and watch them."

Moose shook his head. "No way," he answered. "I'm in big trouble after last night."

"And after the police finish, what kind of trouble will you be in then?"

"Okay. Okay. I'll do it," he muttered. "But I think this whole thing is a big waste of time."

"We're going to trap these gnomes, Moose," I told him. "If it's the last thing we do."

*

Ahhh!

My alarm clock! It didn't go off!

And now it was nearly midnight. And I was late. I'd promised to meet Moose outside at eleven-thirty.

I leaped out of bed, still dressed in my jeans and T-shirt. I grabbed my trainers and ran outside.

No moon. No stars. The front lawn lay blanketed in darkness.

The garden was silent. Too silent.

I glanced around for Moose. No sight of him. He probably went back inside when I didn't show.

What should I do now? Stay out by myself? Or go back to bed?

Something rustled in the bushes. I gasped.

"Joe. Joe. Over here," Moose whispered loudly.

He popped his head out from behind the evergreen shrubs in front of my house. And waved me over.

I slid down next to him.

Moose punched me hard on the arm. "I thought you chickened out."

"No way!" I whispered back. "This was *my* idea!"

"Yeah, your crazy idea," Moose replied. "I can't believe I'm hiding behind a bush. In the middle of the night. Spying on garden ornaments."

"I know it sounds crazy, but —"

"Shhh. Did you hear something?" Moose interrupted.

I heard it. A scraping sound.

I reached into the shrub and parted the thick green branches. The needles clawed at my hands and arms. I jerked my arms out quickly. Too quickly. Blood dripped from my fingers where two needles had pierced right through my skin.

The scraping sound came closer.

My heart pounded in my chest.

Closer.

Moose and I sat there. We exchanged frightened glances.

I had to look. I had to see what was making those sounds.

I parted the needles once again. And stared through the mass of needled branches. Two small, glowing eyes met mine!

"Get it, Moose! Get it!" I cried.

Moose jumped up from behind the bush. Just in time — to see it scamper away.

"A raccoon! It was only a raccoon!"

I let out a long sigh. "Sorry, Moose."

We sat there a while longer. We parted the branches every few minutes to check on the gnomes. My arms were scratched raw from the rough needles.

But the gnomes hadn't budged. They stood

grinning into the night in their silly suits and caps.

I groaned. My legs felt stiff and cramped.

Moose checked his watch. "We've been out here for over two hours," he whispered. "Those gnomes aren't going anywhere. I'm going home."

"Wait a little longer," I begged him. "We'll catch them. I know we will."

"You're a pretty good guy," Moose said as he parted the bushes for the millionth time. "So I hate to tell you this, Joe. But you're as crazy as—"

He didn't finish his sentence. His mouth dropped open, and his eyes nearly popped out of his pudgy head.

I peered into the shrubs—in time to see the gnomes come to life. They stretched their arms over their heads. And stroked their chins.

They shook out their legs. And smoothed out their shirts.

"They—they're *moving*!" Moose cried.

Too loudly.

And then I lost my balance and fell. Right into the bush.

They've seen us, I realized.

Now what?

"No. Oh, man. No!" Moose whispered. He tugged me to my feet. "They're moving. They're really moving!"

Squinting through the branches, we both stared in horror at Hap and Chip.

The gnomes bent their knees, limbering up. Then they each took one stiff step. Then another.

I was right. They are alive, I thought. Very alive.

And they're coming for Moose and me.

We have to run, I told myself. We have to get *out* of here.

But neither of us could take our eyes off the living garden gnomes!

The full moon suddenly appeared low over the trees. The front lawn lit as if someone had turned on a spotlight. The stocky figures swung their short, fat arms and began to run. Their pointed hats cut through the air like sharks' fins.

They scrambled towards us on their stumpy legs. Moose and I dropped to our knees and tried to hide. My whole body was trembling so hard, I was making the bush shake!

The gnomes ran closer. So close that I could see the dark red of their evil eyes and the white gleam of their grins.

I clenched my fists so tightly, my hands ached.

What were they going to do to us?

I shut my eyes—and heard them run past. I heard thudding footsteps. Whistling breaths.

I opened my eyes to see them racing across the cement path and around the side of the house.

"Moose—they didn't see us!" I whispered happily.

We helped each other to our feet. I felt dizzy. The dark ground tilted. My legs felt soft and rubbery like jelly.

Moose wiped his sweaty brow. "Where are they going?" he whispered.

I shook my head. "I don't know. But we have to follow them. Come on."

We gave each other a quick thumbs-up and stepped out from our hiding place. I led the way. We moved across the cement path and past the front porch. Towards the side of the house.

I stopped when I heard their raspy voices, talking low. Just up ahead.

Moose grabbed my shoulder, his eyes wide

open in alarm. "I'm getting out of here. Now!"

I turned around. "No!" I pleaded. "You've got to stay and help me catch them. We have to show our parents what's been going on here."

He heaved a long sigh. It made me feel a little better to know that a big, tough guy like Moose was as frightened as I was. Finally, he nodded. "Okay. Let's go get them."

Keeping in the dark shadow of the house, we made our way around to the back. I saw Buster, sound asleep beside his kennel in the centre of the garden.

And then I saw the two garden gnomes. They were bent over the pile of paint and brushes and dust sheets the painters had left beside the garage.

Moose and I hung back as Hap and Chip picked up two cans of black paint. They prised the cans open with their thick fingers.

Giggling, the two gnomes swung back the open cans, then hurled the black paint at the side of my house. The black paint spattered over the fresh white paint, then dripped down in long, thick streaks.

I clapped a hand over my mouth to keep from screaming.

I knew it. I'd known it all along. But no one would believe me. The gnomes were behind all the trouble around here.

The gnomes returned to the pile for more paint. "We've got to stop them," I whispered to Moose. "But how?"

"Let's just tackle them," Moose suggested. "Tackle them from behind and pin them down."

It sounded simple enough. They were little, after all. Smaller than us. "Okay," I whispered, my stomach fluttering. "Then we'll drag them into the house and show my parents."

I took a deep breath and held it. Moose and I started to inch forward.

Closer. Closer.

If only my legs weren't wobbling like rubber bands!

Closer.

And then I saw Moose go down.

He toppled forward — and hit the ground hard, letting out a loud *"Oooof!"*

It took me a second to see that he had tripped over Buster's rope.

He struggled to get to his feet. But the rope had tangled around his ankle.

He reached down with both hands. Gave it a hard tug.

And woke up Buster!

"Rrrrrowwwwwf! Rrrrrrowwwwwf!" Buster must have seen the gnomes because he started barking his head off.

The gnomes spun around.

And fixed their eyes on us. In the bright moonlight, their faces turned hard and angry.

"Get them!" Chip growled. "Don't let them escape!"

"Run!" I screamed.

Moose and I bolted towards the front of the house.

Buster was still barking his head off.

And over the barking, I heard shrill giggles. The gnomes giggled as they chased after us.

Their feet slapped sharply on the grass. I glanced back, saw their stubby legs moving fast, a blur of motion.

I pumped my legs, gasping for breath, and rounded the side of the house.

I could hear the high-pitched giggles of the two gnomes close behind us.

"Help!" Moose cried. "Somebody—help us!"

My mouth hung open. I struggled to breathe. They were gaining on us.

I knew I had to run faster. But my legs suddenly felt as heavy as bricks.

"Hellllp!" Moose called.

I glanced at the house. Why wasn't anyone waking up in there?

We ran around the house and kept running. Why were Hap and Chip giggling like that?

Because they knew they were going to catch us?

I felt a stab of pain in my side. "Oh, no!" A cramp.

I felt Moose tugging me. "Don't slow down, Joe. Keep going!"

The pain sharpened, like a knife in my side. "Can't run . . ." I choked out.

"Joe—keep going! Don't stop!" Moose cried, frantically pulling my arm.

But I doubled over, holding my side.

It's all over, I thought. They've got me.

And then the front door swung open. The porch light flashed on.

"What's going on out here?" a familiar voice called.

Mindy!

She stepped out, pulling at the belt of her pink dressing gown. I saw her squint into the darkness.

"Mindy!" I called. "Mindy—watch out!"

Too late.

The gnomes grabbed her.

Giggling loudly, they pinned her arms back. Dragged her down the porch steps. Carried her to the street.

Mindy thrashed her arms and kicked her legs. But the giggling gnomes had surprising strength.

"Help me!" Mindy called back to Moose and me. "Don't just stand there—help me!"

I swallowed hard. The pain in my side faded.

Moose and I didn't say a word. We just started chasing after them.

They had already carried Mindy to the street. Their feet slapped on the pavement. In the light from the street lamp, I saw Mindy struggling to free herself.

Moose and I hurtled down the driveway. "Put her down!" I shouted breathlessly. "Put my sister down—now!"

More giggles. They scurried past the McCalls' house. Past the next two houses.

Moose and I ran after them, shouting, begging them to stop.

And then—to our shock—they did stop.

In the shadow of a tall hedge, they set Mindy down and turned to us. "We mean you no harm," Chip said.

The gnomes' expressions were serious now. Their eyes peered at us through the darkness.

"I don't *believe* this!" Mindy cried, straightening her gown. "This is crazy! Crazy!"

"Tell me about it," I muttered.

"Please listen to us," Hap rasped.

"We mean you no harm," Chip repeated.

"No harm!" Mindy shrieked. "No harm! You just dragged me from my home! You — you — "

"We only wanted to get your attention," Hap said softly.

"Well, you've *got* it!" Mindy exclaimed.

"We mean you no harm," Chip said once again. "Please believe us."

"How *can* we believe you?" I demanded, finally finding my voice. "Look at all the trouble you've caused. You've ruined the gardens! You splashed paint everywhere! You — "

"We can't help it," Hap interrupted.

"We really can't," Chip echoed. "You see, we're Mischief Elves."

"You're *what*?" Mindy cried.

"We're Mischief Elves. We do mischief. That's our mission in life," Hap explained.

"Wherever there is mischief in the world, we're there," Chip added. "Mischief is our job. We can't help ourselves."

He bent down and broke off a chunk of the concrete kerb. Then he pulled open the postbox across from us and shoved the piece of concrete inside.

"See? I can't help myself. I have to do mischief wherever I go."

Hap giggled. "Without us, the world would be a pretty dull place—wouldn't it?"

"It would be a much *better* place," Mindy insisted, crossing her arms in front of her.

Moose still hadn't said a word. He just stood and stared at the two talking garden gnomes.

Hap and Chip made pouty faces. "Please don't hurt our feelings," Chip rasped. "Our life isn't easy."

"We need your help," Hap added.

"You want us to help you do mischief?" I cried. "No way! You've already got me into major trouble."

"No. We need you to help get us our freedom," Chip said solemnly. "Please—listen and believe."

"Listen and believe," Hap echoed.

"We lived in a land far from here," Chip began. "In a forest deep and green. We guarded the mines and protected the trees. We performed our mischief innocently. But we also did a lot of good."

"We were hard-working people," Hap told us, scratching his head. "And we were happy in our forest home."

"But then the mines were closed and the forests were cut down," Chip continued. "We were captured. Kidnapped. And taken far from home. We were shipped to your country and forced to work as garden ornaments."

"Slaves," Hap said, shaking his head sadly. "Forced to stand all day and night."

"That's impossible!" Mindy cried. "Don't you get bored? How do you stand so still?"

"We go into a trance," Chip explained. "Time passes without our realizing it. We come out of the trance at night and go about doing our job."

"You mean mischief!" I declared.

They both nodded.

"But we want to be free," Hap continued. "To go where we want. To live where we choose. We want to find another forest where we can be free to live in peace." Two tiny gnome tears rolled down his fat cheeks.

Chip sighed and raised his eyes to me. "Will you help us?"

"Help you do *what*?" I demanded.

"Help our friends and us escape?" Chip replied.

"There are six others," Hap explained. "They're locked in the basement. At the shop where you bought us. We need your help to set them free."

"We can climb into the basement window," his friend continued. "But we are too short to climb back out. And too short to reach the doorknob to let ourselves out through the door."

"Will you help us escape?" Hap pleaded, tugging the bottom of my T-shirt. "You just have to climb down into the basement. Then help our six friends out of the basement."

"Please help us," Chip begged, tears in his eyes. "Then we'll be gone. To a deep forest. And we will never cause you any more mischief."

"That sounds good to me!" Mindy exclaimed.

"So you'll do it?" Hap squealed.

They both began tugging at us, chirping, "Please? Please? Please? Please? Please?"

Moose, Mindy and I exchanged troubled glances.

What should we do?

"Please? Please? Please? Please?"

"Let's help them," Moose said, finally finding his voice.

I turned to Mindy. I didn't usually ask her advice. But she was the oldest. "What do you think?"

Mindy bit her lower lip. "Well, look how much Buster hates to be tied up," she said. "He only wants to be free. I guess everything deserves to be free. Even garden gnomes."

I turned back to the gnomes. "We'll do it!" I declared. "We'll help you."

"Thank you! Thank you!" Chip cried happily. He threw his arms around Hap. "You don't know what this means to us!"

"Thank you! Thank you! Thank you!" Hap squealed. He leaped into the air and clicked the heels of his boots together. "Hurry! Let's go!"

"Now?" Mindy cried. "It's the middle of the night! Can't we wait until tomorrow?"

"No. Please. Now," Hap insisted.

"In the darkness," Chip added. "While the shop is closed. Please. Let's hurry."

"I'm not dressed," Mindy replied. "I really don't think we can go now. I think —"

"If we stay here longer, we'll have to do more mischief," Chip said with a wink.

I sure didn't want that to happen. "Let's do it now!" I agreed.

And so the five of us crept along the dark street and up the steep hill towards Lawn Lovely. Wow, did I feel weird! Here we were, walking around in the middle of the night with a couple of garden ornaments! About to break into the shop and set six more garden ornaments free!

The old pink house was a strange enough place during the day. But at night, it was totally creepy. All those garden animals — deer and seals and flamingos — stared at us through the darkness, with blank, lifeless eyes.

Were they alive, too? I wondered.

Hap seemed to read my mind. "They're only for decoration," he sneered. "Nothing more."

The two excited gnomes made their way quickly across the wide lawn and around the side of Mrs Anderson's house. Moose, Mindy and I followed behind.

Mindy clutched my arm with an ice-cold hand. My legs felt wobbly. But my heart was pounding with excitement — not fear.

Hap and Chip pointed to the long, low window that led down to the basement. I knelt down and peered inside. Total darkness.

"You're sure the other gnomes are down there?" I asked.

"Oh, yes," Chip declared eagerly. "All six. They're waiting for you to rescue them."

"Please hurry," Hap pleaded, shoving me gently to the window. "Before the old woman hears us and wakes up."

I lowered myself to the edge of the open window. And turned back to my sister and Moose.

"We're coming right behind you," Moose whispered.

"Let's rescue them and get *out* of here," Mindy urged.

"Here goes," I said softly.

I crossed my fingers and slid down into the darkness.

I bumped over the window frame and landed on my feet. A few seconds later, I heard Moose and Mindy slide in after me.

I squinted into the darkness that surrounded us. I couldn't see a thing. I licked my dry lips and sniffed the air. A sharp smell, like vinegar, filled the hot, damp basement. Sweat, I thought. Gnome sweat.

I heard a low giggle from outside. Chip and Hap hurtled over the window ledge and thudded to the floor.

"Hey, guys—" I whispered.

But they scampered off into the darkness.

"What's going on here?" Moose demanded.

"We've got to find the light switch," Mindy whispered.

But before we could move, the ceiling lights all flashed on. I blinked in the sudden blaze of brightness.

And then gasped as I stared across the

vast basement — at a sea of garden gnomes!

Not six! Six *hundred*! Row after row of them, jammed against each other, staring at the three of us.

"Whoa!" Moose cried. "It's a mob!"

"Hap and Chip *lied* to us!" I cried.

Their shirts were different colours. But the garden gnomes all looked exactly alike. They all wore pointed caps and black belts. They all had staring red eyes, wide noses, grinning lips and large pointy ears.

I was so startled to see so many of the ugly creatures, it took me a while to spot Hap and Chip. Finally, I saw them at the side of the room.

Hap clapped his hands three times.

And three more times. Short, sharp claps that echoed off the basement walls.

And then the crowd of gnomes came to life, stretching and bending, grinning and giggling, chattering in shrill, excited voices.

Mindy grabbed my arm. "We've got to get out of here."

I could barely hear her over the chattering, giggling mob of gnomes. I glanced up at the basement window. It suddenly seemed so high, so far away.

When I turned back, Hap and Chip had moved in front of us. They clapped their hands for attention.

The hundreds of gnomes instantly fell silent.

"We have brought the young humans!" Hap announced, grinning happily.

"We have kept our promise!" Chip declared.

Giggles and cheering.

And then, to my horror, the gnomes began moving forward. Their eyes flashed excitedly. They reached out their stubby arms towards us. The pointed hats bobbed and slid forward, like sharks on the attack.

Mindy, Moose and I backed up. Backed up to the wall.

The gnomes crowded up against us. Their little hands plucked at my clothes, slapped my face, pulled my hair.

"Stop!" I shrieked. "Get back! Get back!"

"We came to help you!" I heard Mindy scream. "Please — we came to help you escape!"

Loud giggling.

"But we don't *want* to escape!" a grinning gnome declared. "Now that *you're* here, it's going to be so much fun!"

Fun?

What did he mean by *fun*?

Hap and Chip pushed their way back to the front and stepped up beside us. They clapped their hands together to silence the giggling, chattering crowd.

The basement instantly turned silent.

"You tricked us!" Mindy screamed at the two gnomes. "You lied to us!"

They giggled in reply and slapped each other's shoulders gleefully.

"I can't believe you fell for our sad story," Hap said, shaking his head.

"We *told* you we're Mischief Gnomes," Chip sneered. "You should have known we were making mischief!"

"Great joke, guys," I said, forcing a hoarse laugh. "You fooled us. Way to go. So now let us go home, okay?"

"Yeah. Let us go home!" Moose insisted.

The whole room erupted in laughter.

Hap shook his head. "But the mischief has just begun!" he declared.

Cheers and giggles.

Chip turned to the crowd of excited gnomes. "So what shall we do with our lovely prisoners? Any ideas?"

"Let's see if they bounce!" a gnome called from near the back of the room.

"Yeah! Dribble them!"

"A dribbling contest!"

"No—bounce them against the wall. Bounce and catch!"

More cheers.

"No! Fold them into tiny squares! I love it when we fold humans into squares!"

"Yes! A folding contest!" another gnome cried.

"Fold them! Fold them! Fold them!" several gnomes began to chant.

"Tickle them!" a gnome in front suggested.

"Tickle them for hours!"

"Tickle! Tickle! Tickle!"

The room rang out with their excited chants.

"Fold them! Fold them! Fold them!"

"Tickle! Tickle! Tickle!"

"Dribble! Dribble! Dribble! Dribble!"

I turned to Moose. He stared out at the crowd of chanting gnomes, dazed and frightened. His eyes bulged and his chin quivered.

Mindy had her back pressed up against the

basement wall. Her blonde hair was matted to her forehead. Her hands were jammed into the pockets of her dressing gown.

"What are we going to do?" she asked me, shouting over the excited chants.

Suddenly I had an idea.

I raised my arms high over my head. *"Quiet!"* I screamed.

The room instantly grew silent. Hundreds of red eyes glared at me.

"Let us go!" I demanded. "Or the three of us will scream at the top of our lungs. We will wake up Mrs Anderson. And she will be down here in a second to rescue us!"

Silence.

Had I frightened them?

No. The gnomes burst into loud, scornful laughter. They slapped each other's shoulders, hooted, and giggled.

"You'll have to do better than that!" Hap grinned up at me. "We all know that Mrs Anderson can't hear a thing."

"Go ahead and shout," Chip urged. "Shout all you want. We like it when humans shout." He turned to Hap, and the two of them slapped each other's shoulders and fell on the floor, giggling gleefully, kicking their feet in the air.

Over the vast basement, the chants started up again.

"Tickle! Tickle! Tickle!"

"Fold them! Fold them! Fold them!"

"Dribble! Dribble! Dribble!"

With a long sigh, I turned to my frightened sister and friend. "We're doomed," I muttered. "We don't have a chance."

"Tug of War! Tug of War!"

A new chant started in the back of the room and swept up towards the front.

"Yes!" Hap and Chip declared happily.

"Excellent mischief!" Hap cried.

"A Tug of War! We'll tug them till they stretch!" Chip shouted.

"Stretch them! Stretch them!"

"Tug of War! Tug of War!"

"Joe—what are we going to do?" I heard Mindy's frightened voice over the enthusiastic chants.

Think, Joe, I urged myself. Think! There has to be a way out of this basement.

But I felt so dazed. The chants rang in my ears. The grinning faces leered up at us. My thoughts were a jumbled mess.

"Stretch them! Stretch them!"

"Fold them! Fold them!"

"Tickle! Tickle! Tickle!"

Suddenly, over the shrill gnome voices, I heard a familiar sound.

A dog's bark.

Buster's bark.

"Buster!" Mindy cried. "I hear him!"

"I—I did too!" I exclaimed, turning and raising my eyes to the window above our heads. "He followed us! He must be right outside!"

I desperately wished Buster could talk. Could run home and tell Mum and Dad that we were in terrible trouble.

But he could only bark. Or . . . could he do more?

I suddenly remembered how frightened Hap and Chip appeared whenever Buster came around. The terrified expressions on their faces.

My heart fluttered with hope. Maybe the gnomes are afraid of dogs. Maybe Buster can scare them into letting us go. Maybe he can even frighten them back into their trance.

I edged closer to my sister, my back pressed against the wall. "Mindy, I think the gnomes are afraid of Buster. If we get him down here, I think he can save us."

We didn't hesitate. All three of us started shouting up to the window. "Buster! Buster! Come here, boy!"

Could he hear us over the chanting gnomes? Yes!

His big head peered down at us through the window.

"Good boy!" I cried. "Now, come here. Come down here, Buster!"

Buster's mouth opened. His pink tongue drooped from his mouth, and he started to pant.

"Good doggie!" I crooned. "Good doggie —come down here. Fast! Come, boy! Come, Buster!"

Buster poked his head into the window. And yawned.

"Down, Buster!" Mindy ordered. "Come down here, boy!"

He pulled his head out of the window. And settled down on the ground outside. I could see his head resting on his paws.

"No, Buster!" I shrieked, shouting over the chants. "Come, boy! Don't lie down! Come! Buster, come!"

"*Rowf?*" He pushed his head back into the window. Further. Further.

"Come on boy! Come on!" I pleaded. "A little more . . . a little more. If you come down here, I'll feed you doggie treats five times a day."

Buster cocked his head to the side and sniffed at the damp, sweaty air of the basement.

I held my arms out to the dog. "Please, Buster. You're our last chance. Please —hurry! Come down here."

To my dismay, Buster pulled his head out of the window.

Turned.

And trotted away.

Mindy and Moose let out long, disappointed sighs. "Buster deserted us," Mindy said softly. Her shoulders sagged. Moose dropped to his knees on the floor, shaking his head.

"Trampoline! Trampoline!"

The chant had changed.

Hap grinned up at us. "Maybe we'll use you for trampolines! That would be fun!"

"It's almost time for a vote!" Chip added, rubbing his hands together eagerly.

"Trampoline! Trampoline!"

"Tug of War! Tug of War!"

I held my hands over my ears, trying to block out the sound of their shrill voices.

Silence. Please let me have silence, I thought. Silence.

The word gave me an idea.

Silence. Buster's dog whistle was silent!

Suddenly, I knew how to bring Buster back!

"Mindy!" I cried. "The dog whistle! Buster

always comes when I blow the dog whistle!"

Mindy raised her head and brightened. "That's right!" she cried. "Hurry, Joe!"

I grabbed for the shiny metal whistle under my T-shirt. It felt slippery with sweat. This has to work, I thought to myself. It has to bring Buster back.

I pulled the whistle out.

"The whistle!" several gnomes shrieked.

The room instantly grew silent.

I raised the whistle to my lips.

"Quick—blow it!" Mindy screeched.

To my surprise, Hap and Chip both dived at me.

They leaped up and slapped at the whistle.

The whistle spun out of my hands.

"Noooo!" I cried in despair.

I grabbed frantically for it.

But it rolled and tumbled away, sliding across the basement floor.

Mindy, Moose and I all dived for it.

But the gnomes were quicker.

A gnome in a bright blue shirt raised the whistle, clutched tightly in his little fist. "I've got it!"

"No, you don't!" Moose cried. He leaped at the gnome, tackled him around the knees.

The gnome let out a *yelp* as he went toppling to the floor.

The dog whistle fell from his hand.

And bounced across the hard floor towards me.

I scooped it up. Started to raise it to my lips.

Three gnomes leaped on to my shoulders, giggling and grunting.

"Noooo!" I uttered a cry as they batted the whistle from my hand. I dropped to the floor, three gnomes on top of me.

I finally shook them off and jumped to my feet. My eyes searched for the whistle.

I saw a bunch of gnomes diving for the floor, scrambling for it. A few feet away, Moose struggled against four or five gnomes who had formed a line to block him. Mindy was battling another group of gnomes, who held her back, their tiny hands around her legs and waist.

And then I saw Hap raise the whistle high.

The gnomes stepped back, clearing a circle around him.

Hap set the whistle in front of him on the floor. Then he raised his foot high.

He was about to crush it!

"Noooooo!" Another long cry escaped my throat. I scrambled over the floor, half-crawling, half-flying.

As Hap's heavy plaster foot came down, I stretched out my hand.

Fumbled for the whistle.

Grabbed it.

Rolled away as the gnome's foot stamped down heavily. It thudded inches from my head.

I sat up. Raised the whistle to my lips.

And blew as hard as I could.

Now what?

Would the whistle work?

Would Buster come running to rescue us?

I blew the silent whistle again.

And turned to the window. Buster, where *are* you?

The gnomes must have been asking the same question. Because they froze in place, too. The excited chattering, giggling, and chanting stopped.

The only sound I could hear was my own shallow breathing.

I stared up at the window. A rectangle of blackness. No sign of Buster.

"Hey—!" Moose's cry made me turn around.

"Look at them!" Moose's voice echoed through the silence.

"Look—they all froze!" Mindy declared. She placed both hands on the red cap of a gnome—and pushed the gnome over.

It clattered to the floor. And didn't move. A hunk of plaster.

"I don't get it!" Moose scratched his crew cut.

Still gripping the dog whistle tightly, I moved around the room, examining the frozen gnomes, pushing them over. Enjoying the silence.

"Back in their trance state," Mindy murmured.

"But *how*?" Moose demanded. "Buster never showed up. If they weren't terrified of the dog, why did they all freeze up again?"

I suddenly knew the answer. I raised the whistle and blew it again. "It was the whistle," I explained. "It wasn't Buster. I had it wrong. They were afraid of the whistle. Not the dog."

"Let's get out of here," Mindy said softly. "I never want to see another garden gnome as long as I live."

"Wait till I tell my parents about this!" Moose declared.

"Whoa!" I cried, grabbing his shoulder. "We can't tell *anyone* about this. No way!"

"Why not?" he demanded.

"Because no one will believe it," I replied.

Moose stared at me for a long moment. "You're right," he agreed finally. "You're definitely right."

Mindy moved to the wall and stared up at the window. "How do we get out of here?"

"I know how," I told her. I picked up Hap and Chip and stood them beneath the window. Then I climbed on to their caps, lifted my hands to the window, and pulled myself up. "Thanks for the boost, guys!" I called down.

They didn't reply.

I hoped they were frozen for good.

Mindy and Moose followed me out. Of course, Buster was waiting for us in the garden. His stubby tail began to wag as soon as I appeared. He came running over and licked my face till I was sopping wet and sticky.

"Sorry, fella. You're a little late," I told him. "You weren't much help—were you!"

He licked me some more. Then he greeted Mindy and Moose.

"Yaaaay! We're out! We're out!" Moose cried. He slapped me so hard on the back, I thought my teeth were going to fly out!

I turned to my sister. "Tickle! Tickle! Tickle!" I chanted.

"Give me a break!" Mindy cried, rolling her eyes for the thousandth time that day.

"Tickle! Tickle! Tickle!" I made tickling motions with my hands and started to chase her down the street.

"Joe—stop it! Don't tickle me! I'm warning you!"

"Tickle! Tickle! Tickle!"

I knew I'd never forget those high-pitched chants. I knew I'd hear them in my dreams for a long, long time.

*

The next evening, Mindy and I were watching MTV in the den when Dad came home.

"Be nice to your dad," Mum had warned us earlier. "He's very upset that somebody stole his two garden gnomes."

Yes, the two gnomes were missing when he woke up.

Big surprise.

Mindy and I were so happy, we didn't have a single argument all day.

And now we were happy to see Dad —except that he had a strange expression on his face. "Uh . . . I've brought home a little surprise," he announced, glancing guiltily at Mum.

"*Now* what?" she demanded.

"Come and see." Dad led us out to the front lawn.

The sun was disappearing behind the trees, and the sky was grey. But I could still see clearly what Dad had purchased at Lawn Lovely this time.

An enormous, brown plaster gorilla!

At least eight feet tall, with gigantic black eyes and a bright purple chest. The gorilla had paws the size of baseball mitts and a head as big as a basketball.

"It's the ugliest thing I ever saw!" Mum cried, both hands pressed to her face. "You're not really going to put that horrible monster on our front lawn —are you, dear?"

Anything is better than those garden gnomes, I thought. Anything is better than garden gnomes who come alive and do terrible mischief.

I glanced at Mindy. I had a feeling she was thinking the same thing.

"I think it's a beauty, Dad," I said. "It's the best-looking garden gorilla I ever saw!"

"It's great, Dad," Mindy agreed.

Dad smiled.

Mum turned and hurried back to the house, shaking her head.

I glanced up at the gorilla's enormous purple-and-brown painted face. "Be a good gorilla," I murmured. "Don't be like those awful gnomes."

Then, as I started to turn away, the gorilla winked at me.

A Shocker on
Shock Street

"This is creepy, Erin." My friend Marty grabbed my sleeve.

"Let go!" I whispered. "You're hurting me!"

Marty didn't seem to hear. He stared straight ahead into the darkness, gripping my arm.

"Marty, please—" I whispered. I shook my arm free. I was scared, too. But I didn't want to admit it.

It was darker than the darkest night. I squinted hard, trying to see. And then a grey light glowed dimly in front of us.

Marty ducked low. Even in the foggy light, I could see the fear in his eyes.

He grabbed my arm again. His mouth dropped open. I could hear him breathing hard and fast.

Even though I was frightened, a smile crossed my face. I *liked* seeing Marty scared.

I really enjoyed it.

I know, I know. That's terrible. I admit it. Erin Wright is a bad person. What kind of a friend am I?

But Marty always brags that he is braver than me. And he is usually right. He usually *is* the brave one, and I'm the wimp.

But not today.

That's why seeing Marty gasp in fright and grab my arm made me smile.

The grey light ahead of us slowly grew brighter. I heard crunching sounds on both sides of us. Close behind me, someone coughed. But Marty and I didn't turn around. We kept our eyes straight ahead.

Waiting. Watching. . .

As I squinted into the grey light, a fence came into view. A long wooden fence, its paint faded and peeling. A hand-lettered sign appeared on the fence: DANGER. KEEP OUT. THIS MEANS YOU.

Marty and I both gasped when we heard the scraping sounds. Soft at first. Then louder. Like giant claws scraping against the other side of the fence.

I tried to swallow, but my mouth suddenly felt dry. I had the urge to run. Just turn and run as fast as I could.

But I couldn't leave Marty there all alone. And besides, if I ran away now, he would never let me forget it. He'd tease me about it for ever.

So I stayed beside him, listening as the scraping, clawing sounds turned into banging. Loud crashes.

Was someone trying to break through the fence?

We moved quickly along the fence. Faster, faster — until the tall, peeling fence pickets became a grey blur.

But the sound followed us. Heavy footsteps on the other side of the fence.

We stared straight ahead. We were on an empty street. A familiar street.

Yes, we had been here before.

The pavement was puddled with rainwater. The puddles glowed in the pale light from the streetlamps.

I took a deep breath. Marty gripped my arm harder. Our mouths gaped open.

To our horror, the fence began to shake. The whole street shook. The rain puddles splashed against the kerb.

The footsteps thundered closer.

"Marty — !" I gasped in a choked whisper.

Before I could say another word, the fence crumbled to the ground, and the monster came bursting out.

It had a head like a wolf — snapping jaws of gleaming white teeth — and a body like a giant crab. It swung four huge claws in front of it, clicking them at us as its snout pulled open in a throaty growl.

"NOOOOOOO!" Marty and I both let out howls of terror.

We jumped to our feet.

But there was nowhere to run.

We stood and stared as the wolf-crab crawled towards us.

"Please sit down, kids," a voice called out behind us. "I can't see the screen."

"Ssshhhh!" someone else whispered.

Marty and I glanced at each other. I guess we both felt like jerks. I know I did. We dropped back into our seats.

And watched the wolf-crab scamper across the street, chasing after a little boy on a tricycle.

"What's your problem, Erin?" Marty whispered, shaking his head. "It's only a movie. Why did you scream like that?"

"You screamed too!" I replied sharply.

"I only screamed because you screamed!" he insisted.

"Sssshhh!" someone pleaded. I sank low in the seat. I heard crunching sounds all around me. People eating popcorn. Someone behind me coughed.

On the screen, the wolf-crab reached out his big, red claws and grabbed the kid on the trike. SNAP. SNAP. Goodbye, kid.

Some people in the arena laughed. It *was* pretty funny.

That's the great thing about the *Shocker on Shock Street* movies. They make you scream and laugh at the same time.

Marty and I sat back and enjoyed the rest of the movie. We love scary movies, but the *Shock Street* films are our favourites.

In the end, the police caught the wolf-crab. They boiled him in a big pot of water. Then they served steamed crab to the whole town. Everyone sat around dipping him in butter sauce. They all said he was delicious.

It was the perfect ending. Marty and I clapped and cheered. Marty put two fingers in his mouth and whistled through his teeth the way he always does.

We had just seen *Shocker on Shock Street VI*, and it was definitely the best one of the series.

The theatre lights came on. We turned up the aisle and started to make our way through the crowd.

"Great special effects," a man told his friend.

"Special effects?" the friend replied. "I thought it was all real!"

They both laughed.

Marty bumped me hard from behind. He

thinks it's funny to try and knock me over. "Pretty good movie," he said.

I turned back to him. "Huh? *Pretty* good?"

"Well, it wasn't scary enough," he replied. "Actually, it was kind of babyish. *Shocker V* was a lot scarier."

I rolled my eyes. "Marty, you screamed your head off—remember? You jumped out of your seat. You grabbed my arm and—"

"I only did that because I saw how scared you were," he said, grinning. What a liar! Why can't he ever admit it when he's scared?

He stuck his trainer out and tried to trip me.

I dodged to the left, stumbled—and bumped hard into a young woman.

"Hey—look out!" she cried. "You twins should be more careful."

"We're not twins!" Marty and I cried in unison.

We're not even brother and sister. We're not related in any way. But people always think that Marty and I are twins.

I guess we do look a lot alike. We're both twelve years old. And we're both pretty short and kind of chubby. We both have round faces, short black hair and blue eyes. And we both have little noses that sort of turn up.

But we're not twins! We're only friends.

I apologized to the woman. When I turned

back to Marty, he stuck out his shoe and tried to trip me again.

I stumbled, but quickly caught my balance. Then I stuck out my shoe—and tripped him.

We kept tripping each other through the long lobby. People were staring at us, but we didn't care. We were laughing too hard.

"Do you know the coolest thing about this movie?" I asked.

"No. What?"

"That we're the first kids in the world to see it!" I exclaimed.

"Yeah!" Marty and I slapped each other a high five.

We had just seen *Shocker on Shock Street VI* at a special sneak preview. My dad works with a lot of movie people, and he got us tickets for it. The others in the cinema were all adults. Marty and I were the only kids.

"Know what else was really cool?" I asked. "The monsters. All of them. They looked so incredibly real. It didn't look like special effects at all."

Marty frowned. "Well, I thought the Electric Eel Woman was pretty phony-looking. She didn't look like an eel—she looked like a big worm!"

I laughed. "Then why did you jump out of your seat when she shot a bolt of electricity and fried that gang of teenagers?"

"I didn't jump," Marty insisted. "*You* did!"

"Did not! You jumped because it looked so real," I insisted. "And I heard you choke when the Toxic Creep leaped out of the nuclear waste pit."

"I choked on some popcorn, that's all."

"You were scared, Marty, because it was so real."

"Hey—what if they *are* real?" Marty exclaimed. "What if it isn't special effects? What if they're all *real monsters*?"

"Don't be dumb," I said.

We turned the corner into another hall.

The wolf-crab stood waiting for me there.

I didn't even have time to scream.

He opened his toothy jaws in a long wolf howl—and wrapped two giant red claws around my waist.

I opened my mouth to scream, but only a squeak came out.

I heard people laughing.

The big claws slid off my waist. Plastic claws.

I saw two dark eyes staring out at me from behind the wolf mask. I should have known that it was a man in a costume. But I didn't expect him to be standing there.

I was surprised, that's all.

I blinked at a white flash of light. A man had just taken a picture of the creature. I saw a big red and yellow sign against the wall: SEE THE MOVIE — THEN PLAY THE GAME ON CD-ROM.

"Sorry if I scared you," the man inside the wolf-crab costume said softly.

"She scares easily!" Marty declared.

I gave Marty a hard shove, and we hurried away. I turned back to see the creature waving a claw at me. "We've got to go upstairs and see my dad," I told Marty.

"Tell me something I *don't* know."

He thinks he's so funny.

Dad's office is upstairs from the cinema, on the twenty-ninth floor. We jogged to the lifts at the end of the hall and took one up.

Dad has a really cool job. He builds theme parks. And he designs all kinds of rides.

Dad was one of the designers of Prehistoric Park. That's the big theme park where you go back to prehistoric times. It has all kinds of brilliant rides and shows—and dozens of huge dinosaur robots wandering around.

And Dad worked on the Fantasy Films Studio Tour. Everyone who comes to Hollywood goes on that tour.

Dad's idea was the part where you walk through a huge movie screen and find yourself in a world of movie characters. You can star in any kind of movie you want to be in!

I know it sounds as if I'm bragging, but Dad is really smart, and he's an engineering genius! I think he is the world expert on robots. He can build robots that will do anything! And he uses them in all his parks and studio tours.

Marty and I stepped off the lift on the twenty-ninth floor. We waved to the woman at the front desk. Then we hurried to Dad's office at the end of the hall.

It looks more like a playroom than an office. It's a big room. Huge, really. Filled with toys, and stuffed cartoon characters, movie posters and models of monsters.

Marty and I love to roam around the office, staring at all the cool stuff. On the walls, Dad has great posters from a dozen different movies. On a long table, he has a model of The Tumbler, the upside-down roller coaster he designed. The model has little cars that really screech around the tracks.

And he has a lot of cool stuff from *Shock Street*—like one of the original furry paws that Wolf Girl wore in *Nightmare on Shock Street*. He keeps it in a glass case on the windowsill.

He has models of tramcars and little trains and planes and rockets. Even a big, silver plastic airship. It's radio-controlled, and he can make it float round and round his office.

What a great place! I always think of Dad's office as the happiest place in the world.

But today, as Marty and I stepped inside, Dad didn't look too happy. He hunched over his desk with the telephone to his ear. His head was lowered, his eyes down. He kept a hand pressed against his forehead as he mumbled into the phone.

Dad and I don't look at all alike. I'm short and dark. He's tall and thin. And he has blond hair, although there's not much of it left. He's quite bald.

He has the kind of skin that turns red easily.

His cheeks go really pink when he talks. And he wears big, round glasses with dark frames that hide his brown eyes.

Marty and I stopped at the doorway. I don't think Dad saw us. He stared down at the desk. He had his tie pulled down and his shirt collar open.

He muttered for a short while longer. Marty and I crept into the office.

Finally, Dad set down the phone. He raised his eyes and saw us. "Oh, hi, you two," he said softly. His cheeks turned bright pink.

"Dad—what's wrong?" I asked.

He sighed. Then he pulled off his glasses and pinched the bridge of his nose. "I have very bad news, Erin. Very bad news."

"Dad—what is it? *What?*" I cried.

Then I saw the grin slowly spread across his face. I knew I'd been tricked again.

"Gotcha!" he declared. His brown eyes flashed gleefully. His cheeks were bright pink. "Gotcha again. You fall for that gag every time."

"Dad—!" I let out an angry cry. Then I rushed up to the desk, wrapped my hands around his neck and pretended to strangle him.

We both collapsed against each other, laughing. Marty still stood in the doorway, shaking his head. "Mr Wright, that was so lame," he muttered.

Dad struggled to slip his glasses back on. "I'm sorry. You kids are just too easy to fool. I couldn't resist." He smiled at me. "Actually, I've got *good* news."

"Good news? Is this another joke?" I demanded suspiciously.

He shook his head. He picked up something

from his desk. "Check this out, guys. Do you know what this is?" He held it in his palm.

Marty and I came closer to examine it. It was a little, white plastic vehicle with four wheels. "Some kind of train carriage?" I guessed.

"It's a tram," Dad explained. "See? People sit on long benches inside it. Here. It's motor-driven." He pointed to the front of the model to show where the engine went. "But do you know *where* this tram will be used?"

"Dad, we give up. Just *tell* us," I insisted impatiently. "Stop keeping us in suspense."

"Okay, okay." His cheeks reddened. His smile grew wider. "This is a model of the tram that will be used at the Shocker Studio Tour."

My mouth dropped open. "Do you mean the tour is finally going to open?" I knew that Dad had been working on it for years.

Dad nodded. "Yes. We're finally about to open it to the public. But before we do, I want you two to test it out."

"Huh? You *mean* it?" I shrieked. I was so excited, I felt as if I'd burst out of my skin!

I turned to Marty. He was leaping up and down, shooting both fists into the air. "Yes! Yes! Yes!"

"I built this whole tour," Dad said, "and I want you two to be the first kids in the world to go on it. I want to know your opinion. What you like and what you don't like."

"Yes! Yes! Yes!" Marty kept leaping into the air. I thought I might have to tie a rope around his waist and hold on to it to keep him from floating away!

"Dad—the *Shock Street* movies are the *best*!" I cried. "This is awesome!" And then I added, "Is the tour very scary?"

Dad rested a hand on my shoulder. "I hope so," he replied. "I tried to make it as scary and real as I could. You get on the tram and you ride through the whole movie studio. You get to meet all of the characters from the horror movies. And then the tram takes you on a slow ride down Shock Street."

"The *real* Shock Street?" Marty cried. "Do you mean it? You get to ride down the real street where they make the movies?"

Dad nodded. "Yes. The real Shock Street."

"Yes! Yes! Yes!" Marty started pumping his fists in the air again, shouting like a maniac.

"Awesome!" I cried. "Totally awesome!" I was as excited as Marty.

Suddenly Marty stopped leaping. His expression turned serious. "Maybe Erin shouldn't go," he told my dad. "She gets too scared."

"Huh?" I cried.

"She was so scared during the movie sneak preview, I had to hold her hand," Marty told Dad.

What a liar!

"Give me a break!" I cried angrily. "If anyone was a scaredy-cat wimp, it was you, Marty!"

Dad raised both hands to signal *halt*. "Calm down, guys," he said softly. "No arguing. You have to keep together. You know, you two will be the *only* ones on the tour tomorrow. The only ones."

"Yes!" Marty cheered happily. "Yes! Yes!"

"Wow! That's great!" I cried. "It's totally great. It's going to be the *best*!" Then I had an idea. "Can Mum come too? I bet she would really enjoy it."

"Excuse me?" Dad squinted at me through his glasses. His whole face turned bright red. "What did you say?"

"I asked if Mum could come too," I repeated.

Dad kept staring at me for a long time, studying me. "Are you feeling okay, Erin?" he asked finally.

"Yes. Fine," I replied meekly.

I suddenly felt very confused and upset. What had I done wrong?

Was something wrong with Mum?

Why was Dad staring at me like that?

Dad came around the desk and put an arm around my shoulder. "I think you and Marty will have a better time if you go by yourselves," he said softly. "Don't you agree?"

I nodded. "Yeah. I guess."

I still wondered why he was staring at me so suspiciously. But I decided not to ask him. I didn't want him to get angry or something and change his mind about us going on the tour.

"Do you mean you're not coming with us?" Marty asked Dad. "We're really going by ourselves?"

"I want you to go by yourselves," Dad replied. "I think that will make it more exciting for you."

Marty grinned at me. "I hope it's really scary!" he declared.

"Don't worry," Dad replied. A strange smile spread over his face. "You won't be disappointed."

The next afternoon, a grey haze hung in the

air as Dad drove Marty and me to Shocker Studios. I sat up front with Dad, peering out of the car window at the smog. "It's so gloomy out," I murmured.

"Perfect for a horror movie tour," Marty chimed in from the backseat. He was so excited, he could barely sit still. He kept bouncing his legs up and down and tapping his hands on the leather seat.

I had never seen Marty so crazed. If he didn't have his seat-belt to hold him down, he'd probably bounce right out of the car!

The car climbed up the Hollywood hills. The narrow road curved past redwood houses and tree-filled gardens cut into the sides of the hills.

As we climbed, the sky turned even darker. We're driving up into a cloud of fog, I thought. Far in the distance, I could see the HOLLY-WOOD sign, stretching in the haze across a dark peak.

"Hope it doesn't rain," I muttered, watching the fog roll over the sign.

Dad chuckled. "You know it *never* rains in Los Angeles!"

"Which monsters are we going to see?" Marty asked, bouncing in the backseat. "Is Shockro on the tour? Do we really get to walk on Shock Street?"

Dad squinted hard through his glasses, turning the wheel as the road curved and twisted.

"I'm not telling," he replied. "I don't want to spoil it for you. I want it all to be a surprise."

"I just wanted to know so I could warn Erin," Marty said. "I don't want her to get too scared. She might faint or something." He laughed.

I let out an angry growl. Then I turned around and tried to punch him. But I couldn't reach.

Marty leaned forward and messed up my hair with both hands. "Get off me!" I screamed. "I'm warning you —!"

"Take it easy, guys," Dad said softly. "We're here."

I turned and stared out of the windscreen. The road had flattened out. Up ahead, an enormous sign proclaimed SHOCKER STUDIOS in scary, blood-red letters.

We drove slowly up to the huge iron gates in the front. The gates were closed. A guard in a small black booth sat reading a newspaper. I glimpsed gold script letters above the gate. They spelled out one word: BEWARE.

Dad pulled right up to the gate, and the guard peered up. He gave Dad a big smile. Then he pressed a button, and the gates slowly swung open. Dad drove the car into the tall white multistorey car park beside the studio. He parked in the first space next to the entrance. The car park seemed to stretch on for ever. But I could see only three or four other cars inside.

"When we open next week, this car park will

be jammed!" Dad said. "There will be thousands of people here. I hope."

"And today, we're the only ones!" Marty cried excitedly, jumping out of the car.

"We're so lucky!" I agreed.

A few minutes later, we were standing on the platform outside the main building, facing a wide street, waiting for the tram to take us on the tour. The street led to dozens of white studio buildings, spread out all the way down the hill.

Dad pointed to two enormous buildings as big as aeroplane hangars. "Those are the soundstages," he explained. "They film a lot of movie scenes inside those buildings."

"Does the tour go inside them?" Marty demanded. "Where is Shock Street? Where are the monsters? Are they making a movie now? Can we watch them making it?"

"Whoa!" Dad cried. He placed his hands on Marty's shoulders as if to keep him from flying off the ground. I had never seen Marty so totally wired! "Take it easy, fella," Dad warned. "You'll blow a fuse! You won't survive the tour!"

I shook my head. "Maybe we should put him on a leash," I told Dad.

"Arf, arf!" Marty barked. Then he snapped his teeth at me, trying to bite me.

I shivered. The fog rolled in from the hills. The air felt damp and cold. The sky darkened.

Two men in business suits came zooming

along the street in a golf cart. They were both talking at once. One of them waved to Dad.

"Can we ride in one of those carts?" Marty asked. "Can Erin and I each have our own cart?"

"No way," Dad told him. "You have to take the automated tram. And remember—stay in the tram. No matter what."

"You mean we can't walk on Shock Street?" Marty whined.

Dad shook his head. "Not allowed. You have to stay in the tram."

He turned to me. "I'll be waiting for you here on the platform when you get back. I want a full report. I want to know what you like and what you don't like. And don't worry if things don't work exactly right. There are still a few bugs to work out."

"Hey—here comes the tram!" Marty cried, hopping up and down and pointing.

The tram came rolling silently around the corner. I counted six carriages in all. They were shaped like roller-coaster cars, open on top— only much longer and wider. The carriages were black. A grinning white skull was painted on the front of the first car.

A young, red-haired woman wearing a black uniform was seated on the first bench in the front car. She waved to us as the tram rolled up to the platform. She was the only passenger.

She hopped out as the tram stopped. "Hi, I'm

146

Linda. I'm your tour guide." She smiled at my dad. Her red hair fluttered in the wind.

"Hello, Linda," Dad said, smiling back at her. He gently shoved Marty and me forward. "Here are your first two victims."

Linda laughed and asked us our names. We told her.

"Can we ride in front?" Marty asked eagerly.

"Yes, of course," Linda replied. "You can sit anywhere you want. This whole ride is just for you."

"All right!" Marty cried. He slapped me a high five.

Dad laughed. "I think Marty is ready to begin," he told Linda.

Linda pushed her red hair out of her face. "You can start right away, guys. But first, there's something I have to do."

She leaned over the tramcar and tugged out a black canvas bag. "This will only take a second, guys." She pulled a red plastic gun from the bag. "This is a Shocker Stun Ray Blaster."

She gripped the plastic pistol tightly. It looked like something in a *Star Trek* movie. Her smile faded. Her green eyes narrowed. "Be careful with these blasters, guys. They can freeze a monster in its tracks from twenty feet."

She handed the blaster to me. Then she reached into her bag to get one for Marty. "Don't fire them unless you have to." She swallowed

147

hard and bit her lower lip. "I sure hope you don't have to."

I laughed. "You're kidding—right? These are just toys—right?"

She didn't answer. She pulled another blaster from her bag and started to bring it to Marty.

But she stumbled over a cord on the platform. "Ohh!" She let out a startled cry as the blaster went off in her hand.

A loud buzz. A bright ray of yellow light.

And Linda stood frozen on the platform.

"Linda! Linda!" I screamed.

Marty's mouth dropped open. He let out a choked gurgle.

I turned to Dad. To my surprise, he was laughing.

"Dad—she's—she's frozen!" I cried. But when I turned back to Linda, she had a big smile on her face, too.

It took us both a while, but we soon realized the whole thing was a joke.

"That's the first shock on the *Shocker* tour," Linda announced, lowering the red blaster. She put a hand on Marty's shoulder. "I think I really shocked *you*, Marty!"

"No way!" Marty insisted. "I knew it was a joke. I just played along."

"Come on, Marty!" I cried, rolling my eyes. "You nearly dropped your teeth!"

"Erin, I *wasn't* scared," Marty insisted sharply. "Really. I just went along with the joke.

Do you really think I'd fall for a stupid plastic blaster gun?"

Marty is such a jerk. Why can't he ever admit it when he's scared?

"Climb in, you two," Dad urged. "Let's get this show on the road."

Marty and I climbed into the front seat of the tram. I looked for a seat-belt or a safety bar, but there wasn't one. "Are you coming with us?" I asked Linda.

She shook her head. "No. You're on your own. The tram moves automatically." She handed Marty his Stun Blaster. "Hope you don't need it."

"Yeah. Sure," Marty muttered, rolling his eyes. "This gun is so babyish."

"Remember—I'll meet you back here at the end of the ride," Dad said. He waved. "Enjoy it. I want a full report."

"Don't get out of the tram," Linda reminded us. "Keep your head and arms inside. And don't stand up while the tram is moving."

She stepped on a blue button on the platform. The tram started up with a jolt. Marty and I were thrown back against the seat. Then the tram rolled smoothly forward.

"First stop is The Haunted House of Horror!" Linda called after us. "Good luck!"

I turned back to see her waving to us, her long red hair fluttering in the wind. A strong breeze blew against us as the tram made its way down the hill. The sky was nearly as dark as night. Some of the white studio buildings were hidden by the fog.

"Stupid gun," Marty muttered, rolling it around in his hands. "Why do we need this plastic gun? I hope the whole tour isn't this babyish."

"I hope you don't complain all afternoon," I told him, frowning. "Do you realize how awesome this is? We're going to see all the great creatures from the *Shocker* movies."

"Think we'll see Shockro?" he asked. Shockro is his favourite. I guess because he's so incredibly disgusting.

"Probably," I replied, my eyes on the low buildings we were passing. They all stood dark and empty.

"I want to see Wolf Boy and Wolf Girl," Marty said, counting the monsters off on his fingers. "And . . . the Piranha People, and Captain Sick, The Great Gopher Mutant, and—"

"Wow! Look!" I cried, pounding his shoulder and pointing.

As the tram turned a sharp corner, The Haunted House of Horror loomed darkly in front of us. The roof and its tall stone turrets were hidden by fog. The rest of the mansion stood grey against the dusky sky.

The tram took us nearer. Tall weeds choked the front lawn. The weeds bent and swayed in

151

the wind. The grey shingles on the house were chipped and peeling. Pale green light, dim, eerie light, floated out from the tall window in front.

As we rode closer, I could see a rusty iron porch swing—swinging by itself!—on a broken, rotting porch.

"Cool!" I exclaimed.

"It looks a lot smaller than in the movie," Marty grumbled.

"It's exactly the same house!" I cried.

"Then why does it look so much smaller?" he demanded.

What a moaner.

I turned away from him and studied The Haunted House. An iron fence surrounded the place. As we moved around to the side, the rusty gate swung open, squeaking and creaking.

"Look!" I pointed to the dark windows on the second floor. The shutters all flew open at once, then banged shut again.

Lights came on in the windows. Through the window shades, I could see the silhouettes of skeletons hanging, swinging slowly back and forth.

"That's kind of cool," Marty said. "But not too scary." He raised his plastic gun and pretended to shoot at the skeletons.

We circled The Haunted House of Horrors once. We could hear screams of terror from inside. The shutters banged again and again.

The porch swing continued to creak back and forth, back and forth, as if taken by a ghost.

"Are we going inside or not?" Marty demanded impatiently.

"Sit back and stop complaining," I said sharply. "The ride just started. Don't spoil it for me, okay?"

He stuck his tongue out at me. But he settled back against the seat. We heard a long howl, and then a shrill scream of horror.

The tram made its way silently to the back of the house. A gate swung open and we rolled through it. We moved quickly through the over-grown, weed-choked backyard.

The tram picked up speed. We bounced over the lawn. Up to the back door. A wooden sign above the door read: ABANDON ALL HOPE.

We're going to crash right into the door! I thought. I ducked and raised my hands to shield myself.

But the door creaked open, and we burst inside.

The tram slowed. I lowered my hands and sat up. We were in a dark, dust-covered kitchen. An invisible ghost cackled, an evil laugh. Battered pots and pans covered the wall. As we passed, they clattered to the floor.

The oven door opened and closed by itself. The teapot on the stove started to whistle. Dishes on the shelves rattled. The cackling grew louder.

"This is pretty creepy," I whispered.

"Ooh. Thrills and chills!" Marty replied sarcastically. He crossed his arms in front of him. "Bor-ring!"

"Marty—give me a break." I shoved him away. "You can be a bad sport if you want. But don't ruin it for me."

That seemed to get to him. He muttered, "Sorry," and slid back up next to me.

The tram moved out of the dark kitchen, into an even darker hallway. Paintings of goblins and ugly creatures hung on the hallway walls.

As we approached a closet door, it sprang open—and a shrieking skeleton popped out in front of us, its jaws open, its arms jutting out to grab us.

I screamed. Marty laughed.

The skeleton snapped back into the closet. The tram turned a corner. I saw flickering light up ahead.

We rode into a large, round room. "It's the living room," I whispered to Marty. I raised my eyes to the flickering light and saw a chandelier above our heads, with a dozen burning candles.

The tram stopped beneath it. The chandelier began to shake. Then, with a hiss, the candles all flickered out at once.

The room plunged into darkness.

Then a deep laugh echoed all around us.

I gasped.

"Welcome to my humble home!" a deep voice suddenly boomed.

"Who is that?" I whispered to Marty. "Where is it coming from?"

No reply.

"Hey—Marty?"

I turned to him. "Marty—?"

He was gone.

"Marty?"

My breath caught in my throat. I froze, staring into the darkness.

Where did he go? I asked myself. He knows we aren't supposed to leave the tram. Did he climb out?

No.

If he had, I would have heard him.

"Marty?"

Someone grabbed my arm.

I heard a soft laugh. Marty's laugh.

"Hey—where are you? I can't see you!" I cried.

"I can't see you, either," he replied. "But I didn't move. I'm still sitting right next to you."

"Huh?" I reached out and felt the sleeve of his shirt.

"This is cool!" Marty declared. "I'm waving my arms, but I can't see a thing. You really can't see me?"

"No," I replied. "I thought — "

"It's some kind of trick with the lights," he said. "Black light or something. Some kind of neat movie special effect."

"Well, it creeped me out," I confessed. "I really thought you'd disappeared."

"Sucker," he sneered.

And then we both jumped.

A fire suddenly blazed in the big brick fireplace. Bright orange light filled the room. A big black armchair spun around to reveal a grinning skeleton.

The skeleton raised its bony yellowed head. The jaws moved. *"I hope you like my house,"* its voice boomed. *"Because you will never leave!"*

It tossed back its head and let out an evil cackle.

The tram jolted to a start. We rumbled out of the living room. Into a long, dark hallway. The skeleton's laugh followed us into the hall.

I fell back against the seat as we picked up speed.

We whirred around a corner. Down another long hall, so dark I couldn't see the walls.

Faster. Faster.

We whipped around another corner. Made another sharp turn.

We were climbing now. And then we took a sharp dip that made both of us throw up our hands and scream.

Around another sharp turn. Up, up, up. And then we came crashing down.

A wild roller-coaster ride in total darkness.

It was awesome. Even better because we didn't expect it. Marty and I screamed our heads off. We bumped hard against each other as the tram whirled around in the black halls of The Haunted House of Horrors. Up, up, again — then we tilted sharply down.

I hung on to the front of the car for dear life. I gripped it so hard, both hands ached. There was no seat-belt, no safety bar.

What if we tumbled out? I wondered.

The car tilted sharply sideways, as if reading my frightened thoughts. I let out a shriek and lost my grip. I slid against the side of the car. Marty fell on top of me.

I frantically reached out for something to hold on to.

The car tilted back level. I took a deep breath and slid back into place on the long seat.

"Whoa! That was *excellent*!" Marty cried, laughing. "Excellent!"

Gripping the front of the car, I took another deep breath and held it. I was trying to slow my racing heart.

A door swung open in front of us, and we burst through it.

The car bounced hard. I saw trees. The grey-fogged sky.

We were back outside. Racing through the backyard. Both of us were tossed from side to side as we roared over the weeds, zigzagging through the dark trees.

"Whoa! Stop!" I choked out. I couldn't catch my breath. The wind blew hard against my face. The tram clattered and squealed as we bumped over the rough ground.

We were out of control. Something had definitely gone wrong with the tram.

Bouncing hard on the plastic seat, holding on tightly, I searched for someone who could help us.

No one in sight.

We bumped on to the road. The tram started to slow. I turned to Marty. His hair was blown over his face. His mouth hung open. His eyes rolled around in his head. He was totally dazed.

The tram slowed, slowed, slowed, until we were creeping smoothly along.

"That was *great*!" Marty declared. He smoothed back his hair with both hands and grinned at me. I knew he had been scared, too. But he was pretending that he'd enjoyed the crazy, wild ride.

"Yeah. Great." I tried to pretend, too. But my voice came out weak and shaky.

"I'm going to tell your dad that the roller-coaster ride through the halls was the *best*!" Marty declared.

"It was kind of fun," I agreed. "And kind of scary."

Marty turned away from me. "Hey. Where are we?"

The tram had come to a stop. I pulled myself up and peered around. We had parked between two rows of tall evergreen bushes. The bushes were slender, shaped like spears reaching up to the sky.

Above us, the afternoon sun was trying to break through the fog. Rays of pale light beamed down from the grey sky. The tall, thin shadows of the bushes fell over our tram car.

Marty stood up and turned to the back of the tram. "There's nothing around here," he said. "We're in the middle of nowhere. Why did we stop?"

"Do you think —?" I started. But I stopped talking when I saw the bush move.

It wiggled. Then the bush next to it wiggled, too.

"Marty —" I whispered, tugging his sleeve. I saw two glowing red circles behind the bush. Two glowing red *eyes*!

"Marty — there's someone there."

Another pair of eyes. And then another pair of eyes. Staring out at us from behind the evergreen bushes.

And then two dark claws.

And then rustling sounds. The bush tilted as

a dark figure leaped out. Followed by another.

Snarling, growling.

I gasped. Too late to run.

We were surrounded by ugly creatures. Snuffling, wheezing creatures, who staggered out from the bushes. Reaching out, reaching out for us, they began to climb into the tram.

Marty and I jumped to our feet.

"Ohhhhhh." I heard Marty let out a frightened moan.

I started to back away. I thought maybe I could scramble out of the other side of the car.

But the snarling, growling monsters came at us from both sides.

"L-leave us alone!" I stammered.

A monster covered in tangled brown fur opened his jaws to reveal long, jagged rows of yellow teeth. His hot breath exploded in my face. He stepped closer. Then he swiped at me with a fat paw and uttered a menacing roar. "Would you like an autograph?" he growled.

I gaped at him, my mouth hanging down to my knees. "Huh?"

"Autographed photo?" he asked. He raised his furry paw again. He held a black-and-white snapshot in it.

"Hey—you're Ape Face!" Marty cried, pointing.

The hairy creature nodded his head. He raised the photo to Marty. "Want a photo? This is the autographing part of the tour."

"Yeah! Okay," Marty replied.

The big ape pulled a marker from behind his ear and bent to sign the photo for Marty.

Now that my heartbeat was returning to normal, I began to recognize some of the other creatures. The guy covered in purple slime was The Toxic Wild Man. And I recognized Sweet Sue, the walking-talking baby doll with real hair you can brush. Sweet Sue was really a mutant murderer from Mars.

The frog-faced guy covered from head to toe with purple and brown warts was The Fabulous Frog, also known as The Toadinator. He starred in *Pond Scum* and *Pond Scum II*, two of the scariest movies ever made.

"Frog—can I have your autograph?" I asked.

"Grrrbbit. Grrbit." He croaked and slipped a pen into his wart-covered hand. I leaned forward eagerly and watched him sign his photo. It was hard for him to write. The pen kept slipping in his slimy frog hands.

Marty and I collected a lot of autographs. Then the creatures went snarling and wheezing back into the bushes.

When they were gone, we both burst out laughing. "That was so dumb!" I cried. "When I saw them creeping out from behind the bushes,

I thought I'd have a cow!" I glanced back at the photos. "But it's kind of cool to get their autographs."

Marty made a disgusted face. "It's just a bunch of actors in costumes," he sneered. "It's for babies."

"But—but—they looked so real," I stammered. "It didn't look as if they were wearing fancy dress costumes—did it? I mean, The Toadinator's hands were really slimy. And Ape Face's fur was so real. The masks were awesome. I couldn't tell they were masks."

I brushed the hair out of my eyes. "How do they get into those costumes? I didn't see any buttons or zippers, or anything!"

"That's because they're movie costumes," Marty explained. "They're better than normal costumes."

Mr Know-It-All.

The tram started to back out. I settled down into the seat. I watched the two rows of evergreen bushes fade into the distance.

Down the long, sloping hill, I could see the white studio buildings. I wondered if they were making a movie on one of the soundstages. I wondered if the tram would take us to watch them shoot.

I could see two golf carts moving along the road. They were carrying people down to the soundstage buildings.

The sun still struggled to shine through the fog. The tram bounced over the grass, up the hill.

"Whoa!" I cried out as we turned sharply and headed back towards the trees.

"Please remain in the car at all times." A woman's voice burst from a speaker in the tram car. "Your next stop will be The Cave of The Living Creeps."

"'The Cave of The Living Creeps?' Wow! That sounds scary!" Marty exclaimed.

"Sure does!" I agreed.

We had no idea just how scary it would turn out to be.

The tram zigzagged its way through the trees. Their shadows rolled over us like dark ghosts.

We moved so silently. I tried to imagine what the ride would be like if the tram was packed with excited kids and adults. I decided it would be a lot less scary with a crowd.

But I wasn't complaining. Marty and I were really lucky to be the first kids ever to try out this ride.

"Wow!" Marty grabbed my arm as The Cave of The Living Creeps loomed in front of us. The mouth of the cave was a huge dark hole, cut into the side of the hill. I could see pale, silvery light flickering past the entrance.

The tram slowed down as we approached the dark opening. A sign above the entrance had one word carved roughly into it: FAREWELL.

The tramcar lurched forward. "Hey—!" I cried out and ducked my head. What a tight squeeze!

Into the dim, flickering light.

The air instantly grew colder. And damp. A sour, earthy smell rose to my nostrils, making me gasp.

"Bats!" Marty whispered. "What do you think, Erin? Think there are bats in here?" He leaned close and let out an evil laugh in my ear.

Marty *knows* that I hate bats!

I know, I know. Bats aren't really evil creatures. And they aren't dangerous. Bats eat mosquitoes and other insects. And they don't attack people or get tangled in your hair or try to suck your blood. That's only in the movies.

I know all that. But I don't care.

Bats are ugly and creepy and disgusting. And I hate them.

One day, I told Marty how much I hate bats. And so he's been teasing me about them ever since.

The tram moved deeper into the cave. The air grew colder. The sour aroma nearly choked me.

"Look — over there!" Marty screamed. "A vampire bat!"

"Huh? Where?" I couldn't help myself. I cried out in alarm.

Of course it was one of Marty's dumb jokes. He laughed like a maniac.

I growled at him and punched him hard on the shoulder. "You're not funny. You're just dumb."

That made him giggle even harder. "I'll bet there *are* bats in this cave," he insisted. "You can't go into a deep, dark cave like this one without seeing bats."

I turned away from his grinning face and listened hard. I was listening for fluttering bat wings. I didn't hear any.

The cave narrowed. The walls seemed to close in on us. The side of the car scraped against the dirt wall. I could feel that we were heading down.

In the dim, silvery light, I saw a long row of pointy icicle-type things hanging down from the cave ceiling. I know they have a name, but I can never remember which one it is—stalagmites or stalactites.

I ducked my head again as the tram shot under them. Up close, they looked like pointed elephant tusks.

"We're getting closer to the bats!" Marty teased.

I ignored him. I kept my eyes straight ahead. The cave grew wide again. Dark shadows shifted and danced over the walls as we rolled past.

"Ohhh." I uttered a groan as I felt something cold and slimy drop on to the back of my neck.

I jerked away and turned sharply to Marty. "Cut it out!" I snapped. "Get your cold hands off me!"

"Who—me?"

He wasn't touching me. Both of his hands gripped the front of the car.

Then *what* was on the back of my neck? So cold and wet. Icy wet. I shuddered. My whole body shook.

"M-Marty!" I stammered. "H-Help!"

Marty stared at me, confused. "Erin — what's your problem?"

"The back of my neck — " I choked out.

I could feel the cold, wet thing start to move. I decided not to wait for Marty to help me.

I reached back and pulled it off. It felt sticky and cold between my fingers. It slithered and wriggled, and I dropped it on the seat.

A worm!

A huge, long white worm. So cold, so wet and cold.

"Weird!" Marty exclaimed. He leaned close to examine it. "I've never seen a worm that big! And it's white."

"It — it dropped from the ceiling," I said, watching it wiggle next to me. "It's ice-cold."

"Huh? Let me touch it," Marty said. He raised his hand and slowly lowered his index finger to the worm.

His finger poked the worm in its middle.

And then Marty opened his mouth in a scream of horror that echoed through the cave.

"What is it? Marty—what's *wrong*?" I shrieked.

"I—I—I—" He couldn't speak. He could only utter, "I—I—I—!" His eyes bulged. His tongue flopped out.

He reached up and pulled a white worm off the top of his head. "I—I—I got one too!"

"Yuck!" I cried. His worm was nearly as long as a shoelace!

We both tossed our worms out of the tram.

But then I felt a soft, damp *plop* on my shoulder. And then a cold *plop* on top of my head. Another on my forehead, like a cold slap.

"Ohhh—help!" I moaned. I started thrashing my arms, grabbing at the worms, struggling to pull them off me.

"Marty—please!" I turned to him for help.

But he was battling them, too. Twisting and ducking. Trying to dodge, as more and more white worms fell from the ceiling.

I saw one fall on his shoulder. I saw another one begin to wrap itself around his ear.

As fast as I could, I pulled the sticky, wet creatures off me and tossed them over the side of the slow-rolling tram.

Where are they coming from? I wondered.

I glanced up — and a fat, wet one fell over my eyes.

"Yeowwww!" I let out a shriek, grabbed it, flung it away.

The tram turned sharply, sending us both sliding over the seat. The cave narrowed again as we entered a different tunnel. The silvery light glowed dimly around us as we bounced forward.

Two white worms, each at least a foot long, wriggled across my lap. I tugged them off and heaved them over the tram.

Breathing hard, I searched for more. My whole body itched. The back of my neck tingled. I couldn't stop shaking.

"They've stopped falling," Marty announced in a shaky voice.

Then why did I still itch?

I rubbed the back of my neck. Stood up and searched the seat, then the floor. I found one last worm, climbing over my shoe. I kicked it away, then dropped back on to the seat with a loud sigh.

"That was totally gross!" I wailed.

Marty scratched his chest, then rubbed his face with both hands. "I guess that's why they call it The Cave of The Living Creeps," he said. He swept a hand back through his black hair.

I shivered. I couldn't stop itching. I knew the worms were gone, but I could still feel them. "Those disgusting white worms — do you think they were alive?"

Marty shook his head. "Of course not. They were fakes." He sniggered. "I guess they fooled you, huh?"

"They sure felt real," I replied. "And the way they wriggled around — "

"They were robots or something," Marty said, scratching his knees. "Everything here is fake. It has to be."

"I'm not so sure," I said, my whole body still itchy and tingling.

"Well, just ask your father," Marty replied grumpily.

I had to laugh. I knew why Marty was suddenly so grouchy. Whether the worms were real or fake, they had scared him. And he knew that I knew that he had been frightened.

"I don't think *little* kids will like the worms," Marty said. "I think they'll get too scared. I'm going to tell that to your dad."

I started to reply — and felt something drop over me. Something scratchy and dry.

It covered my face, my shoulders — my entire body.

I shot both hands up and tried to push it away. It's some kind of a net, I thought.

I grabbed at it, desperate to get it off my face. As I struggled, I turned and saw Marty squirming and batting his arms, caught under the same net.

The tram bounced through the dim cave tunnel. The sticky net felt like cotton candy on my skin.

Marty let out a yelp. "It — it's a big spider's web!" he stammered.

I tugged and grabbed and pulled. But the sticky threads clung to my face, my arms, and my clothes. "Yuck! This is so gross!" I choked out.

And then I saw the black dots scurrying through the net. It took me a few seconds to realize what they were. Spiders! Hundreds of them!

"Ohhhh." A low moan escaped my throat.

I batted the spider's web with both hands. I rubbed my cheeks frantically, trying to scrape away the sticky threads. I pulled a spider off my forehead. Another one off the shoulder of my T-shirt.

"The spiders — they're in my hair!" Marty wailed.

He suddenly forgot about acting cool. He

began raking his hair with both hands, slapping himself in the head, pinching and swiping at the spiders.

As the tram rolled silently on, we both twisted and squirmed, struggling to flick away the black spiders. I pulled three of them out of my hair. Then I felt one climb into my nose!

I opened my mouth in a horrified scream — and *sneezed* it out.

Marty plucked a spider off my neck and sent it soaring through the air. The last spider. I couldn't see — or feel — any more.

We both dropped down in the seat, breathing hard. My heart pounded in my chest. "Still think everything is fake?" I asked Marty, my voice weak and small.

"I — I don't know," he replied softly. "The spiders could be puppets maybe. You know. Radio-controlled."

"They were *real*!" I cried sharply. "Face it, Marty — they were real! This is The Cave of The Living Creeps — and they were *living*!"

Marty's eyes grew wide. "You really think so?"

I nodded. "They had to be real spiders."

A smile spread over Marty's face. "That's so *cool*!" he declared. "Real spiders! That is totally cool!"

I let out a long sigh and slumped lower in the seat. I didn't think it was cool at all. I thought it was creepy and disgusting.

These rides are supposed to be *fake*. That's what makes them fun. I decided to tell my dad that the worms and spiders were too scary. He should get rid of them before the studio tour opens to the public.

I crossed my arms in front of me and kept my eyes straight ahead. I wondered what we would run into next. I hoped there weren't any other disgusting insects waiting to fall on us and climb all over our faces and bodies.

"I think I hear the bats!" Marty teased. He leaned close to me, grinning. "Hear those fluttering sounds? Giant vampire bats!"

I shoved him back to his side of the seat. I wasn't in any mood for his joking around.

"When do we get out of this cave?" I asked impatiently. "This isn't any fun."

"I think it's cool," Marty repeated. "I like exploring caves."

The narrow tunnel opened into a wide cavern. The ceiling appeared to be a mile high. There were giant rocks scattered over the cavern floor. Rocks piled on rocks. Rocks everywhere.

Somewhere ahead of us, I heard water dripping. *Plunk plunk plunk.*

Eerie green light glowed from the cave walls. The tram pulled up to the back wall—and then stopped.

"Now what?" I whispered.

Marty and I turned in our seat, letting our

eyes explore the huge cavern. All I could see were rocks. Smooth rocks, some round, some square.

Plunk plunk plunk. Water dripped somewhere to our right. The air felt cold and damp.

"This is kind of boring," Marty murmured. "When do we get going?"

I shrugged. "I don't know. Why did we stop here? It's just a big empty cave."

We waited for the tram to back up and take us out of there.

And waited.

A minute went by. Then another few minutes.

We both turned around and got up on our knees, peering to the back of the tram. Nothing moved. We listened to the steady drip of water, echoing off the high stone walls. No other sound.

Leaning forward against the back of the seat, I cupped my hands around my mouth and shouted. "Hey—can anybody hear us?"

I waited, listening. No reply.

"Can anybody hear us?" I tried again. "I think we're stuck here!"

No reply. Just the steady *drip drip drip*.

I waited, squinting hard into the glow of green light.

Why wouldn't the tram get moving? Had it broken down? Were we really stuck here?

I turned to Marty. "What's up with this tram? Do you think we're—HEY!"

I gasped as I stared at the empty seat beside me.

I reached both hands out. I grabbed for Marty.

Another lighting trick? Another optical illusion?

"Marty? Hey — Marty?" I croaked.

A cold shiver rolled down my back.

This time Marty was really gone.

"Marty —?"

A scraping sound beside the tram made me jump.

I spun around and saw Marty grinning at me from the cave floor. "Gotcha."

"You creep!" I shouted. I swung my fist, but he dodged away, laughing. *"You're* The Living Creep!" I cried. "You deliberately tried to scare me."

"It isn't too hard a job!" he shot back. His smile faded. "I climbed down to check things out."

"But the tram might start up any second!" I told him. "You know what that tour guide told us. She said we should never leave the tram."

Marty squatted down and studied the tyres. "I think the tram is stuck or something. Maybe it came off its tracks." He raised his eyes to me and shook his head fretfully. "But there *aren't* any tracks."

"Marty—get back in," I pleaded. "If it starts up and leaves you standing there—"

He grabbed the side of the car with both hands and shook it. The tram bounced on its tyres. But it didn't move.

"I think it broke down," Marty said softly. "Your father said that some things might not work."

I felt a stab of fear in my chest. "You mean we're *stranded* here? All by ourselves in this creepy cave?"

He stepped to the front of the car and squeezed between the tram and the cave wall. Then he tried to push the tram back, shoving with both hands as hard as he could.

It wouldn't budge.

"Oh, wow," I muttered, shaking my head. "This is horrible. This isn't any fun at all."

I got back up on my knees on the seat and tried shouting again, as loud as I could: "Is anybody in here? Does anybody work here? The tram is stuck!"

Plunk plunk plunk. The dripping water was my only reply.

"Can somebody *help* us?" I shouted. "Please—can somebody help?"

No answer.

"Now what?" I cried.

Marty was still shoving with all his might against the front of the tram. He gave one last hard push, then gave up with a sigh. "You'd better climb down," he said. "We have to walk."

"Huh? Walk? In this creepy dark cave? No way, Marty!"

He came around to my side of the car. "You're not afraid —*are* you, Erin?"

"Yes, I am," I confessed. "A little." I glanced around the huge cavern. "I don't see any exits. We'd have to walk back through those tunnels. With all the spiders and worms and everything."

"We can find a way out," Marty insisted. "There's got to be a door somewhere. They always build emergency exits in these theme park rides."

"I think we should stay in the tram," I said uncertainly. "If we stay here and wait, someone will come and find us."

"It could take days," Marty declared. "Come on, Erin. I'm going to walk. Are you coming with me?"

I shook my head, my arms crossed tightly in front of me. "No way," I insisted. "I'm staying here."

I knew he wouldn't go off by himself. I knew he wouldn't go unless I joined him.

"Well. Bye then," he said. He turned and started walking quickly across the cave floor.

"Hey, Marty —?"

"Bye. I'm not waiting here all day. See you later."

He was really leaving. Leaving me alone in the stalled tram, in the scary cave. "But, Marty—wait!"

He turned back to me. "Are you coming or not, Erin?" he called back impatiently.

"Okay, okay," I murmured. I saw that I had no choice. I climbed over the side of the tram and dropped to the cave floor.

The dirt was smooth and damp. I started walking slowly towards Marty.

"Hurry it up," he called. "Let's get out of here." He was walking backwards now, motioning for me to catch up with him.

But I stopped and my mouth dropped open in horror.

"Don't look at me like that!" he shouted. "Don't stare at me as if I'm doing something wrong!"

But I wasn't staring at Marty.

I was staring at the thing creeping up behind Marty.

"Uh . . . uh . . . uh . . ." I struggled to warn Marty, but only frightened grunts escaped my throat.

He kept backing up, backing right into the enormous creature.

"Erin, get a move on. What's your *problem*?" he demanded.

"Uh . . . uh . . . uh . . ." I finally managed to point.

"Huh?" Marty spun around—and saw it, too. "Whoa!" he screamed. His trainers slid on the soft cave floor as he came running back to me. "What is *that* thing?"

At first, I thought it was some kind of machine. It looked like one of those tall steel cranes you see on construction sites. All silvery and metallic.

But as it rose up on its wire-thin back legs, I saw that it was *alive*!

It had round black eyes the size of billiard balls. They spun wildly in its skinny silver skull.

Two slender antennae bobbed at the top of the head. Its mouth appeared soft, mushy. A grey tongue darted out between long, bristly whiskers.

Its long body stretched back like a folded-up leaf. As it stood, it waved its front legs, short white sticks.

The whole creature looked like some kind of gross stick figure. Its long back legs bent and sprang forward, bent then sprang forward. The thick tongue swung from side to side. The black eyes stopped whirling and focused on me.

"Is it—is it a *grasshopper*?" I choked out.

Marty and I had both backed up to the tram.

Waving its stick arms, the creature sprang closer, its antennae circling slowly on top of its head.

Marty and I pressed our backs against the cold cave wall. We couldn't move back any further.

"I think it's a praying mantis," Marty replied, staring up at it. The insect had to be at least three times as tall as us. As it moved forward, its head nearly scraped the cave ceiling.

The tongue licked its soft, mushy mouth. The mouth puckered and made loud sucking sounds. My stomach lurched. The sound was so *sick*!

The round black eyes stared down at Marty and me. The giant praying mantis, its body shin-

183

ing like aluminium, took another hopping step towards us. It started to lower its head.

"Wh-what's it going to do?" I stammered, pressing my back hard against the cave wall.

To my surprise, Marty suddenly started to laugh.

I turned to him and grabbed his shoulder. Was he totally losing it?

"Marty—are you okay?"

"Of course!" he replied. He pulled away from me and took a step towards the towering insect. "Why should we be scared, Erin? It's a big robot. It's programmed to walk up to the tram."

"Huh? But, Marty—"

"It's all on a computer," he continued, staring up as the big head bobbed lower on its stick body. "It isn't real. It's part of the ride."

I stared up at the creature. Big drops of saliva rolled off its fat tongue and hit the cave floor with a *splat*.

"It's . . . uh . . . really lifelike," I murmured.

"Your dad is a genius at this stuff!" Marty declared. "We'll have to tell him what a good job he did on the praying mantis." He laughed. "Your dad said there were still some bugs, remember? This must be one of them!"

The insect rubbed its front legs together. It made a shrill whistling sound.

I covered my ears. The high-pitched note made my ears ache!

I was still holding my ears as a second giant praying mantis hopped out from behind a tall rock.

"Look—another one!" Marty cried, pointing. He tugged my arm. "Wow. They move so smoothly. You can't even tell that they're machines."

The two silvery insects chittered at each other, a sharp shrill, metallic sound. Their black eyes twirled. Their antennae rotated rapidly, excitedly.

Gobs of saliva rolled off their tongues and splattered to the floor. The second one flashed silvery wings on its back, then quickly closed them up again.

"Great-looking robots!" Marty declared. He turned to me. "We'd better get back in the tram. It'll probably start up again now that we've seen these giant bugs."

The two insects chittered to each other. They hopped closer, their sticklike legs springing hard, bouncing off the smooth cave floor.

"I hope you're right," I told Marty. "Those insects are *too* real. I want to get out of here!"

I started to follow him to the tram.

The first mantis leaped forward quickly. It hopped between us and the tram, blocking our path.

"Hey—!" I cried.

We tried to step around it. But it took a big hop to stay in front of us.

"It—it won't let us pass!" I stammered.

"Ohhh!" I cried out as the big creature suddenly swung down and slammed its head against my chest. The powerful head-butt sent me sprawling backwards.

"Hey—stop that!" I heard Marty shout. "That machine must be broken!"

Its black eyes glowing, the mantis lowered its head again—and gave me another hard push towards the centre of the cave.

Its partner moved quickly to trap Marty. It lowered its body and prepared to head-butt Marty. But Marty quickly backed away, raising his hands in front of him like a shield. He hurried to join me.

I heard scraping sounds. Shrill chirps and chittering.

I spun around to discover two more huge, ugly mantises climbing out from behind rocks. Then two more, their antennae twisting excitedly. Their fat grey tongues rolling around their open mouths.

Marty and I huddled together in the middle of the cavern as the creatures hopped and scraped around us. Then they rose up high on their hind legs, their black eyes gleaming, their short stick arms waving.

"We—we're surrounded!" I cried.

The giant insects all began chittering at once. They scraped their front legs together excitedly. The shrill whistle rose through the cave, echoing off the stone walls.

They formed a circle around us, leaning back on their spindly hind legs. Moving closer. Tightening the circle. Their tongues whipped back and forth. Thick gobs of mantis saliva hit the floor.

"They're out of control!" Marty shrieked.

"What are they going to do to us?" I cried, covering my ears against their excited chirps and the deafening whistle.

"Maybe they are voice-controlled," Marty shouted. He tilted back his head and shouted up at them: "Stop! Stop!"

They didn't stop.

One of them tilted its silvery head, opened its ugly mouth wide, and spat out a black gob. It splattered on to Marty's trainer.

He jumped back. His trainer stuck to the floor. He struggled to tug it free. "Yuck! Watch out! That black stuff—it's like glue!" he cried.

THOOOM.

Another mantis opened its mouth wide and spat out a big black gob of sticky goo. It splotched the shoulder of my T-shirt.

"Oww!" I wailed. It was so hot—it burned me right through my shirt.

The others chittered shrilly and scraped their hairy stick arms. Their tongues darting back and forth, they began to lower their heads to us.

"The stun guns!" I cried, grabbing Marty's arm. "Maybe the guns will work against these bugs!"

"Those guns are only toys!" he wailed.

THUPPP.

Another black gob missed Marty's foot by inches.

"Besides, the guns are in the tram," Marty continued, staring up at the ugly creatures. "No way they'll let us get to the tram."

"Then what are we going to do?" I cried.

As I asked the question, an idea flashed into my mind.

"Marty—" I whispered. "How do you normally get rid of bugs?"

"Huh? Erin—what are you *talking* about?"

"You step on them—right? Don't you usually step on them?"

"But, Erin—" he protested. "These bugs are big enough to step on *us*!"

"It's worth a try!" I cried.

I raised my trainer—and stamped as hard as I could on the foot of the nearest mantis.

The giant insect let out a shrill hiss and hopped backwards.

Beside me, Marty stomped on another insect, bringing the heel of his trainer down hard on its spindly foot. That creature fell back, too, raising its head in a shrill hiss of pain. Its eyes spun wildly. Its antennae shot straight up.

I stomped down hard again. With a hoarse choking sound, the big mantis fell on to its side. All four stick legs thrashed the air.

"Let's go!" I shouted.

I turned and burst through the circle of insects. I didn't know where to run. I only knew I had to get away.

The cave erupted in hisses and shrill whistles, angry chittering and croaks. I glimpsed Marty lurching after me.

I ignored the echoing, ringing sounds and ran.

Ran to the tram.

Leaned over the side and grabbed both plastic stun guns into my arms.

Then I pushed away from the tram and hurtled along the stone cave wall.

Where could I go?

How could I escape?

The chittering and hissing grew louder, more frantic. The tall shadows of the giant insects danced on the wall as I ran. I had the feeling that the shadows could reach out and grab me.

I glanced back.

Marty came running behind me at full speed.

The mantises were hopping, scrabbling, limping across the dirt floor after us.

Where to run? Where?

And then I saw the narrow opening in the cave wall. Just a crack, really.

But I dived for it. Slipped into it. Squeezed myself into the dark hole between the stone.

And burst out the other side. Into the misty daylight.

Outside!

I could see trees tilting down the hill. The road that led down to the studio buildings.

Yes! Outside! I made it!

I felt so happy. So *safe*.

But I didn't have long to enjoy the feeling.

As I started to catch my breath, I heard Marty's terrified cry: "Erin—help! Help! They've *got* me! They're *eating* me!"

With a gasp, I spun around.

How could I help Marty? How could I get him out of the cave?

To my surprise, he was leaning against the cave wall, one elbow against the rock, his legs crossed. A big grin on his round face.

"April Fool," he said.

"YAAAIIIII!" I let out an angry scream. Then I dropped the two plastic pistols and rushed at him, ready to pound him with my fists. "You jerk! You scared me to death!"

He laughed and dodged to the side as I came at him. I swung my fist and hit air.

"Don't play any more dumb jokes like that!" I cried breathlessly. "This place is too scary! Those big insects—"

"Yeah. They were scary," he agreed, his smile fading. "They were so real! How do you think they made them spit like that?"

I shook my head. "I don't know," I muttered.

I had a heavy feeling in my stomach. I knew it was a crazy idea. But I was beginning to think these creatures we were seeing *were* real.

Maybe I've seen too many scary movies. But the big praying mantises and the white worms and all the other creatures and monsters really seemed to be alive.

They didn't move like mechanical creatures. They appeared to breathe. And their eyes focused on Marty and me as if they could really see us.

I wanted to tell Marty what I was thinking. But I knew he would only laugh at me.

He was so sure that they were all robots and that we were seeing some awesome movie special effects. Of course, that made sense. We were on a movie studio tour, after all.

I hoped Marty was right. I hoped it was all tricks. Movie magic.

My dad was a genius when it came to designing mechanical creatures and building theme park rides. And maybe that's all we were seeing. Maybe Dad had really outdone himself this time.

But the heavy feeling in my stomach wouldn't go away. I had the feeling that we were in danger. Real danger.

I had the feeling that something had gone wrong here. That something was out of control.

I suddenly wished we weren't the first two kids to try out the tour. I knew it was supposed to be a thrill to be the only ones here. But it was too quiet. Too empty. Too scary. It would be so much more fun if hundreds of other people were along with us.

I wanted to tell Marty all this. But how could I?

He was so eager to prove that he was braver than me. So eager to prove that he wasn't afraid of anything.

I couldn't tell him what I was really thinking.

I picked up the two plastic stun guns and handed him one. I didn't want to carry them both.

He tucked the barrel of his gun into his jeans pocket. "Hey, Erin—look where we are!" he cried. He jogged past me, his eyes straight ahead. "Check it out!"

He started running across the grass. I turned and started to follow him. I didn't want him to get too far ahead.

The sky had darkened. The sun had disappeared behind a heavy blanket of clouds. Wisps of grey fog hung low in the cool air. It was nearly evening.

We crossed the road and stepped into a town. I mean, it was a movie set of a town. A small town with low, one- and two-storey buildings, small shops, a country-looking general store.

Big, old houses in the block beyond the stores.

"Do you think this is a set they really use in the movies?" I asked, hurrying to catch up with Marty.

He turned to me, his dark eyes flashing with excitement. "Don't you recognize it? Don't you know where you are?"

And then my eyes fell on the crumbling, old mansion half-hidden by the twisted trees. And across from it, I saw the crooked picket fence that ran around the old cemetery.

And I knew we were on Shock Street.

"Wow!" I exclaimed, spinning around, trying to take it all in at once. "This really is Shock Street. This is where they filmed all the movies!"

"It doesn't look the way I imagined it," Marty said. "It looks even scarier!"

He was right. As the sky darkened to evening, long shadows fell over the empty buildings. The wind made a moaning sound as it swept around the corner.

Marty and I made our way down the street, trying to see *everything*. We kept crossing from side to side, peering into a dark, dust-covered shop window—then running to examine the front yard of a rundown old mansion.

"Check out that empty lot," I said, pointing. "That's where The Mad Mangler hung out. Remember? In *Shocker III?* Remember—he mangled everyone who walked by?"

"Of course I remember," Marty snapped. He stepped into the empty lot. Tall weeds bent low, blown by the moaning wind. Shadows moved against the fence at the back.

I stayed on the pavement and squinted hard, trying to see what cast the shadows.

Did The Mad Mangler still lurk back there?

The lot was totally empty. So how could there be tall, shifting shadows on the fence?

"Marty—come back," I pleaded. "It's getting dark."

He turned back. "Scared, Erin?"

"It's just an empty lot," I told him. "Let's keep walking."

"People *always* thought it was just an empty lot," Marty replied in a low, scary voice. "Until The Mad Mangler jumped out and mangled them!" He let out a long, evil laugh.

"Marty—you're losing it," I murmured, shaking my head.

He came trotting out of the lot, and we crossed the street. "I wish I had a camera," he said. "I'd really like a picture of me standing in The Mad Mangler's lot." His eyes lit up. "Or even better—!"

He didn't finish his sentence. Instead, he took off, running full speed.

"Hey—wait up!" I cried.

A few seconds later, I saw where he was heading. The old cemetery.

195

He ran up to the cracked and peeling wooden gate and turned back to me. "Even better, I'd like a photo of me standing in the cemetery. The actual set where they filmed *Cemetery on Shock Street*."

"We don't have a camera," I called from the street. "Get away from there."

He ignored me and started to open the gate. The bottom was stuck in the grass. Marty tugged hard. Finally, the gate started to pull open, creaking and groaning as it moved.

"Marty — let's go," I insisted. "It's getting late. Dad is probably waiting for us, wondering what happened to us."

"But this is part of the tour!" he insisted. He tugged the heavy gate open just wide enough to squeeze inside the cemetery.

"Marty — please! Don't go in!" I begged. I ran up beside him.

"Erin, it's just a movie set," he replied. "You didn't used to be such a total wimp!"

"I — I just have a bad feeling about this cemetery," I stammered. "A very bad feeling."

"It's part of the tour," he repeated.

"But this gate was *closed*!" I cried. "It was closed so that people don't go in." I raised my eyes to the cemetery. I saw the old gravestones tilting up from the ground like crooked teeth. "I have such a bad feeling . . ."

Marty ignored me. He tugged the gate open

a little wider and slipped into the cemetery.

"Marty—please—!" I gripped the low fence tightly with both hands and watched him.

He took three steps towards the old graves. Then his hands shot straight up in the air—and he dropped out of sight.

I stared into the darkness, blinking hard.

I swallowed. Once. Twice.

I couldn't believe that he was gone, that he had vanished so quickly.

The wind moaned between the jagged, tilting gravestones.

"Marty—?" My voice came out in a choked whisper. "Marty?"

I gripped the picket fence so hard, my hands ached. I knew I had no choice. I had to go in there and see what had happened to him.

I took a deep breath and pushed myself through the opening. The ground was soft. My trainers sank into the tall grass.

I took one step.

Then another.

I stopped when I heard Marty's voice. "Hey— be careful."

"Huh?" I gazed around. "Where are you?"

"Down here."

I peered down—into a deep, dark hole. An open grave. Marty stared up at me. He had dirt on his cheeks and down the front of his T-shirt. He raised both hands. "Help me out. I fell!"

I had to laugh. He looked ridiculous, standing in that hole, covered in dirt.

"It's not funny. Help me out," he repeated impatiently.

"I warned you," I said. "I had a bad feeling."

"It smells down here," Marty complained.

I leaned down. "What does it smell like?"

"Like dirt. Get me out!"

"Okay, okay." I grabbed his hands and tugged. He kicked his feet, digging the toes of his trainers into the soft dirt.

A few seconds later, he was back on the ground, frantically brushing himself off. "That was cool!" he declared. "Now I can tell people I was in a grave in The Shock Street Cemetery."

A chill ran down my back as the wind picked up. "Let's get out of here," I pleaded.

Something grey floated silently between two old gravestones. A wisp of fog? A grey cat?

"Check out these graves," Marty said, still brushing dirt off his jeans. "They're all cracked and faded. I can barely read the names. That's so cool. And look how they sprayed cobwebs over that row of stones. Creepy, huh?"

"Marty—can we go?" I begged again. "Dad is

probably worried by now. Maybe the tram's started up again. Maybe we can find it."

He ignored me. I watched him lean over a tombstone to read the words cut into it. "Jim Socks," he read. "Eighteen forty to eighteen eighty-seven." He laughed. "Jim Socks. Get it? And look at the ones next to it. Ben Dover. Sid Upp. These are all funny!"

I laughed. Ben Dover and Sid Upp were pretty funny.

My laugh was cut short when I heard a soft cry from the back of the graveyard. I saw another grey wisp dart behind a tombstone.

I held my breath and listened hard. The wind whistled through the tall grass.

Rising above the wind came another shrill cry.

A cat? I wondered. Is the cemetery filled with cats? Or is it a child?

Marty heard it, too. He moved down the row of stones until he stood beside me. His dark eyes glowed excitedly. "This is so cool. Did you hear the sound effects? There must be a speaker hidden in the ground."

Another shrill cry.

Definitely human. A girl?

I shivered. "Marty, I really think we should try to get back to my dad. We've been here all afternoon. And —"

"But what about the rest of the tour?" he argued. "We have to see everything!"

I heard another cry. Louder. Closer. A cry of terror.

I tried to ignore it. Marty was probably right. The cries had to be coming from a loudspeaker somewhere.

"How can we finish the tour?" I demanded. "We were supposed to stay on the tram — remember? But the tram — OHH!"

I cried out as a hand shot up from the ground in front of us. A green hand. Its long fingers unfolded, as if reaching for us.

"Whoa!" Marty cried, stumbling back.

Another green hand shot up from the dirt. Then two more.

Hands reaching up from graves.

I let out a frightened gasp. Hands were bursting up through the grass. Hands all around us. Their fingers twisting and arching, reaching out.

Marty started to laugh. "This is totally awesome! Just like in the movie!"

He stopped laughing as a hand poked up beside him and grabbed his ankle. "Erin — help!" he cried.

But I couldn't help.

Two green hands had wrapped around my ankles and were pulling me down, down into the grave.

"*Come dowwwwwnnnnn,*" a soft voice moaned. "*Come dowwwwwnnnn with us.*"

"Nooo!" I shrieked.

My arms thrashed the air. I tried to kick, but the hands gripped me so tightly, so firmly.

My whole body frantically jerked and tilted back and forth, as I struggled not to fall. If I fell, I knew they would grab my hands, too. And pull me face down into the earth.

"*Come dowwwwwwwnnnnnnn. Come dowww-wwnnnn with us.*"

This isn't a joke, I thought. These hands are *real*. They are really trying to pull me underground.

"Help! Oh, help!" I heard Marty's cry. Then I saw him fall. He toppled to the grass, on to his knees.

Two hands gripped his ankles. Two more green hands poked up from the dirt to grab his wrists.

"*Come dowwwwwwwnnnnnn. Come doww-wwwnnnn with us*," the sad voice moaned.

"Noooo!" I shrieked, tugging wildly, desperately.

To my surprise, I pulled free.

One foot sank into the soft grass. I glanced down. My trainer had slid off. The hand still gripped the trainer—but my foot was free.

With a happy cry, I bent down. Pulled off the other trainer.

I was free now. Free!

Breathing hard, I bent and quickly pulled off my socks. I knew it would be easier to run barefoot. I tossed the socks away. Then I hurried over to Marty.

He was flat on his stomach. Six hands held him down, tugging at him, tugging hard. His whole body twisted and shook.

He raised his head when he saw me. "Erin—help me!" he gasped.

I dropped to my knees. Reached for his trainers. Tugged them off.

The green hands gripped the trainers tightly. Marty kicked his feet free and tried to climb to his knees.

I grabbed a green hand and pulled it off his wrist. The hand slapped at me. A cold, hard slap that made my hand ring with pain.

Ignoring it, I grabbed for another green hand.

Marty rolled over. Rolled free. Jumped to his

feet, gasping, trembling, his mouth hanging open, his dark eyes bulging.

"Your socks —" I cried breathlessly. "Pull them off! Hurry!"

He clumsily tore them off his feet.

The hands grabbed wildly for us. Dozens of hands stretching up from the dirt. Hundreds of hands reaching up for us from the tall graveyard grass.

"*Come dowwwwwwwnnnnnnn. Come dowwwwwwnnnn with us*," the voice moaned.

"*Come dowwwwwwwnnnnnnn. Come dowwwwwwnnnn*," a dozen other soft voices called from beneath the ground.

Marty and I froze. The soft, sad voices seemed to hypnotize me. My legs suddenly felt as if they were made of stone.

"*Come dowwwwwwwnnnnnnn. Come dowwwwwwnnnn*."

And then I saw a green head pop up from the dirt. And then another head. Another. Bald green heads with empty eye sockets and open, toothless mouths.

I saw shoulders, then arms. More heads poking up. Bright-green bodies pulling up from beneath the ground.

"M-Marty —" I choked out. "They're coming up after us!"

The cemetery rang out with grunts and groans as the ugly green figures pulled themselves up from the ground.

I took one last glance at their tattered, shredded clothing, at their blackened eye sockets, their toothless, grinning mouths.

And then I started to run.

Marty and I both ran without saying a word. Side by side, we darted across the tall grass between the rows of crooked tombstones.

My heart thudded in my chest. My head throbbed. My bare feet sank into the cold dirt, slipped on the tall, damp grass.

Marty reached the wooden gate first. He was running so hard, he banged into the fence. He let out a cry—then slipped through the gate on to Shock Street.

I could hear moans and groans and eerie calls from the disgusting green people behind me. But I didn't look back. I dived for the gate. Squeezed through. Then I shoved it shut behind me.

Running into the street, I stopped to catch my breath. I bent over and pressed my hands against my knees. My side ached. I sucked in breath after breath.

"Don't stop!" Marty cried frantically. "Erin — keep going!"

I took a deep breath and followed him down the street. Our bare feet slapped the pavement.

I could still hear the moans and calls behind us. But I was too scared to glance back.

"Marty — where *is* everybody?" I called breathlessly.

Shock Street was empty, the houses and shops all dark.

Shouldn't there be people around? I wondered. This is a big movie studio. Where are the people who work for Shocker Studios? Where are the people who work on the studio tour?

Why isn't anyone around to help us?

"Something is wrong!" Marty choked out, running at full speed. We passed The Horror Hardware Store and Shock City Electronics. "The robots are out of control or something!"

At last! Marty agreed with me. He finally agreed that something was terribly wrong.

"We've got to find your dad," Marty said, running across the street to the next block of dark houses. "We've got to tell him there's a problem."

"We have to find the tram," I called, struggling to keep up with him. "Ow!"

My bare foot came down on something hard. A rock or something. Pain shot up my leg. But I hobbled on.

"If we can get back to the tram, it will take us back to Dad," I called.

"There *has* to be a way out of Shock Street," Marty said. "It's only a movie set."

We ran past the tall mansion with two turrets. It looked like an evil castle. I didn't remember it from any of the *Shocker* movies.

Beyond the mansion stretched a big, empty dirt lot. At the back of the lot stood a low brick wall, just a foot or two taller than Marty and me.

"Cut through here!" I told Marty. "If we can climb up on that wall, we can probably see the studio road."

I was just guessing. But it was worth a try.

We both turned into the empty lot.

My bare feet thudded over the soft dirt.

The dirt felt cold and wet. As we crossed the field, our feet tossed up big clumps of mud.

I pumped my legs harder as the mud grew softer. My bare feet were sinking into it. As I ran, the cold mud rose up over my ankles.

Marty and I were nearly to the brick wall when we ran into the sink-hole.

"Yaaaaaiiii!" We both uttered hoarse cries as the ground gave way beneath us.

The mud made a sick *splussssh* as we sank.

I tossed up both hands. Tried to grab on to something.

But there was nothing to grab.

The mud oozed around me. Over my ankles. My legs. Up over my knees.

It's sucking me down, I thought. I tried to cry out again—but panic choked my throat.

I glimpsed Marty beside me. His arms were waving wildly. His whole body twisted and squirmed as he sank. The mud was up over his waist—and he was still sinking fast.

I kicked hard. Tried to raise my knees.

But I was trapped. Trapped and dropping down, down into the dark, wet ooze.

My mud-covered arms slapped against the surface.

I couldn't stop myself.

The mud bubbled up over my neck. And I was sinking fast.

I held my breath. The mud rose up to my chin.

In a second, it will be over my head, I thought.

A sob escaped my throat.

The mud crept higher, up over my chin. I started to spit as it reached my mouth.

And then I felt something grab my arm. Strong hands slipped under my arms. I felt the hands slide in the mud.

They gripped me harder.

I felt myself being tugged up, tugged by someone very strong.

The mud made a loud *plop* as I rose up. I felt the mud roll down my chest, my legs, my knees.

And then I was standing on the surface, still held by the two powerful hands.

"Marty—!" I called, tasting the sour mud on my lips. "Are you—?"

"I'm up!" I heard his hoarse reply. "Erin, I'm okay!"

The strong hands finally let go. My legs

trembled. I wobbled but remained standing.

I turned to see who had rescued me.

And stared into the glowing red eyes of a wolf.

A human with the face of a wolf. Clawed hands covered in black fur. A long, brown snout curved in an open, toothy grin. Sharp, pointed ears above a thick tuft of black wolf fur.

A female. She wore a silvery catsuit. Sleek and tight-fitting. As I stared in shock, she opened her mouth in a throaty growl.

I recognized her at once. Wolf Girl!

I turned to see her companion — Wolf Boy. He had pulled Marty out of the mud hole. Marty's whole body was caked in mud. He tried to wipe his face, but only managed to smear more mud over his cheeks.

"You — saved us! Thank you!" I cried, finally finding my voice.

The two werewolves uttered low growls, in reply.

"We — we lost the tram," I explained to Wolf Girl. "We need to get back. You know. Back to where the ride began."

She let out a sharp growl. Then she snapped her toothy jaw hard.

"Please — " I begged. "Can you help us get back to the tram? Or can you take us to the main building? My dad is waiting for me there."

Wolf Girl's red eyes flashed. She growled again.

"We know you're just actors!" Marty blurted out shrilly. "But we don't want to be scared any more. We've had enough scares for today. Okay?"

The two werewolves growled. A long white string of saliva drooled over Wolf Boy's black lips.

Something inside me snapped. I totally lost it. "Stop it!" I screamed. "Just stop it! Marty is right! We don't want to be scared now. So stop the werewolf act — and help us!"

The werewolves growled again. Wolf Girl snapped her jaws. A long pink tongue slid out, and she licked her jagged teeth hungrily.

"That's *enough!*" I shrieked. "Stop the act! Stop it! Stop it!"

I was so angry, so *furious* — I reached up with both hands. I grabbed the fur on the sides of Wolf Girl's mask.

And I tugged the mask with all my strength.

Tugged. Tugged with both hands as hard as I could.

And felt real fur. And warm skin.

It wasn't a mask.

"Ohh." I let out a gasp, and jerked my hands away.

The werewolf's red eyes glowed. Her black lips parted. Once again, her tongue flicked hungrily over her yellow, pointed teeth.

My whole body trembled as I backed up against the brick wall. "M-Marty—" I stammered. "It's not an act."

"Huh?" Marty stood stiffly in front of Wolf Boy, his dark eyes wide in his mud-caked face.

"They're not actors," I whispered. "Something is wrong here. Something is terribly wrong."

Marty's mouth dropped open. He took a step back.

Both werewolves uttered low growls. They lowered their heads as if preparing to attack.

"Do you believe me?" I cried. "Do you finally believe me?"

Marty nodded. He didn't say a word. I think he was too terrified to talk.

Saliva poured from the werewolves' mouths. Their eyes glowed like fire in the darkness. Their furry chests began to heave in and out. Their breath came loud and hoarse.

I jumped back against the wall as both werewolves raised their heads and let out long, frightening howls.

What were they going to do to us?

I grabbed Marty and tugged him to the wall. "Up!" I cried. "Get up! Maybe they can't reach us up there!"

Marty leaped high, stretching up his arms. His hands slapped the top of the wall, then slid back down. He tried again. He bent his knees. Jumped. Grabbed for the top of the wall. Slipped back down.

"I can't!" he wailed. "It's too high."

"We've got to!" I shrieked.

I turned back and saw the two werewolves lean back on their hind legs and then spring up. They were snarling and growling now, thick gobs of saliva running over their snapping teeth.

"Up!" I cried.

As Marty leaped for the wall again, I reached down and grabbed his muddy foot. "Up!" I gave him a hard boost.

His hands thrashed the air. Caught the top of the brick wall. Held on.

His bare feet kicked the air. But he held on and tugged himself up.

On his knees on top of the wall, he turned and grabbed my hands. He pulled and I jumped. I struggled to scramble up beside him.

But I couldn't get my knees up. Couldn't get them on to the wall.

My bare feet thrashed wildly. My knees scraped against the wall as Marty tugged.

"I can't do it! I can't!" I gasped.

The werewolves howled again.

"Keep trying!" Marty choked out. He tugged my arms. Tugged with all his strength.

I was still struggling as the two werewolves leaped.

I heard the snap of jaws.

I felt hot breath on the bottom of my foot.

The two werewolves thudded against the wall.

With a desperate cry, I sprang to the top. Gasping for air, I pressed myself flat against the bricks.

I raised my head in time to see the two snarling werewolves leap again. Jaws snapped in front of my face. Red eyes gleamed hungrily at me.

"No!" With a cry, I scrambled to my feet.

The werewolves raised their heads in angry howls and prepared to attack again.

Marty and I stood pressed close together, staring down at them.

They jumped.

Their claws scraped against the bricks. The shrill screech sent chills down my back. Their teeth snapped.

They dropped down. Prepared another leap, snarling excitedly.

"We can't stay up here for ever!" Marty cried. "What do we do?"

I squinted into the darkness. Was that the studio road on the other side of the wall?

Too dark to tell.

The werewolves leaped again. Jagged teeth scraped against my ankle.

I jumped back. Nearly toppled off the wall.

Marty and I bumped into each other, our eyes on the two growling creatures preparing another leap.

The gun! The plastic stun gun!

Mine had fallen from my hand. It was probably buried in that mud hole. But my eyes fell on Marty's gun. Its handle poked out from his jeans pocket.

Without saying a word, I grabbed the handle and tugged the plastic pistol from Marty's jeans.

"Hey—!" he cried. "Erin—what are you doing?"

"They gave us the guns for a reason," I explained, shouting over the frightening howls of the two werewolves. "Maybe this will stop them."

"It—it's only a *toy*!" Marty stammered.

I didn't care. It was worth a try.

Maybe it would frighten them. Maybe it would hurt them. Maybe it would chase them away.

216

I raised the plastic gun. Aimed it as the two werewolves made another leap of attack.

"One—two—three—FIRE!"

I squeezed the trigger. Again. Again.

Again!

The gun made a loud buzzing sound. It shot out a beam of yellow light.

Yes! I thought. Yes! I prayed.

The light will stop them.

It's a stun gun — right? The buzzing sound and the bright light will stun them. It will freeze them in place so Marty and I can make our escape.

I squeezed the trigger hard. Again. Again.

It didn't stop the werewolves. It didn't even seem to surprise them.

They leaped higher. I felt sharp claws scrape my leg. I cried out in pain.

And the plastic gun flew out of my hand.

It clattered against the top of the wall, then slid to the ground.

Just a toy. Marty was right. It wasn't a real weapon. It was just a stupid toy.

"Look out!" Marty opened his mouth in a shrill shriek as the snarling creatures made another high leap at the wall.

Claws scraped the brick—and held on. Red eyes glared up at me. Hot wolf breath tingled my skin.

"Ohhh." My arms flew up as I lost my balance. I struggled to stay up. But my knees bent. My feet slipped.

I grabbed for Marty. Missed.

And toppled off. Landed hard on my back on the other side of the wall.

Gazing up in horror, I saw Marty leap down beside me.

The two werewolves were on the top of the wall now. They glared down at us, red eyes glowing, tongues out, breathing hard.

Preparing to pounce.

Marty dragged me to my feet. "Run!" he cried hoarsely, his eyes wide with panic.

The werewolves growled above us.

The ground tilted. I still felt dizzy, a little dazed from my fall. "We—we can't outrun them!" I moaned.

I heard a rumbling sound. A clatter.

Marty and I both turned. And saw two yellow eyes, glowing against the dark sky.

Yellow eyes of a creature roaring towards us.

No. Not a creature.

As it drew nearer, I could make out its long, sleek shape.

The tram!

The tram bouncing over the road behind yellow headlights. Coming closer. Closer.

Yes!

I turned to Marty. Did he see it, too? He did.

Without saying a word, we both began running to the road. The tram was rolling fast. Somehow we had to climb on it. We *had* to!

Behind us, I heard the werewolves howl. I heard a hard *thump*, then another as they dropped off the wall.

The twin yellow headlights of the tram swept over us.

The werewolves snarled and howled angrily as they chased after us.

A few feet ahead of me, Marty was hurtling forward, his head down, his legs pumping furiously.

The tram bumped closer. Closer.

The howling werewolves were inches behind us. I could almost feel their hot breath on the back of my neck.

A few more seconds. A few more seconds — and Marty and I would make our jump.

I watched the tram speed around a curve, the yellow headlights washing over the dark road. I kept my eyes on the front car. Took a deep breath. Prepared to jump.

And then Marty fell.

I saw his hands shoot out. Saw his mouth open wide in surprise. In horror.

He stumbled over his own bare feet and dropped to the ground, landing hard on his stomach.

I couldn't stop in time.

I ran right into him. Stumbled over him.

Fell heavily on top of him.

And watched the tram speed past us.

"Owoooooooo!"

The two werewolves uttered long howls of triumph.

My heart pounding, I scrambled to my feet. "Get up!" I frantically pulled Marty up by both arms.

We took off after the tram, our bare feet pounding the hard road. The last car bounced a few feet ahead of us.

I reached it first. Shot out my right hand. Grabbed the back of the car.

With a desperate leap, I hoisted myself up. Up. And into the last seat.

Struggling to catch my breath, I turned back to find Marty running behind the tram. His hands reached for the back of the tram. "I—I can't make it!" he gasped.

"Run! You've *got* to!" I screamed.

Behind him, I could see the werewolves scampering close behind.

Marty put on a burst of speed. He grabbed the back of the car with both hands. It dragged him for several feet—until he swung himself around and dropped into the seat beside me.

Yes! I thought happily. We made it! We got away from those howling werewolves.

Or did we?

Would they jump into the tram after us?

I spun around, my whole body trembling. And I watched the werewolves fade into the distance. They ran for a while, then gave up. They both stood in the road, hunched over in defeat, watching us escape.

Escape.

What a wonderful word.

Marty and I grinned at each other. I slapped him a high five.

We were both breathing hard, covered in mud. My legs ached from running. My bare feet throbbed. My heart still thudded from the frightening chase.

But we had escaped. And now we were safe in the tram, on our way back to the starting platform. Back to my dad.

"We've got to tell your dad that this place is messed up," Marty said breathlessly.

"Something is horribly wrong here," I agreed.

"Those werewolves—they weren't kidding around," Marty continued. "They—they were real, Erin. They weren't actors."

I nodded. I felt so glad that Marty finally agreed with me. And he wasn't pretending to be brave any more. He wasn't pretending that it was all robots and special effects.

We both knew that we had faced *real* dangers. *Real* monsters.

Something was terribly wrong at Shocker Studios. Dad had told us he wanted a full report. Well, he was going to get one!

I settled back in the seat, trying to calm down.

But I shot straight up again when I realized we weren't alone. "Marty—look!" I pointed to the front of the tram. "We aren't the only passengers."

In fact, every tramcar appeared to be filled with people.

"What's going on?" Marty murmured. "Your dad said we were the only ones on the tour. And now the tram is—OH!—"

Marty never finished his sentence. His mouth fell open in a gasp. His eyes bulged open wide.

I gasped, too.

The other passengers on the tram all turned around at the same time. And I saw their grinning jaws, their dark, empty eye sockets, the grey bones of their skulls.

Skeletons.

The other passengers were all grinning skeletons.

Their jaws opened in dry laughter. Cruel

laughter that sounded like the wind screeching through bare trees. Bones rattled and clattered as they raised their yellowed, skeletal hands to point at us.

Their skulls bobbed and bounced as the tram carried us, faster, faster, through the darkness.

Marty and I slumped low in the seat, trembling, staring at the grinning skulls, the pointing fingers.

Who *were* they?

How did they get on this tram?

Where were they taking us?

The skeletons laughed their wheezing laugh. Their bones clanked and rattled. Their yellowed skulls bounced loosely on their clattering shoulder bones.

The tram picked up speed. We were flying through the darkness.

I forced myself to turn away from the grinning skulls and peered out. Beyond the trees, I could see the low buildings of the movie studio. As I stared, they grew smaller, faded into the blackness of the night.

"Marty—we're not going back to the main platform," I whispered. "We're heading the wrong way. We're going *away* from all the buildings."

He swallowed hard. I could see the panic in his eyes. "What can we do?" he choked out.

"We've got to get off!" I replied. "We've got to jump."

Marty had slumped all the way down in the

seat, as low as he could get. I think he was trying to hide from the skeletons.

Now he raised his head and peeked over the side of the tram. "Erin—we can't jump!" he cried. "We're going too fast."

He was right.

We were rocketing along the road. And the tram kept picking up speed. The trees and shrubs whirred past in a dark blur.

And then as we squealed into a sharp curve, a tall building seemed to jump into our path.

A castle, bathed in swirling spotlights. All grey and silver. Twin towers reached up to the sky. A solid stone wall rose up from the road.

The road.

It curved straight into the castle wall. The road ended at the wall.

And we were roaring down the road, still picking up speed.

Roaring towards the castle.

The skeletons rattled and clattered and laughed their dry, screeching laugh. They bounced in their seats, bones cracking, jumping in excitement as we zoomed at the castle.

Closer. Closer.

Right up to it now. Up to the solid stone wall.

About to smash right into it.

My legs trembled. My heart pounded. But somehow I managed to stand up on the seat.

I took a deep breath. Held it. Closed my eyes — and jumped.

I landed hard on my side, and rolled.

I saw Marty hesitate. The tram bounced. Marty dived over the side.

He hit the ground on his stomach. Rolled on to his back. And kept rolling.

I came to a stop under a tree. And turned to the castle — in time to see the tram plunge into the stone wall.

Without a sound.

The first car hit the castle wall and flew through it.

Silently.

I could see the skeletons bobbing and bouncing.

And I saw the next car and the next and the next — all shoot into the castle wall and disappear through it without making a sound.

A few seconds later, the tram disappeared.

A heavy silence fell over the road.

The spotlights on the castle wall dimmed.

"Erin—are you okay?" Marty called weakly.

I turned to find him on his hands and knees on the other side of the road. I scrambled to my feet. I had scraped my side, but it didn't hurt too badly.

"I'm okay," I told him. I pointed to the castle. "Did you see that?"

"I saw it," Marty replied, standing up slowly. "But I don't believe it." He stretched. "How did the tram go through the wall? Do you think the castle isn't really there? That it's an optical illusion? Some kind of trick?"

"There's an easy way to find out," I said.

We walked side by side on the road. The wind rustled the trees, making them whisper all around us. The pavement felt cold under my bare feet.

"We've got to find my dad," I said quietly. "I'm sure he can explain everything to us."

"I hope so," Marty murmured.

We stepped up to the castle wall. I stuck out both hands, expecting them to go right through.

But my hands slapped solid stone.

Marty lowered his shoulder and shoved it

against the castle wall. His shoulder hit the wall with a *thud*.

"It's solid," Marty said, shaking his head. "It's a real wall. So how did the tram go through it?"

"It's a ghost tram," I whispered, rubbing my hand against the cold stone. "A ghost tram filled with skeletons."

"But we *rode* in it!" Marty cried.

I slapped the wall with both hands and spun away from it. "I'm sick of mysteries!" I wailed. "I'm sick of being scared! I'm sick of werewolves and monsters! I'm never going to another scary movie as long as I live!"

"Your dad can explain it all," Marty said softly, shaking his head. "I'm sure he can."

"I don't want him to explain it!" I cried. "I just want to get *away* from here!"

Keeping close together, we made our way around to the side of the castle. I could hear strange, animal howls behind us. And a frightening cackle cut through the air somewhere above our heads.

I ignored all the sounds. I didn't want to think about whether they were being made by real monsters or fakes. I didn't want to think about the frightening creatures we had run into—or the close calls Marty and I had had.

I didn't want to think.

At the back of the castle, the road appeared again. "I hope we're going in the right direction," I murmured, following it as it curved into the hill.

"Me, too," Marty replied in a tiny voice.

We picked up our pace, walking quickly in the middle of the road. We tried not to pay attention to the sharp animal calls, the shrill cries, the howls and moans that seemed to follow us everywhere.

The road sloped uphill. Marty and I leaned forward as we climbed. The frightening cries and howls followed us up the hill.

As we neared the top, I saw several low buildings.

"Yes!" I cried. "Marty—look! We must be heading back to the main platform." I started jogging towards the buildings. Marty trotted close behind.

We both stopped when we realized where we were.

Back on Shock Street.

Somehow we had made a circle.

Past the old houses and small shops, The Shock Street Cemetery came into view. Staring at the fence, I remembered the green hands poking up from the ground. The green shoulders. The green faces. The hands pulling us, pulling us down.

My whole body shuddered.

I didn't want to be back here. I never wanted to see this terrifying street again.

But I couldn't turn away from the cemetery. As I stared at the old gravestones from across the street, I saw something move.

A wisp of grey. Like a tiny cloud.

It rose up between two crooked, old stones. Floated silently into the air.

And then another puff of grey lifted off the ground. And another.

I glimpsed Marty. He stood beside me, hands pressed against his waist, staring hard. He saw them, too.

The grey puffs rose silently, like snowballs or cotton. Dozens of them, floating up from the graves.

Floating over the cemetery and out over the street.

Floating above Marty and me. Hovering so low.

And then as we stared up at them, they started to grow. To inflate, like grey balloons.

And I saw faces inside them. Dark faces, etched in shadow like the Man in the Moon. The faces scowled at us. Old faces, lined and creased. Eyes narrowed to dark slits. Frowning faces. Sneering faces inside the billowing, white puffs.

I grabbed Marty's shoulder. I wanted to run, to get away, to get out from under them.

But, like smoke, the wisps of mist with their

evil faces, swirled down, swirled around us. Trapped us. Trapped us inside.

The faces, the ugly, scowling faces, spinning around us. Spinning faster, faster, holding us in the swirling, choking mist.

I pressed my hands over my eyes, trying to shut them out.

I froze in total panic. I couldn't think. I couldn't breathe.

I could hear the shrill rush of wind as the ghostly clouds swirled around us.

And then I heard a man's voice, shouting over the wind: "Cut! Print that one! Good scene, everyone!"

I lowered my hands slowly and opened my eyes. I let out my breath in a long whoosh.

A man came striding up to Marty and me. He wore jeans and a grey sweatshirt under a brown leather jacket. He had a blue-and-white Dodgers cap sideways on his head. A blond pony-tail tumbled out from under it.

He carried a clipboard in one hand. He had a silver whistle around his neck. He smiled at Marty and me and flashed us a thumbs-up.

"Hey, what's up, guys? I'm Russ Denver. Good job! You looked really scared."

"Huh?" I cried, my mouth dropping open. "We *were* really scared!"

"I'm so glad to see a real live human!" Marty cried.

"This tour—it's totally messed up!" I shrieked. "The creatures—they're alive! They tried to hurt us! They really did! It wasn't any fun! It wasn't like a ride!" The words spilled out of me in a rush.

"It was really gross! The werewolves snapped at us and chased us up a wall!" Marty exclaimed.

The two of us started talking at once, telling this guy Denver all of the frightening things that had happened to us on the tour.

"Whoa! Whoa!" A smile crossed his handsome face. He raised his clipboard as if to shield himself from us. "It's all special effects, guys. Didn't they explain to you that we're making a movie here? That we were filming your reactions?"

"No. No one explained that, Mr Denver!" I replied angrily. "My dad brought us here. He designed the studio tour. And he told us we were the first to try it out. But he didn't tell us about any movie being filmed. I really think—"

I felt Marty's hand on my shoulder. I knew Marty was trying to calm me down. But I didn't *want* to be calmed down.

I was really angry.

Mr Denver turned back to a group of crew

members behind him in the street. "Take thirty, guys. Let's break for dinner."

They moved away, talking among themselves. Mr Denver turned back to us. "Your father should have explained to you—"

"It's okay. Really," Marty interrupted. "We just got a little scared. All of the creatures seemed so real. And we didn't see any other people anywhere. You're the first real person we've seen all afternoon."

"My dad must be really worried," I told the movie director. "He said he'd be waiting for us on the main platform. Can you tell us how to get there?"

"No problem," Mr Denver replied. "See that big house there with the open door?" He pointed with his clipboard.

Marty and I stared at the house across the street. A narrow path led up to the house. A pale yellow light shone inside the open front door.

"That's Shockro's House of Shocks," the director explained. "Go right in that door and straight through the house."

"But won't we get shocked in there?" Marty demanded. "In the movie, anyone who goes into Shockro's house gets jolted with twenty million volts of electricity!"

"That's just in the movie," Mr Denver replied. "The house is just a set. It's perfectly safe. Go through the house. Then out the back, and you will see the main building on the other side of the street. You can't miss it."

"Thank you!" Marty and I called out at once.

Marty turned and started running full speed towards the house.

I turned back to Mr Denver. "I'm sorry for yelling before," I told him. "I was just so scared, and I thought—"

I gasped.

Mr Denver had turned away. And I saw the long power cord—the power cord that was plugged into his back.

He wasn't a real human. He wasn't a movie director. He was some kind of robot.

He was fake like all the others. He was lying to us. Lying!

I turned and cupped my hands around my mouth. I started to run, frantically calling after Marty: "Don't go in there! Marty—stop! Don't go in that house!"

Too late.

Marty was already running through the door.

"Marty—wait! Stop!" I shouted as I ran.

I had to stop him.

The director was a fake. I knew he wasn't telling the truth.

"Marty—*please!*"

My bare feet pounded the hard pavement. I plunged up the path as Marty trotted into the doorway.

"Stop!"

I flew to the doorway. Reached out both hands. Made a wild dive to tackle him.

And missed.

I skidded across the walk on my stomach.

As soon as Marty entered the house, I saw the flash of white light. I heard a loud buzz. Then the sharp crackle of electricity.

The room exploded in a flash of lightning. So bright I had to shield my eyes.

When I opened them, I saw Marty sprawled face down on the floor. "Nooooo!" I let out a terrified wail.

Scrambling to my feet, I dived into the house.

Would I get shocked, too?

I didn't care. I had to get to Marty. I had to help him out of there.

"Marty! Marty!" I screamed his name again and again.

He didn't move.

"Marty—please!" I grabbed his shoulders and started to shake him. "Wake up, Marty! Snap out of it! Marty!"

He didn't open his eyes.

I suddenly felt a chill. A dark shadow slid over me.

And I realized I wasn't alone in the house.

I spun around with a gasp.

Was it Shockro? Some other scary creature?

A tall figure leaned over me. I squinted into the darkness, struggling to see his face.

"Dad!" I cried as he came into focus. "Dad! Oh, I'm so glad to see you!"

"Erin, what are you doing here?" he asked in a low voice.

"It—it's Marty!" I stammered. "You've got to help him, Dad. He's been shocked and he—he—"

Dad leaned closer. Behind his eyeglasses, his brown eyes were cold. His face set in a troubled frown.

"*Do* something, Dad!" I pleaded. "Marty is hurt. He isn't moving. He won't open his eyes. The studio tour was so *awful*, Dad! Something is wrong. Something is *terribly* wrong!"

He didn't reply. He leaned closer.

And as his face came into the soft light, I saw that he wasn't my father!

"Who *are* you?" I shrieked. "You're not my dad! Why aren't you helping me? Why aren't you helping Marty? Do something—please! Where's my dad? Where *is* he? Who *are* you? Help me! Somebody? Help me AAAAAARRRRRRRR. Help MRRRRRRRRRRRR. Dad—MARRRRRR-RRRRRRR. DRRRMMMMMMMMmmmmm."

Mr Wright stood staring down at Erin and Marty. He shook his head unhappily. He shut his eyes and let out a long sigh.

Jared Curtis, one of the studio engineers, came running into The House of Shocks. "Mr Wright, what happened to your two kid robots?" he demanded.

Mr Wright sighed again. "Programming problems," he muttered.

He pointed to the Erin robot, frozen in place on her knees beside the Marty robot. "I had to shut the girl off. Her memory chip must be bad. The Erin robot was supposed to think of me as her father. But just now, she didn't recognize me."

"And what about the Marty robot?" Jared asked.

"It's totally down," Mr Wright replied. "I think the electrical system shorted out."

"What a shame," Jared said, bending to roll

the Marty robot over. He pulled up the T-shirt and fiddled with some dials on the back. "Hey, Mr Wright, it was a great idea to make robot kids to test the park. I think we can fix them."

Jared opened up a panel on Marty's back and squinted at the red and green wires. "All the other creatures, and monsters, and robots worked perfectly. Not a single bug."

"I should have known there was a problem yesterday," Mr Wright said. "We were in my office. The Erin robot asked about her mother. I built her. She doesn't have a mother."

Mr Wright tossed up his hands. "Oh, well. No problem. We'll re-program these two. Put in new chips. They'll be good as new in no time. Then we'll try them out once again on the Shocker Studio Tour, before we open the park to real kids."

He took the Marty robot from Jared and slung it over his shoulder. Then he picked up the Erin robot. He tossed it over his other shoulder. Then, humming to himself, he carried them to the engineering building.

The Haunted Mask II

I don't know if you have ever spent any time with first graders. But there is only one word to describe them. And that word is ANIMALS.

First graders are animals.

You can quote me.

My name is Steve Boswell, and I am in the sixth grade. I may not be the smartest guy at Walnut Avenue Middle School. But I know one thing for sure: first graders are animals.

How do I know this fact? I learned it the hard way. I learned it by coaching the first-grade soccer team after school every day.

You might want to know *why* I chose to coach their soccer team. Well, I didn't *choose* it. It was a punishment.

Someone set a squirrel loose in the girls' locker room. That someone was me. But it wasn't my idea.

My best friend, Chuck Green, caught the

squirrel. And he asked me where I thought he should set it free.

I said, "How about the girls' locker room before their basketball game on Thursday?"

So maybe it was partly my idea. But Chuck was just as much to blame as I was.

Of course, I was the one who got caught.

Miss Curdy, the gym teacher, grabbed me as I was letting the squirrel out of its box. The squirrel ran across the gym to the stands. The kids on the stands all jumped up and started running and screaming and acting crazy.

It was just a dumb squirrel. But all the teachers started chasing after it. It took hours to catch it and get everyone calmed down.

So Miss Curdy said I had to be punished.

She gave me a choice of punishments. One: I could come into the gym after school every day and inflate basketballs—by mouth—until my head exploded. Or two: I could coach the first-grade soccer team.

I chose number two.

The wrong choice.

My friend Chuck was supposed to help me coach the team. But he told Miss Curdy he had an after-school job.

Do you know what his after-school job is? Going home and watching TV.

A lot of people think that Chuck and I are

best friends because we look so much alike. We're both tall and thin. We both have straight brown hair and dark brown eyes. We both wear baseball caps most of the time. Sometimes people think we're brothers!

But that's not why I like Chuck and Chuck likes me. We're best friends because we make each other laugh.

I laughed really hard when Chuck told me what his after-school job was. But I'm not laughing now.

I'm praying. Every day I pray for rain. If it rains, the first graders don't have soccer practice.

Today, unfortunately, is a bright, clear, beautiful October day. Standing on the playground behind school, I searched the sky for a cloud — any cloud — but saw only blue.

"Okay, listen up, Hogs!" I shouted. I wasn't making fun of them. That's the name they voted for their team. Do you believe it? The Walnut Avenue Hogs.

Does that give you an idea of what these kids are like?

I cupped my hands around my mouth and shouted again. "Line up, Hogs!"

Andrew Foster grabbed the whistle I wear around my neck and blew it in my face. Then Duck Benton stamped on my new trainers. Everyone calls him Duck because he quacks all the time. He and Andrew thought that was a riot.

Then Marnie Rosen jumped up behind me, threw her arms around my neck, and climbed on my back. Marnie has curly red hair, freckles all over her face and the most evil grin I ever saw on a kid. "Give me a ride, Steve!" she shouted. "I want a ride!"

"Marnie—get off me!" I cried. I tried to loosen her grip on my neck. She was *choking* me. The Hogs were all laughing now.

"Marnie—I . . . can't . . . breathe!" I gasped.

I bent down and tried to throw her off my back. But she hung on even tighter.

Then I felt her lips press against my ear.

"What are you *doing*?" I cried. Was she trying to kiss me or something?

Yuck! She spat her bubble gum into my ear.

Then, laughing like a crazed fiend, she hopped off me and went running across the grass, her curly red hair bouncing behind her.

"Give me a *break*!" I cried angrily. The purple gum stuck in my ear. It took me a while to scrape it all out.

By the time I finished, they had started a practice game.

Have you ever watched six-year-olds play soccer? It's chase and kick, chase and kick. Everybody chase the ball. Everybody try to kick it.

I try to teach them positions. I try to teach

them how to pass the ball to each other. I try to teach them teamwork. But all they want to do is chase and kick, chase and kick.

Which is fine with me. As long as they leave me alone.

I blow my whistle and act as referee. And try to keep the game going.

Andrew Foster kicked a big clump of dirt on my jeans as he ran by. He acted as if it were an accident. But I knew it was deliberate.

Then Duck Benton got into a shoving fight with Johnny Myers. Duck watches hockey games on TV with his dad, and he thinks you're *supposed* to fight. Some days Duck doesn't chase after the ball at all. He just fights.

I let them chase and kick, chase and kick for an hour. Then I blew the whistle to call practice to an end.

Not a bad practice. Only one bloody nose. And for once it wasn't mine!

"Okay, Hogs—see you tomorrow!" I shouted. I started to trot off the playground. Their parents or babysitters would be waiting for them in front of the school.

Then I saw that a bunch of the kids had formed a tight circle in the middle of the field. They all wore grins on their faces, so I decided I'd better see what they were up to.

"What's going on, guys?" I asked, trotting back to them.

Some kids stepped back, and I spotted a soccer ball on the grass. Marnie Rosen smiled at me through her freckles. "Hey, Steve, can you kick a goal from here?"

The other kids stepped away from the ball. I glanced to the goal. It was really far away, at least half the field.

"What's the joke?" I demanded.

Marnie's grin faded. "No joke. Can you kick a goal from here?"

"No way!" Duck Benton called.

"Steve can do it," I heard Johnny Myers say. "Steve can kick it further than that."

"No way!" Duck insisted. "It's too far even for a sixth grader."

"Hey—that's an easy goal," I bragged. "Why don't you give me something *hard* to do?"

Every once in a while I have to do something to impress them. Just to prove that I'm better than they are.

So I moved up behind the ball. I stopped about eight or ten steps back. Gave myself plenty of running room.

"Okay, guys, watch how a pro does it!" I cried.

I ran up to the ball. Got plenty of leg behind it.

Gave a tremendous kick.

Froze for a second.

And then let out a long, high wail of horror.

On my way home a few minutes later, I passed my friend Chuck's house. Chuck came running down the gravel driveway to greet me.

I didn't really feel like talking to anyone. Not even my friend.

But there he was. So what could I do?

"Yo—Steve!" He stopped halfway down the driveway. "What happened? Why are you limping?"

"Concrete," I groaned.

He pulled off his black-and-red Cubs cap and scratched his thick brown hair. "Huh?"

"Concrete," I repeated weakly. "The kids had a concrete football."

Chuck squinted at me. I could see he still didn't understand.

"One of the kids lives across the street. He had his friends help roll a ball of concrete to the school," I explained. "Painted white and black to look like a football. Solid concrete. They had it there on the field. They asked me to kick a goal and — and — " My voice caught in my throat. I couldn't finish.

I hobbled over to the big beech tree beside Chuck's driveway and leaned back against its cold, white trunk.

"Wow. That's not a very funny joke," Chuck said, replacing his cap on his head.

"Tell me about it," I groaned. "I think I broke every bone in my foot. Even some bones I don't have."

"Those kids are *animals!*" Chuck declared.

I groaned and rubbed my aching foot. It wasn't really broken. But it hurt. A lot. I shifted my rucksack on my shoulders and leaned back against the tree.

"Know what I'd like to do?" I told Chuck.

"Pay them back?"

"You're right!" I replied. "How did you know?"

"Lucky guess." He stepped up beside me. I could see that he was thinking hard. Chuck always scrunches up his face when he's trying to think.

"It's almost Hallowe'en," he said finally. "Maybe we could think of some way to scare them. I mean, *really* scare them." His dark eyes lit up with excitement.

"Well . . . maybe." I hesitated. "They're just little kids. I don't want to do anything mean."

My rucksack felt weird—too full. I pulled it off my shoulder and lowered it to the ground.

I leaned over and unzipped it.

And about ten million feathers came floating out.

"Those kids—!" Chuck exclaimed.

I pulled open the bag. All of my notebooks, all of my textbooks—covered in sticky feathers. Those animals had glued feathers to my books.

I threw the bag down and turned to Chuck. "Maybe I *do* want to do something mean!" I growled.

A few days later, Chuck and I were walking home from the playground. It was a cold, windy afternoon. Dark storm clouds rose up in the distance.

The storm clouds were too late to help me. I had just finished afternoon practice with the Hogs.

It hadn't been a bad practice. It hadn't been a *good* practice, either.

Just as we had started, Andrew Foster lowered his head and came at me, full speed. He weighs about half a tonne, and he has a very hard head. He ploughed into my stomach and knocked the wind out of me.

I rolled around on the ground for a few minutes, groaning and choking and gasping.

The kids thought it was pretty funny. Andrew claimed it was an accident.

I'm going to get you lot back, I vowed to myself. *I don't know how. But I'm going to get you lot.*

Then Marnie Rosen jumped on my back and tore the collar off my new winter coat.

Chuck met me after practice. He'd started doing that now. He knew that after one hour with the first graders, I usually needed help getting home.

"I hate them," I muttered. "Do you know how to spell hate? H-O-G-S." My torn coat collar flapped in the swirling wind.

"Why don't you make all of them practise with a concrete ball?" Chuck suggested. He adjusted his Cubs cap over his hair. "No. Wait. I've got it. Let them take turns *being* the ball!"

"No. No good," I replied, shaking my head. The sky darkened. The trees shook, sending a shower of dead leaves down around us.

My trainers crunched over the leaves. "I don't want to hurt them," I told Chuck. "I just want to scare them. I just want to scare them to death."

The wind blew colder. I felt a cold drop of rain on my forehead.

As we crossed the street, I noticed two girls from our class walking on the other side. I recognized Sabrina Mason's black ponytail swinging behind her as she hurried along the pavement.

And next to her, I recognized her friend Carly Beth Caldwell.

"Hey—!" I started to call out to them, but I stopped.

An idea flashed into my mind.

Seeing Carly Beth, I knew how to scare those first graders.

Seeing Carly Beth, I knew exactly what I wanted to do.

I started to call to the girls. But Chuck clamped his hand over my mouth and dragged me behind a wide tree.

"Hey—get your clammy paws off me. What's the big idea?" I cried when he finally pulled his hand away.

He pushed me against the rough bark of the tree trunk. "Ssshhh. They haven't seen us." He motioned with his eyes towards the two girls.

"So?"

"So we can sneak up and scare them," Chuck whispered, his dark eyes practically glowing with evil excitement. "Let's make Carly Beth scream."

"You mean for old times' sake?"

Chuck nodded, grinning.

For many years, making Carly Beth scream had been our hobby. That's because she was a really good screamer, and she would scream at just about anything.

One day in the lunchroom last year, Chuck tucked a worm inside his turkey sandwich. Then he gave the sandwich to Carly Beth.

She took one bite and knew that something tasted a bit weird. When Chuck showed her the big bite she had taken out of the worm, Carly Beth screamed for a week.

Chuck and I took bets on who could scare Carly Beth the most and who could make her scream. I suppose it was a bit mean. But it was funny too.

And sometimes when you know that people are really easy to scare, you have no choice. You *have* to scare them as often as you can.

Anyway, that all changed last Hallowe'en.

Last Hallowe'en Chuck and I had a horrible scare. Carly Beth wore the most frightening mask I had ever seen. It wasn't a mask. It was like a living face.

It was so ugly, so real. It glared at us with evil, living eyes. Its mouth sneered at us with real lips. The skin glowed a sick green. And Carly Beth's normally soft voice burst out in a terrifying animal growl.

Chuck and I ran for our lives.

No joke. We were terrified.

We ran for blocks, screaming the whole way. It was the worst night of my life.

Everything changed after that.

Nearly a whole year has gone by, and we

259

haven't tried to scare Carly Beth once. I don't think Carly Beth *can* be scared. Not any more.

After last Hallowe'en, I don't think anything scares her.

She is totally fearless. I haven't heard her shriek or scream once the entire year.

So I didn't want to try to scare her now. I needed to talk to her. About that scary mask of hers.

But Chuck kept pressing me back against the tree trunk. "Come on, Steve," he whispered. "They haven't seen us. We'll duck down behind the hedges and get ahead of them. Then when they come by, we'll jump out and grab them."

"I don't really—" I started. But I could see that Chuck had his heart set on scaring Carly Beth and Sabrina. So I let him pull me down out of sight.

A light rain had started to fall. The gusting wind blew the raindrops into my face. I crept along the hedge, bent low, following Chuck.

We passed by the girls and kept moving. I could hear Sabrina's laugh behind us. I heard Carly Beth say something else. Then Sabrina laughed again.

I wondered what they were talking about. I stopped to glance through the hedge. Carly Beth had a weird expression on her face. Her dark eyes stared straight ahead. She was moving stiffly. She had the collar of her blue down jacket pulled up high around her face.

I ducked down low again as the girls came closer. I turned and saw that Chuck and I were standing on the wide front lawn of the old Carpenter mansion.

I felt a chill as I stared across the weed-choked lawn at the gloomy old house, covered in a deep darkness. Everyone said that the house was haunted—haunted by people who had been murdered inside it a hundred years ago.

I don't believe in ghosts. But I don't like standing so close to the creepy old Carpenter mansion, either.

I pulled Chuck into the patch of waste ground next door. Rain pattered the ground. I wiped raindrops off my eyebrows.

Carly Beth and Sabrina were only a few metres away. I could hear Sabrina talking excitedly about something. But I couldn't make out her words.

Chuck turned to me, an evil grin spreading across his face. "Ready?" he whispered. "Let's get 'em!"

We leaped to our feet. Then we both jumped out, screaming at the top of our lungs.

Sabrina gasped in shock. Her mouth dropped to her knees. Her hands flew up in the air.

Carly Beth stared at me.

Then her head tilted against the blue jacket collar — tilted and fell.

Her head fell off her shoulders.

It dropped to the ground and bounced on to the grass.

Sabrina lowered her eyes to the ground. She gaped at Carly Beth's fallen head in disbelief.

Then Sabrina's hands began to flail the air crazily. She opened her mouth in a scream of horror. And screamed and screamed and screamed.

I swallowed hard. My knees started to buckle.

Carly Beth's head stared up at me from the grass. Sabrina's shrieks rang in my ears.

And then I heard soft laughter. Laughter from inside Carly Beth's jacket.

I saw a clump of brown hair poke up through the raised collar. And then Carly Beth's laughing face shot up from under the jacket.

Sabrina stopped her wild cries and started to laugh.

"Gotcha!" Carly Beth cried. She and Sabrina fell all over each other, laughing like lunatics.

"Oh, wow," Chuck groaned.

My knees were still shaking. I don't think I had taken a breath the whole time.

I bent down and picked up Carly Beth's head. Some sort of dummy head. A sculpture, maybe. I rolled it around between my hands. It was amazing. It looked just like her.

"It's plaster of Paris," Carly Beth explained,

grabbing it away from me. "My mum made it."

"But — it's so real-looking!" I choked out.

She grinned. "Mum is getting pretty good. She keeps doing my head over and over. This is one of her best."

"It's okay. But it didn't fool us," Chuck said.

"Yeah. We knew it was a fake," I quickly agreed. But my voice cracked when I said it. I was still kind of in shock.

Sabrina shook her head. Her black ponytail waved behind her. Sabrina is very tall, taller than Chuck and me. Carly Beth is a shrimp. She only comes up to Sabrina's shoulder.

"You should have seen the looks on your faces!" Sabrina exclaimed. "I thought *your* heads were going to fall off!"

The two girls hugged each other again and had another good laugh.

"We saw you a mile away," Carly Beth said, twirling the head in her hands. "Luckily, I brought this head in to show off in art class today. So I pulled my jacket over my head, and Sabrina tucked the plaster head into the collar."

"You guys scare pretty easy," Sabrina smirked.

"We *weren't* scared. Really," Chuck insisted. "We were just playing along."

I wanted to change the subject. The girls

would talk all day and night about how dumb Chuck and I were. If we let them. I didn't want to let them.

The rain kept pattering down, blown by the gusting wind. I shivered. We were all getting pretty wet.

"Carly Beth, you know that mask you wore last Hallowe'en? Where did you get it?" I asked. I tried to sound casual. I didn't want her to think it was any big deal.

She hugged her plaster head against the front of her jacket. "Huh? What mask?"

I groaned. She is such a jerk sometimes!

"Remember that really scary mask you had last Hallowe'en? Where did you get it?"

She and Sabrina exchanged glances. Then Carly Beth said, "I don't remember."

"Give me a break!" I groaned.

"No. Really — " she insisted.

"You remember," Chuck told her. "You just don't want to tell."

I knew why Carly Beth didn't want to tell. She was probably planning to get another truly terrifying mask at the same store for this Hallowe'en. She wanted to be the scariest kid in town. She didn't want me to be scary too.

I turned to Sabrina. "Do you know where she bought that mask?"

Sabrina made a zipper motion over her lips. "I'm not telling, Steve."

"You don't want to know," Carly Beth declared, still hugging the head. "That mask was *too* frightening."

"You just want to be scarier than me," I replied angrily. "But I need a really scary mask this year, Carly Beth. There are some kids I want to scare and—"

"I'm serious, Steve," Carly Beth interrupted. "There was something totally weird about the mask. It wasn't just a mask. It came alive. It clamped on to my head, and I couldn't get it off. The mask was haunted or something."

"Ha-ha," I said, rolling my eyes.

"She's telling the truth!" Sabrina cried, narrowing her dark eyes at me.

"The mask was evil," Carly Beth continued. "It started giving me orders. It started talking all by itself, in a horrible, harsh growl. I couldn't control it. And I couldn't get it off. It was attached to my head! I—I was so scared!"

"Oh, wow," Chuck murmured, shaking his head. "You've got a good imagination, Carly Beth."

"Good story," I agreed. "Save it for English class."

"But it's the *truth!*" Carly Beth cried.

"You just don't want me to be scary," I grumbled. "But I need a good, scary mask like that one. Come on," I begged. "Tell."

"Tell us," Chuck insisted.

"Tell us," I repeated, trying to sound tough.

"No way," Carly Beth replied, shaking her fake round, little head. "Let's go home. It's raining really hard."

"Not till you tell!" I cried. I stepped in front of her to block her path.

"Grab the head!" Chuck cried.

I grabbed the plaster head from Carly Beth's hands.

"Give it back!" she shrieked. She swiped at it, but I swung it out of her reach. Then I tossed it to Chuck.

He backed away. Sabrina chased after him. "Give that back to her!"

"We'll give it back when you tell us where you bought that mask!" I told Carly Beth.

"No way!" she cried.

Chuck tossed the head to me. Carly Beth made a wild grab for it. But I caught it and heaved it back to Chuck.

"Give it back! Come on!" Carly Beth cried, running after Chuck. "My mum made that. If it gets messed up, she'll *kill* me!"

"Then tell me where you bought the mask!" I insisted.

Chuck tossed the head to me. Sabrina jumped up and batted it down. She made a wild dive for it, but I got there first. I picked it up off the grass and heaved it back to Chuck.

"Stop it! Give it back!"

Both girls were screaming angrily. But Chuck and I kept up our game of keep-away.

Carly Beth made a frantic leap for the head and fell on her stomach on to the grass. When she stood up, the front of her jacket and her jeans were soaked, and she had grass stains on her forehead.

"Tell!" I insisted, holding the head high in the air. "Tell me, and you can have the head back!"

She growled at me.

"Okay," I warned her. "I guess I have to drop-kick it on to that roof."

I turned towards the house at the top of the lawn. Then I held the head in front of me in both hands and pretended I was going to punt it on to the roof.

"Okay, okay!" Carly Beth cried. "Don't kick it, Steve."

I kept the head in front of me. "Where did you get the mask?"

"You know that weird little party shop a couple of blocks from school?"

I nodded. I had seen the shop, but I had never gone in.

"That's where I bought it. There's a back room. It was filled with weird, ugly masks. That's where I got mine."

"All right!" I cried happily. I handed Carly Beth back her head.

"You guys are creeps," Sabrina muttered,

268

pulling her collar up against the rain. She pushed me out of the way and wiped the grass stain off Carly Beth's forehead.

"I really didn't want to tell you," Carly Beth moaned. "I wasn't making that story up about the mask. It was so terrifying."

"Yeah. Sure." I rolled my eyes again.

"Please, don't go there!" Carly Beth begged. She grabbed my arm tightly. "Please, Steve. Please, don't go to that party shop!"

I pulled my arm away. I narrowed my eyes at her. And I laughed.

Too bad I didn't take her seriously.

Too bad I didn't listen to her.

It might have saved me from a night of endless horror.

"Get off me! Get off me, Marnie! I *mean* it!" I shouted.

The little red-headed pest hung on to my back, laughing and digging her pudgy fingers into my neck. Why did she think I was some kind of funfair ride?

"Get off! This is my best jumper!" I cried. "If you wreck it—"

She laughed even harder.

It had rained all night and all morning. But the clouds had parted at lunchtime. Now the sky was blue and clear. I had no choice. I had to have soccer practice with the Hogs.

Across the playground, I saw Duck Benton fighting with Andrew Foster. Andrew picked up the football and heaved it with all his might into Duck's stomach.

Duck's mouth shot open. He let out a whoosh of breath, and a huge wad of bubble gum went flying into the air.

"Get off!" I pleaded with Marnie. I tried spinning and twirling as fast as I could, trying to throw her off my back. I knew if anything happened to this jumper, Mum would have a fit.

You might ask why I was wearing my best, blue wool jumper to soccer practice. Good question.

The answer is: it was Class Photo Day. And Mum wanted me to get a really good picture to send to all my aunts and uncles. She made me wear the jumper. And she made me shampoo my hair before school and not wear my Orlando Magic cap over it.

So I looked like an idiot all day. And now, here was soccer practice. And I had forgotten to bring a sweatshirt or something to replace my good jumper.

"Whoooooa!" Marnie gave me a final kick in the side as she hopped off my back.

I pulled down my jumper, hoping it wasn't stretched too badly. I heard angry shouts and glanced up to find Andrew and Duck swinging their fists at each other and butting heads across the field.

I reached for my whistle.

And grabbed air.

Marnie had swiped it. She held it high above her head and ran, laughing, over the grass.

"Hey, you—!" I screamed, chasing after the little thief.

I took three steps—and my trainers slid in the mud. My feet flew out from under me. With an angry cry, I fell forward. And landed on my stomach in deep, wet mud.

"Noooooo!" I let out a howl of dread. "Please. Nooooo!"

But when I pulled myself up, the mud came with me. My entire body was caked in thick, wet mud. My beautiful blue jumper? It was now an ugly *brown* jumper.

With a sad groan, I sank back on to the ground. I just wanted to disappear, to sink from sight into the big mud hole.

My faithful team, the Horrible Hogs, were laughing and yelling. They thought it was a riot. Nice kids, huh?

At least my mud dive had stopped Andrew and Duck from fighting.

The mud weighed me down as I climbed slowly to my feet. I felt like Andrew. I felt as if I weighed half a tonne. Maybe I did!

I wiped mud off my eyes with both hands— and saw Chuck standing over me. He tsk-tsked a few times. "You look really bad, man."

"Tell me something I don't know," I muttered.

"Why did you do that?" he asked.

I squinted through five centimetres of mud at him. "Excuse me?"

"You look like Mud Monster or something." Chuck sniggered.

"Ha-ha," I said glumly.

"You told me to meet you here, Steve. You said we were going straight to that party shop to buy the you-know-what."

He glanced back at my team of first graders. They weren't listening to our conversation. They were too busy flinging mud balls at each other.

I scooped my hand along the front of my sweater and scraped off about five kilograms of glop. "I . . . uh . . . I think I'd better go home after practice and get changed first," I told Chuck.

Talk about a *long* afternoon!

I had to break up the mud ball fight. Then I had to hand over all of the little angels to their parents and babysitters.

Then I had to explain to their angry parents and babysitters why they had practised mud ball fighting instead of soccer.

I crept home. Chuck waited for me outside. I hid my mud-caked clothes in the back of my wardrobe. I didn't have time to explain to my mum.

Then I changed into a clean pair of jeans and a grey-and-red Georgetown Hoyas sweatshirt one of my uncles had sent me. I don't know anything about the Hoyas. I don't even know what a Hoya is. But it is a cool sweatshirt.

I pulled my cap down over my mud-drenched hair. Then I hurried to meet Chuck.

"Steve—is that you?" Mum called from the living room.

"No, it isn't!" I called back. I closed the front door behind me and ran down the driveway before she could stop me from going out again.

I was really eager to find that party shop and check out the weird masks. So eager, I forgot to take any money with me.

Chuck and I walked two blocks before I reached into my jeans pocket and realized it was empty. We jogged back to my house, and I crept up to my room once again.

"This just isn't my day," I muttered to myself.

But I knew that buying a really disgusting, frightening mask would instantly cheer me up. Then I could go ahead with my plan to terrify the Hogs, to get my revenge.

Revenge!

What a beautiful word.

When I'm older and have my own car, that's what I want it to say on my number plate.

I pulled all of my pocket money out of the dressing-table drawer where I hide it. I counted it quickly—about twenty-five dollars. Then I jammed the bills into my jeans pocket and hurried back downstairs.

"Steve—are you going out again?" Mum called from the living room.

"Be right back!" I shouted. I slammed the

front door and ran down the driveway to meet Chuck.

Our trainers slid over fat, wet leaves as we walked. A pale full moon hung low over the trees. The streets and pavements still glistened from all the rain.

Chuck had his hands stuffed into the pockets of his hooded sweatshirt. He leaned into the wind as we walked. "I'm going to be late for dinner," he grumbled. 'I'm probably going to get into major trouble."

"It'll be worth it," I told him, feeling a little more cheerful. We crossed the street that led to the party shop. A small grocery stood on the corner. Other small shops came into view.

"I can't wait to see these masks!" I exclaimed. "If I find one just *half* as scary as Carly Beth's. . ."

There it stood! In the darkness above a small, square shop, I could make out the sign: THE PARTY PLACE.

"Let's check it out!" I cried.

I leaped over a fire hydrant.

Flew over the pavement. Up to the big front window.

And peered in the window.

"Oh, wow!" Chuck cried breathlessly, stepping up beside me.

We both pressed our faces against the window glass and stared in.

Stared into total darkness.

"Is it closed?" Chuck asked softly. "Maybe it's just closed for the night."

I uttered an unhappy sigh. "No way. It's closed for good. The shop's gone."

Peering through the dust-smeared glass, I could see empty shelves and display racks inside. A tall metal shelf lay on its side across the centre aisle. A waste-paper basket, overflowing with paper and empty cans, stood on top of the counter.

"There's no 'Out of Business' sign on the door," Chuck said. He's a good friend. He saw how disappointed I looked. He was trying to stay hopeful.

"It's empty," I sighed. "Totally cleaned out. It

isn't going to open up again tomorrow morning."

"Yeah. Guess you're right," Chuck murmured. He slapped my shoulder. "Yo—snap out of it. You'll find a scary mask at some other shop."

I pushed myself away from the window. "I wanted one like Carly Beth's," I complained. "You remember that mask. You remember those glowing eyes, right? And the way the mouth moved. The way it growled at us with those long, dripping fangs. It was so gross. And it looked totally real. Like a real monster!"

"They probably have masks like that at K-Mart," Chuck said.

"Give me a break," I muttered. I kicked at a sweet wrapper that blew across the pavement.

A car rumbled past slowly. Its headlights rolled over the front of the shop, lighting up the bare shelves, the empty counters inside.

"We'd better get home," Chuck warned, pulling me away from the shop. "I'm not allowed to wander around town after dark."

He said something else, but I didn't hear him. I was still picturing Carly Beth's mask, still unable to get over my disappointment.

"You don't understand how important this is to me," I told Chuck. "Those first graders are ruining my life. I have to pay them back this Hallowe'en. I have to."

"They're just first graders," he replied.

"No, they're not. They're monsters. Vicious, man-eating monsters."

"Maybe we can *make* a scary mask," Chuck suggested. "You know. Out of papier-mache and stuff."

I didn't even bother to answer him. Chuck is a good guy, but sometimes he has the dumbest ideas ever thought up by a human.

I could just see Marnie Rosen and Duck Benton when I popped out on Hallowe'en: *"Ooh, we're scared! We're scared! Papier-mache!"*

"I'm hungry," Chuck grumbled. "Come on, Steve. Let's get out of here."

"Yeah. Okay," I agreed. I started to follow him down the street—then stopped.

Another car had turned on to the street. Its headlights rolled over a narrow alley beside the party shop.

"Whoa, Chuck! Check it out!" I grabbed the shoulder of his sweatshirt and spun him around. "Look!" I pointed into the alley. "That door is open!"

"Huh? What door?"

I dragged Chuck into the alley. A large black trapdoor in the pavement had been left up. It caught the light from a streetlamp on the pavement.

Chuck and I peered in through the door. Steep concrete steps led down to a basement.

The basement of the party shop!

Chuck turned to me, a confused expression on his face. "So? They left the basement door open. So what?"

I grabbed the open trapdoor and leaned over the steps, squinting into the dim light from the streetlamp. "There are boxes down there. A whole load of crates."

He still didn't understand.

"Maybe all the masks and costumes and party things are packed up in those crates. Maybe the stuff hasn't been shipped away yet."

"Whoa. What are you thinking about?" Chuck demanded. "You're not going down there — are you? You're not going to sneak down to that dark basement and try to steal a mask — *are you?*"

I didn't answer him.

I was already halfway down the stairs.

My heart began to pound as I made my way down. The steps were narrow and slippery. Slick from all the rain.

"Ohh!" I let out a cry as one foot slid over the concrete step and I felt myself start to fall. I shot out both hands in search of a railing—but there wasn't one.

I landed on the hard basement floor with a loud *thud*—luckily, on both feet. Feeling shaken, I took a deep breath and held it.

Then I turned back to the trapdoor and called up to Chuck. "I'm okay. Get down here."

In the light from the streetlamp, I could see his unhappy face peering down at me. "I—I really don't want to," he called softly.

"Chuck—hurry," I insisted. "Get out of the alley. If someone drives by and sees you, they'll get suspicious."

"But it's so late, Steve," he whined. "And it isn't right to break into basements and—"

"We're not breaking in," I called up to him impatiently. "The door was open—right? Hurry up. If the two of us search the boxes, we can do it in five minutes."

He leaned down over the opening. "It's too dark," he complained. "We don't have a torch or anything."

"I can see fine," I replied. "Get down here. You're wasting time."

"But it's against the law—" he started. Then I saw his expression change. His mouth dropped open as car headlights washed over him. With a low gasp, Chuck ducked through the opening, and bolted down the stairs.

He stepped up close beside me, breathing hard. "I don't think they saw me." His eyes darted around the large basement. "It's too dark, Steve. Let's go home."

"Give your eyes a chance to adjust," I instructed him. "I can see okay."

I gazed slowly around the basement. It was bigger than I'd thought. I couldn't really see the walls. They were hidden in darkness.

The ceiling was low, only about half a metre over our heads. Even in the dim light, I could see the thick cobwebs in the rafters.

The boxes had been stacked in two rows near the steps. Somewhere way across the room, I could hear the steady *drip drip drip* of water.

"Oh!" I jumped when I heard a clattering sound.

It took me a few seconds to figure out that it was the wind blowing against the metal trap-door up in the alley.

I made my way over to the nearest box and bent over to examine it. The flaps were folded over each other. But the box wasn't sealed.

"Let's have a look," I murmured, reaching for the flaps.

Chuck had his arms crossed tightly in front of his chest. "This isn't right," he protested. "It's stealing."

"We haven't taken anything," I protested. "And even if we do find a good, scary mask and take it, we'll just borrow it. We'll return it after Hallowe'en."

"Aren't you . . . a little scared?" Chuck asked softly, his eyes moving all around the dark room.

I nodded. "Yeah, I'm a little scared," I admitted. "It's cold and creepy down here." The wind clattered the trapdoor above us again. I heard the faint *drip* of water against the concrete floor.

"Let's hurry," I urged. "Help me."

Chuck stepped beside me, but he just stared down at the box and didn't try to help.

I pulled open the first box, pushed back the cardboard flaps, and peered inside. "What *is* this stuff?" I reached in and pulled out a cone-shaped party hat. The box was stuffed with party hats.

"This is great!" I whispered happily to Chuck. I dropped the hat back in the box. "I was right. All the stuff from the store is packed up down here. We're going to find the scary masks. I know we will!"

Boxes were stacked on top of boxes. I pulled down another one and started to pull it open. "Chuck, you take the bottom one," I instructed.

He hesitantly reached for the box. "I have a bad feeling about this, Steve," he murmured.

"Just find the masks," I replied. My heart was thudding. My hands were shaking as I pulled open the second box. I was really excited.

"This one is filled with candles," Chuck reported.

My box had piles of party place mats, napkins, and paper cups. "Keep going," I urged. "The masks have got to be down here."

Above our heads, the wind shook the trapdoor. I hoped it wouldn't suddenly slam shut on us. I didn't want to be trapped down in this cold basement in the dark.

Chuck and I slid two more boxes into the pale square of light from outside. My box was taped shut. I struggled to pull off the tape.

I stopped when I heard the creaking sound above my head.

Creaking floorboards?

I froze, my hands over the box. "What was that?" I whispered.

Chuck frowned at me. "What was what?"

"Didn't you hear that noise upstairs? It sounded like a footstep."

Chuck shook his head. "I didn't hear anything."

I listened for a few more seconds. Silence now. So I went back to work on the box.

I pulled it open and peered eagerly inside.

Greeting cards. Dozens of greeting cards. I sifted through them. Birthday cards. Valentines. A whole box full of cards.

Disappointed, I shoved the box to the side and turned to Chuck. "Any luck?"

"Not yet. Let's see what's in this one."

He pulled open the box with both hands. Then he leaned over it and peered inside.

"Oh, *yuck!*" he cried.

"It's so disgusting!" Chuck groaned.

"What is? What?" I demanded. I leaped over my box to get to him.

"Check it out." A grin spread over Chuck's face as he pulled something out of the box.

I gasped as I saw an ugly purple face with broken teeth and a long, fat worm poking out of a hole in its cheek.

"You found them!" I shrieked.

Chuck let out a gleeful laugh. "A whole box of masks! And they're all totally gross!"

I grabbed the ugly mask from his hand and studied it. "Hey—it feels warm!"

It was so cold down in that basement. Why did the mask feel warm?

The worm bobbed out of the ugly face, as if it were alive.

I dropped the mask, plunged my hand into the box, and pulled out another one. A disgusting pig face with thick gobs of green stuff dripping from its snout.

"That one looks like Carly Beth!" Chuck joked.

"These are scarier than the mask Carly Beth had last year," I said.

I pulled another one from the box. A furry animal face, sort of like a gorilla, except that it had two long pointed fangs sliding down past its chin.

I dropped it and grabbed another mask. Then another. A hideous bald head with one eye hanging down by a thread and an arrow through the forehead.

I tossed it to Chuck and pulled out another one.

"This is amazing!" I cried happily. "These will terrify those kids. How will I ever choose the best one?"

Chuck let out a disgusted groan and dropped the mask he was holding into the box. "They feel like real skin. They're so warm."

I didn't pay any attention to him. I was busy digging down to the bottom of the box. I wanted to check out each mask before I made my choice.

I wanted the scariest, grossest mask in the box. I wanted a mask that would give those first graders more nightmares than they had given me!

I pulled out a mask of a girl's face with a lizard's head poking out from her mouth.

No. Not scary enough.

I pulled out a mask of a snarling wolf, its lips pulled back to show two jagged rows of pointed teeth.

Too wimpy.

I pulled out an ugly mask of a leering old man, his mouth twisted in an evil grin. One long, crooked tooth stuck down over his lower lip.

The mask had long, stringy yellow hair that dropped down over the old man's craggy forehead. I could see big black spiders climbing in the hair and in the ears. A chunk of forehead was missing, revealing a patch of grey skull beneath.

Not bad, I thought.

This one even *smelled* bad!

I started to put it back when I heard a creaking sound again.

Louder this time.

The ceiling above my head groaned.

I gasped. It really sounded like a footstep. Someone walking around up there.

But the shop had appeared dark and empty. Chuck and I had both stared into the window for a long time. If anyone was hiding there in the darkness, we would have seen them.

Another *creak* made me suck in a mouthful of air.

I froze, listening hard. I could hear the steady *drip drip* of water across the dark basement. I could hear the trapdoor rattling outside.

And I could hear my own shallow breathing.

The ceiling squeaked. I swallowed hard.

It's an old building, I told myself. All old buildings squeak and creak. Especially on a windy night.

A scraping footstep made me gasp out loud.

"Chuck—did you hear that?"

Gripping the old-man mask, I listened hard.

"Did you hear that?" I whispered. "Do you think someone else is in the building?"

Silence.

Another scraping footstep.

"Chuck?" I whispered. "Hey—Chuck?"

My heart pounding, I turned to him.

"Chuck?"

He had gone.

"Chuck?"

A stab of fear made my breath catch in my throat.

I heard the hard thud of trainers against concrete, and turned to the stairs. In the dim light, I saw Chuck disappear out through the trapdoor.

As soon as he reached the alley, he poked his head back in. "Steve — get *out!*" he called down in a loud whisper. "Hurry! Get *out* of there!"

Too late.

A ceiling light flashed on.

As I blinked against the bright light, I saw a man move quickly across the basement. He swept along the wall, pulled a long, black cord — and the trapdoor slammed shut with a deafening *clang*.

"Oh!" I uttered a weak cry as he turned angrily to me.

I was trapped.

Chuck had got out. But I was trapped. Trapped in the basement with this guy.

And what a weird-looking guy! To begin with, he wore a long black cape that swept behind him as he crossed the room to me.

Is that a Hallowe'en costume? I wondered.

Does he wear a black cape all the time?

Beneath the billowing cape, he wore a black suit, kind of old-fashioned looking.

He had shiny black hair, parted in the middle and slicked down with some kind of hair grease, and a pencil-thin, black moustache that curled over his upper lip.

As he stood over me, his black eyes glowed like two burning coals.

Like vampire eyes! I thought.

My whole body was shaking. I gripped the sides of the box and tried to return his stare.

Trapped, I thought, waiting for him to speak. Trapped with a vampire.

"What are you doing here?" he asked finally. He pushed back his cape and crossed his arms in front of him. The glowing eyes glared down at me sternly.

"Uh . . . just looking at masks," I managed to choke out. I was still on my knees on the floor. I knew that my legs were shaking too hard to stand up.

"The shop is closed," the man said through gritted teeth.

"I know," I admitted, lowering my eyes to the floor. "I — "

"The shop went out of business. We're closed for good."

"I . . . I'm sorry," I murmured.

Was he going to let me go? What was he going to do with me?

If I started to scream, no one would hear me.

Would Chuck try to get help for me? Or was he halfway home by now?

"I live upstairs," the man explained, still glaring at me angrily. "I heard scraping sounds down here. Boxes being moved around. I was going to call the police."

"I'm not a burglar," I blurted out. "Please don't call the police. The trapdoor was open and my friend and I came down."

His eyes moved quickly around the room. "Your friend?"

"He ran away when he heard you coming," I told him. "I just wanted to see if there were any masks. You know. For Hallowe'en. I wasn't going to steal anything. I just — "

"But the shop is closed," the man repeated. He glanced at the open box in front of me. "Those masks are very special. They're not for sale."

"N-not for sale?" I stammered.

"You shouldn't break into shops," the man replied, shaking his head. His slicked-down hair gleamed under the low ceiling light. "How old are you?"

I drew a blank. My mouth dropped open, but no answer came out. I was so terrified, I forgot how old I was!

"Twelve," I answered finally. I took a deep breath, trying to calm myself.

"Twelve and you're already breaking into shops," the man said softly.

"I don't break into shops!" I protested. "I mean, I never did before. I came to buy a mask. Look. I brought money."

I jammed my trembling hand into my jeans pocket and pulled out a wad of bills. "Twenty-five dollars," I said, holding up the money so he could see it. "Here. Is it enough for one of these masks?"

He rubbed his chin. "I told you, young man. These masks are special. They cannot be sold. Believe me—you do not want one of these."

"But I do!" I cried. "They're awesome! They're the best masks I've ever seen. Hallowe'en is only a few days away. I need one. I need one desperately. Please—!"

"No!" the man shouted sharply. "Not for sale."

"But why not?" I wailed.

He eyed me thoughtfully. "Too real," he replied. "The masks are too real."

"But that's why they're so awesome!" I exclaimed. "Please? *Please?* Take my money.

292

Here." I pushed the wad of bills towards him.

He didn't reply. Instead, he turned away. His cape swirled behind him. "Come with me, young man."

"Huh? Where?" Cold fear ran down my back. I was still holding the money out in front of me.

"Come upstairs with me. I'm going to call your parents."

"No!" I shrieked. "Please —!"

If my mum and dad found out I had been caught breaking into the basement of a shop, they would go totally ballistic! They'd ground me for life! I'd miss this Hallowe'en — and the next thirty Hallowe'ens to come!

The man eyed me coldly. "I don't want to call the police," he said softly. "I'd rather call your parents."

"Please. . ." I murmured again, climbing to my feet.

I suddenly had an idea.

I could make a run for it.

I glanced quickly at the concrete stairs leading up to the trapdoor. If I took off — and really flew — I could get up those stairs before the man could reach me.

The trapdoor was shut. But it probably wasn't locked. I could push it open from underneath, and just keep running.

I glanced again at the steps. It was worth a try, I decided.

I took a deep breath and held it.

Then I silently counted to three.

One ... two ... THREE!

On three, I took off. My heart thudded louder than my trainers on the hard floor. But I made it to the stairs in about a second and a half!

"Hey—stop!" I heard the caped man cry out in surprise. I could hear his heavy steps as he plunged after me.

"Stop, young man! Where are you going?"

I didn't slow down or glance back.

I took the stairs two at a time.

Yes! Yes! I'm getting away! I thought.

As I reached the top, I shot out both hands — and pushed up on the trapdoor with all of my might.

It didn't budge.

"Ohh!" I let out a terrified moan.

The caped man had reached the bottom of the steps. I could practically feel his breath on the back of my neck.

The door has *got* to open! I told myself. It's *got* to!

I took a deep breath. Then I heaved my shoulder against the door. I uttered a desperate groan as I pushed.

Pushed.

The caped man made a grab for me.

I felt his hand brush my ankle.

I kicked the hand away. Then I shoved my shoulder hard against the trapdoor.

And it opened.

"Yes!" A happy cry escaped my throat as I scrambled out into the alley.

The cold air rushed against my hot face. I stumbled over something hard—a stone or a brick. I didn't stop to look. I ran through the narrow alley, to the pavement in front of the shop.

My eyes swept back and forth. I searched for Chuck. No sign of him.

Had the caped man followed me out of the trapdoor? Was he chasing after me?

I turned back to the alley. And saw only darkness.

Then I took off, running fast, my feet practically flying over the pavement. I shot across the street. Bright lights washed over me. A car horn honked, making me jump about a mile! The car roared past.

"Hey, Steve —!"

Chuck stepped out from behind a tall evergreen shrub. "You made it!"

"Yeah. I made it," I replied, gasping for breath.

"I —I didn't know what to do!" he stammered.

I shook my head. "So you just stood here?"

"I waited for you," he said. "I was kind of scared."

Big help.

"Get going," I urged, glancing back across the street. "He may be chasing us."

We ran side by side, our breath steaming up into the cold night air. The houses and dark lawns whirred past in a grey-black blur. We didn't say another word to each other.

Three blocks later, I slowed down as we

reached Chuck's house. I leaned over and tried to shake away the sharp pain in my side. I always get a pain like that when I run more than a few blocks.

"See you!" Chuck cried breathlessly. "Sorry you didn't get your mask."

"Yeah. It's too bad," I murmured glumly.

I watched him run along the side of his house until he disappeared around the back. Then I took a deep breath and took off again, jogging now, towards my house on the next block.

My heart was still racing in my chest. But I was starting to feel calmer. The man in the black cape hadn't chased after us. In a few seconds, I would be safe in my own home.

Halfway up our driveway, I slowed to a stop. The pain in my side had faded to a dull ache.

I stepped into the yellow light from the front porch. I could hear my dog Sparky barking inside the house. Sparky knew I was home.

As I climbed on to the front doorstep, a smile crossed my face.

A very wide smile.

I was pleased with myself. In fact, I was overjoyed. I felt like leaping in the air. Or maybe doing a wild, crazy dance. Or crowing like a rooster. Or tilting back my head and howling at the moon.

The evening had been a total success.

I didn't tell Chuck. I didn't want Chuck to know.

But when the caped man clicked on the basement light—in that split second before he saw me and I saw him—I grabbed a mask from the box. And I shoved it under my sweatshirt.

I had a mask!

It hadn't been easy. In fact, being trapped in that eerie basement with that strange man had been the scariest time of my life.

But I had a mask! Safely tucked under my sweatshirt.

I could feel it against my chest as I ran. And I could feel it now, warm against my skin as I reached for the front door.

I was so happy. So pleased with myself.

And then I felt the mask start to move.

And I screamed as something sharp bit into my chest.

I grabbed the front of my sweatshirt. I pressed both hands tight against the bulge of the mask.

"Whoa," I murmured, holding the mask in place under the sweatshirt.

Stop imagining things, Steve, I scolded myself.

Calm down. The mask started to slip down your chest. That's all. It wasn't moving. It didn't bite you.

Get in the house, I ordered myself. Hide the thing in a drawer in your room. And pull yourself together.

Why was I so nervous?

The scary part was over. I had escaped with one of the great masks. Now it was my turn to scare *other* people. Why was I standing there scaring myself?

Still holding the front of my sweatshirt, I pushed open the front door and stepped into the house. "Down, boy! Get down, Sparky!" I cried as the little black terrier greeted me. He leaped high off the floor, bouncing off me, barking and whining as if he hadn't seen me in twenty years.

"Get down, Sparky! Down!"

I wanted to sneak into the house, run up to my room, and stash the mask away before my parents heard me return. But Sparky ruined that plan.

"Steve—is that you?" Mum stormed into the living room, a fretful frown on her face. She glared at me and angrily blew a curl of blonde hair from in front of her eyes. "Where on earth were you? Your father and I went ahead and ate dinner. Yours is ice-cold by now!"

"Sorry, Mum," I said, still holding the front of my sweatshirt to keep the mask in place as I tried to push Sparky away.

The lock of hair fell back over her forehead. She blew at it again. "Well? Where *were* you?"

"I . . . well. . ."

Think fast, Steve.

You can't tell her you sneaked out to steal a Hallowe'en mask from the basement of a shop.

"I had to help Chuck with something," I finally answered.

Sure, it was a lie. But it wasn't a serious lie.

I'm usually a very honest guy. But right then, all I cared about was having the mask! I had it, and I was desperate to get it out from under my sweatshirt and hidden in a safe place in my room.

"Well, you should have told me where you were going," Mum scolded. "Your father has gone out to do the grocery shopping. But he's very angry, too. You should have been home for dinner."

I lowered my head. "Sorry, Mum."

Sparky gazed up at me. Was he staring at the bulge in my sweatshirt?

If the dog could see it, Mum could see it too.

"I'll take off my coat and come right down," I told her.

I didn't give her a chance to reply. I spun around, leaped on to the stairs, and ran up two at a time. I flew down the hall, burst into my room, and slammed the door behind me.

I took a few seconds to catch my breath. I listened hard, making sure that Mum hadn't followed me upstairs.

No. I could hear her banging around in the kitchen, getting my dinner ready.

I couldn't *wait* to check out the mask!

Which one had I taken? When the light came on in the shop basement, I'd grabbed a mask without looking. I'd stuffed it under my sweatshirt before I could see it.

Now I eagerly reached under the sweatshirt and pulled out my hard-won prize.

"Wow!" I raised it in both hands and admired it.

The old-man mask. I had taken the mask of the creepy old man.

I smoothed out its long strings of yellow-white hair. Holding it by the big, pointy ears, I lifted it in front of my face and examined it closely.

A single white tooth hung down over the bottom lip. A brown wormhole poked through the centre of the tooth.

Outside on the front doorstep, the big tooth had scraped my chest, I realized. That's what made me think the mask was biting me.

The mouth was twisted in an evil sneer. The lips curled like two brown worms.

The long nose had gobs of green dripping from each nostril. A square patch of skin was missing just above the forehead. I could see grey skull bone in the hole.

The whole face was creased and lined. The flesh was sickly green. The skin appeared to be peeling off the face. Dark scabs bulged from the sunken cheeks.

Black spiders appeared to crawl through the stringy, yellow hair. Spiders poked out of the two ears.

"Yuck!" I cried.

Was I holding the scariest Hallowe'en mask in the world?

No. In the universe!

I began to feel a little queasy just holding it. I rubbed the scabby cheek with one finger. The skin felt warm, like real skin.

"Heh-heh-heh." I practised laughing like an old man. "Heh-heh-heh." I tried a dry cackle.

Look out, Hogs! I told myself. When I come leaping out at you on Hallowe'en night in this mask, you will jump out of your skins!

"Heh-heh-heh."

I raked the ugly, long hair back over the head. My fingers bumped over the spiders tangled in the hair. The spiders didn't feel rubbery. They felt soft and warm like the skin.

I gazed down happily at the disgusting, old face. It sneered back at me. The brown worm lips quivered.

Should I try it on?

I carried it over to the mirror on my wardrobe door. I was dying to see what I'd look like.

I'll slip it on for just a second, I decided. Long enough to see how ugly and frightening I look.

Holding it in both hands, I raised the mask over my head.

Then slowly, carefully . . . very carefully . . . I began to pull the mask down, down, down over my face.

"Steve—!"

Mum's loud cry from downstairs startled me.

"Steve—where are you? Get down here for your dinner!"

"Coming!" I shouted back. I lowered the mask. I'd try it on later, I decided.

I walked quickly to the dressing-table and pulled open my sock drawer. Smoothing the long, spidery hair over the ugly face, I set the mask down carefully in the drawer. Then I hid it under several pairs of socks and closed the drawer.

I hurried down to the kitchen. Mum had a salad on the table and a plate of warmed-up macaroni-and-cheese.

My stomach growled. I suddenly realized that I was starving! I sat down, pushed the salad aside, and started forking up the macaroni as fast as I could.

I glanced down to see Sparky staring up at

me with his big, black, soulful eyes. He saw me looking at him and tilted his head.

"Sparky," I said, "you don't like macaroni — remember?"

He tilted his head the other way, as if trying to understand. I slipped him a spoonful. He sniffed it and left it on the floor.

Behind me, Mum busily cleaned out the refrigerator, making room for the groceries Dad was out buying. I was *dying* to tell her about the scary mask. I wanted to show it to her. Maybe put it on and make her scream.

But I knew she'd ask too many questions about where I'd bought it, and how much it cost, and how much of my pocket money I'd used up to pay for it.

All questions I couldn't answer.

So I bit my tongue and forced myself not to blurt out the exciting news that I wouldn't have to be a tramp again this Hallowe'en.

That was my costume for the past five years. A tramp. Actually, it wasn't much of a costume. I wore one of Dad's baggy old suits with patches on the trousers. Mum rubbed charcoal on my face to make me look dirty. And I carried a knapsack on a fishing rod over my shoulder.

Bor-ing!

This Hallowe'en will be different, I promised myself. This Hallowe'en will not be boring.

I was so happy. As I sat gobbling down

macaroni-and-cheese, I couldn't get that creepy mask out of my mind.

I'm not going to tell *anyone* about it, I decided. I'm going to scare everyone I know.

I'm not even going to tell Chuck. After all, he ran away and left me down in that dark basement.

Look out, Chuckie Boy! I told myself, grinning so hard some macaroni slipped out of my mouth. I'm going to get you too!

I had soccer practice for my first graders after school the next day. It was a sunny, cold October afternoon. The sunlight made the yellow and brown falling leaves glitter like gold. Puffs of white cloud floated like soft cotton across the blue sky.

Everything looked beautiful to me. Because Hallowe'en was only one day away.

I was staring up at the clouds when Marnie Rosen drop-kicked the soccer ball into my stomach.

I grabbed my stomach and doubled over in pain. Duck Benton and two other kids jumped on my back and drove me face down into the mud.

I didn't care.

In fact, I laughed.

Because I knew that I had only one day to wait.

I tried to show them how to pass. As I ran

along the touchline, Andrew Foster stuck out his foot. I tripped and went sailing into the bike rack. A handlebar caught me under the chin as I fell, and I actually saw stars.

But I didn't care.

I picked myself up with a grin on my face.

Because I had a secret. I had an evil secret that the kids didn't know. I knew that trick-or-treat night was going to be a *special* treat for me!

At four o'clock, I called an end to practice. I was too weak to blow the whistle. My clothes were soaked with mud, I walked with a limp, and I had cuts and bruises in twenty different places.

A typical practice with the Horrible Hogs.

But did I care?

You know the answer.

I gathered them in a circle around me. They were shoving each other, and pulling hair and calling each other horrible names. I told you — they're total animals.

I raised my hands to quieten them down. "Let's have a special Hogs' Hallowe'en party tomorrow," I suggested.

"YEAAH!" they cheered.

"We'll meet in our costumes after practice," I continued. "The whole team. And we'll all go trick-or-treating together. I'll take you."

"YEAH!" they cheered again.

"So tell your parents to drop you off," I told

them. "This is going to be our special party. We'll meet in front of the old Carpenter mansion."

Silence. This time they didn't cheer.

"Why do we have to meet there?" Andrew asked.

"Isn't that old house supposed to be haunted?" Marnie asked softly.

"That place is too creepy," Duck added.

I narrowed my eyes at them, challenging them. "You guys aren't *scared*—are you?" I demanded.

Silence. They exchanged nervous glances.

"Well? Are you all too wimpy to meet me there?" I asked.

"No way!" Marnie insisted.

"No way! We're not scared of a stupid old house!"

They all began to tell me how brave they were. They all said they would meet me there.

"I saw a ghost once," Johnny Myers bragged. "Behind my garage. I shouted 'Boo!' and it floated away."

These kids are animals, but they have great imaginations.

The other kids all started teasing Johnny. He stuck to his story. He insisted he'd seen a ghost. So they pushed him to the ground and got his jacket all muddy.

"Hey, Steve—what are you going to be for Hallowe'en?" Marnie asked.

309

"Yeah. What's your costume?" Andrew demanded.

"He's going to be a pile of toxic waste!" someone joked.

"No. He's going to be a ballerina!" someone else declared.

They all hooted and jeered.

Go ahead and laugh, guys, I thought. Have a good laugh now. Because when you see me on Hallowe'en, I'll be the only one laughing.

"Uh . . . I'm going to be a tramp," I told them. "You'll recognize me. I'll be wearing a tattered old suit. And my face will be all dirty. I'll be dressed like a down-and-out!"

"You *are* a down-and-out!" one of my loyal team members shouted.

More wild laughing and hooting. More shoving and hair-pulling and wrestling on the ground.

Luckily, their parents and babysitters showed up to take them home. I watched them go with a big smile on my face. A big, evil smile.

Then I grabbed my rucksack and hurried home. I ran all the way. I was eager to take another look at my mask.

Chuck stepped out as I jogged past his house. "Hey, Steve . . . what's up?" he called.

"Not much!" I called back. "Later, man!"

I kept running. I didn't want to hang out with Chuck. I needed to check that mask. I needed to remind myself of how awesome it was. How totally terrifying.

I burst through the front door. Then I ran straight up the stairs to my room, taking the stairs three at a time.

I raced down the long hall. I turned into my room and tossed my bag on to the bed. Then I hurried across the room to my dressing-table and eagerly jerked open my sock drawer.

"Huh?"

I peered inside. With a trembling hand, I shoved several balled-up pairs of socks out of the way.

The mask had gone.

"No!"

I began pawing frantically through the drawer, tossing all the socks on to the floor.

No mask. Gone.

The balled-up socks bounced all over the room. My heart was bouncing too.

Then I remembered that I had moved the mask. Before school that morning. I was worried that my mum might do the laundry. And open my sock drawer. And see it there.

So I had shoved it to the back of my wardrobe, behind my rolled-up sleeping bag.

Letting out a long whoosh of air, I dropped to my hands and knees. I quickly collected all the socks and stuffed them back into the drawer. Then I opened the wardrobe door and pulled down the mask from the top shelf.

Steve, you've got to calm down, man, I told myself. It's just a Hallowe'en mask, after all. You've got to stop scaring yourself like that.

Sometimes it helps to scold yourself, to give yourself advice.

I started to feel a little calmer. I smoothed back the stringy yellow hair and rubbed my hand over the craggy, scab-covered skin of the mask.

The brown lips sneered at me. I poked my little finger through the disgusting wormhole in the teeth. I squeezed the spiders hiding inside the ears.

"This is *so cool*!" I declared out loud.

I couldn't wait a whole day till Hallowe'en. I had to show it to someone.

No. I had to *scare* someone with it.

Chuck's face popped instantly into my mind. My old friend Chuck was the perfect victim. I knew that he was home. I had seen him there a few minutes ago.

Wow. Will he be shocked! I told myself. Chuck thought that I'd run out of that shop's basement empty-handed. When I sneak into his house and creep up on him wearing this disgusting mask, he'll *faint*!

I glanced at the clock. I had an hour before dinnertime. Mum and Dad weren't even home yet.

Yes, I'll do it! I decided.

"Heh-heh-heh." I practised my old-man cackle. "Heh-heh-heh." The scariest, most evil cackle I could do.

Then I grasped the wrinkled neck of the mask in both hands. Stepping in front of the mirror, I raised the mask over my head.

And tugged it down.

It slid easily over my hair. It felt soft and warm as I pulled it over my face.

Down over my ears. Over my cheeks.

Down, down.

Until I felt the top of the mask settle on to my hair. I twisted it until I could see out of the narrow eyeholes.

Then I lowered my hands to my sides and stepped closer to the mirror to check myself out.

So warm.

I suddenly felt too warm.

The rubbery mask pressed tightly against my cheeks and forehead.

Warmer.

"Hey—!" I cried out as my face began to burn.

So hot. . .

So hard to breathe.

"Hey . . . what is *happening* to me?"

I could feel the skin of the mask tightening around my face.

My cheeks burned. A sour odour swept over me, choked me.

I gagged. I sucked in a deep breath through my mouth. But the mask was so tight, I could hardly breathe.

I grabbed the ears with both hands. The outside of the mask felt normal. But inside, I was burning up!

I tried to tug the mask off. But it wouldn't slide up. The hot rubber stuck to my face.

I groaned as the putrid odour washed over me again.

I tugged harder. The mask didn't budge.

I gasped for breath.

I grabbed the stringy hair — and pulled. I slid my hands under the chin — and pushed.

"Ohhh." A sick groan escaped my throat. My hands dropped limply to my sides.

I suddenly felt so tired. So weak.

So totally weak.

Every breath was a struggle. I bent over. My body began to tremble.

I felt so weak. And old.

Old.

Was this how an old man felt?

Calm down, Steve. I scolded myself. It's just a rubber mask. It fits a little too snugly, that's all.

It's stuck to your face. But you'll pull it off, and you'll be fine.

Calm down. Count to ten. Then examine the mask in the mirror. Grab it from the bottom, and you'll be able to pull it up. No problem.

I counted to ten. Then I stepped up close to the mirror.

I nearly cried out when I saw my reflection. The mask really was awesome! So real. So gross.

With my eyes staring out of it, the face seemed to come alive. The brown lips sneered back at me. When I moved *my* lips, they appeared to move too. The green gobs of goo trembled inside the big nostrils. The spiders appeared to be crawling through the tangled, yellow hair.

It's only a mask. A really cool mask, I said to myself.

I started to feel a little calmer.

But then a cackle escaped my throat. "Heh-heh-heh."

Not my cackle!

Not in my voice! An old man's cackle.

How did that happen? How did I utter such a strange sound?

I clamped my lips shut. I didn't want to make that sound again.

"Heh-heh-heh."

Another frightening cackle! In a shrill, high-pitched voice. More like a dry croak than a laugh.

I tightened my jaw. Clenched my teeth. Held my breath so I wouldn't cackle again.

"Heh-heh-heh."

I wasn't doing it!

Who was cackling like that?

Where was the shrill, dry laugh coming from?

I gaped at the old face in the mirror, suddenly frozen in fear.

And then I felt a strong hand grab my leg.

With a choked gasp, I whirled around.

And peered down through the tight eyeholes of the mask.

I instantly saw that it wasn't a hand on my leg. It was teeth.

Dog teeth.

"Sparky—it's you!" I cried. But my voice came out in a dry whisper.

Sparky backed away.

I cleared my throat and tried again. "Don't be afraid, Sparky. It's only me." My voice! It sounded more like a dry cough.

It sounded like my grandpa!

I had an old man's face—and an old man's voice.

And I felt so tired. So totally weak and tired.

As I reached to pet Sparky, my arms drooped as if they weighed half a tonne. Both of my knees cracked as I bent down.

The dog gazed up at me and tilted his head. His short stub of a tail wagged furiously.

"Don't be scared, Sparky," I croaked. "I was just trying out this mask. Pretty scary, huh?"

I lowered my face and tried to pick Sparky up.

But as I leaned forward, I could see the dog's eyes go wide with terror. Sparky let out a shrill *yip*—jumped out of my hands, and went tearing across the room, barking at the top of his lungs. Barking in total fright.

"Sparky—it's me!" I cried. "I know I sound different. But it's me—Steve!"

I wanted to chase after him. But my legs felt so weak, and my knees refused to bend.

It took me three tries to pull myself up to a standing position. My head ached. I was too out of breath to run after Sparky.

Too late, anyway. I could hear him barking his head off, already downstairs.

"Weird," I muttered, rubbing my aching back. I hobbled back to the mirror. Sparky has seen masks before. He knew it was me. Why was he so scared? Was it my weird voice?

How had the mask dried up my voice? And why did I suddenly feel one hundred and ten?

At least my face no longer felt on fire. But the skin of the mask still pressed so tightly against my face, I could barely move my lips.

I have to get out of this thing, I decided. Chuck

will have to wait until Hallowe'en night to be scared out of his skull.

I raised both hands to my neck and searched for the bottom of the mask. My neck felt scraggy and wrinkled. The skin was dry.

Where was the bottom of the mask?

I leaned close to the mirror on my wardrobe door and narrowed my eyes at my reflection. I stared hard at the neck of the mask.

Wrinkled skin flecked with ugly brown patches.

But where was the bottom? Where did the mask end and my neck begin?

My hands began to tremble as they fumbled up and down my throat. I could feel my heart begin to race.

I moved my hands slowly, carefully, up and down my neck.

Again. And again.

Finally, I let my hands drop to my side and uttered a weary, frightened sigh.

There *was* no mask bottom. No line at all between the mask and my neck.

The wrinkled, spotted mask skin had become *my* skin.

"Nooooo! Nooooo!" I wailed in my old man's voice. I had to get the thing off me! There had to be a way!

I squeezed the cheeks of the mask and tugged with all my might.

"Ow!" Sharp pain ran down my face.

I pulled the hair. That sent a wave of pain shooting down my scalp. Frantically, I grabbed at the mask, slapped at it, pulled it, tore at it.

I felt each move. Each slap and tug made my skin hurt. Every touch hurt me as if it were my own skin.

"The eyeholes!" I croaked.

I reached for the eyeholes. Maybe I could slip my fingers inside the eyeholes and lift the mask off.

My hands fumbled around my eyes. My trembling fingers searched, poking and rubbing.

No eyeholes. There were no eyeholes.

The rutted, scab-covered skin had melted on to me. It had become *my* skin.

The ugly, disgusting mask had become *my* face!

I looked like a horrifying, spider-infested, decaying old man. And I felt as old and weird as I looked!

My throat tightened in terror. I sank against the mirror, pressing my ugly, craggy forehead against the glass.

I shut my eyes. What can I do? What can I do? The question repeated like an unhappy chant in my mind.

And then I heard the front door slam. And I heard Mum's voice at the bottom of the stairway. "Steve—are you home? Steve?"

What can I do? What can I do? The question repeated and repeated.

"Steve?" Mum called. "Come down here. I want to show you something."

No! I thought, swallowing hard, my dry throat making a sick clicking sound. *No! I can't come down! I can't! I don't want you to see me like this!*

"Oh, never mind!" Mum called. "I'm coming up there!"

I heard her footsteps on the stairs.

A shock of panic made me lurch towards the door. I nearly fell over. My old legs were stiff, too stiff to move quickly.

I hobbled to the door and closed it just as Mum reached the first floor. Then I leaned against the door, my hand on my throbbing chest, trying to catch my breath.

Trying to think. Trying to decide what to say.

I couldn't let her see me like this. I couldn't let her see the mask. She'd start asking questions. And I couldn't let her see how the mask had changed me.

A few seconds later, she knocked gently on the door. "Steve, are you in there? What are you doing?"

"Uh . . . nothing, Mum."

"Well, may I come in? I've brought you something."

"Not right now," I croaked.

323

Please don't open the door! I begged silently. *Please don't come into my room!*

"Steve, why do you sound so strange?" Mum demanded. "What's wrong with your voice?"

"Uh. . ." *Think fast, Steve. Think fast.*

"Uh . . . sore throat, Mum. A really bad sore throat."

"Let me take a look at you. Are you sick?" Glancing down, I saw the doorknob turn.

"No!" I screamed, pressing my back against the door.

"You're not sick?"

"I mean, yes," I croaked in my shaky, old-man voice. "I'm not feeling well, Mum. I'm going to lie down for a while. I'll come down later, okay?"

I stared at the doorknob, listening to her breathing on the other side of the door. "Steve, I've bought you those black-and-white biscuits that you love. Your favourites. Do you want one? Maybe it'll make you feel better."

My stomach growled. Those biscuits are my favourites. Dripping with chocolate icing on one side and vanilla icing on the other. "Maybe later," I moaned.

"But I drove two miles out of my way to buy them for you," Mum said.

"Later. I'm really not feeling well." I was telling the truth. My temples throbbed. My whole body ached. I felt so weak, I could barely stand up.

"I'll call you for dinner," Mum said. I listened to her make her way back down the stairs. Then I hobbled over to the bed and slumped my old man's body on to the edge.

"Now what?" I asked myself. I pressed my hands against my scabby cheeks. "How do I get out of this thing?"

I shut my tired, burning eyes and tried to think. After a few minutes, Carly Beth's face floated into my mind.

"Yes!" I croaked. "Carly Beth is the one person in the world who can help me."

Carly Beth wore a mask from the same shop last Hallowe'en. Maybe the same thing had happened to her. Maybe her mask had stuck to her face and changed her.

She had got her mask off. She will know how I can get my mask off too.

The phone stood across the room beside the computer on my desk. Normally, I'd be over there in three seconds. But it took me three minutes of grunting and straining to get my old body to stand up. Then it took another five minutes to drag myself across the room.

By the time I dropped into my desk chair, I was exhausted. It took all my strength to raise my hand and punch in Carly Beth's number on the phone.

I can't go on like this, I told myself. She's got

to help me. She's *got* to know how to get this mask off.

After the third ring, Carly Beth's father answered. "Hello?"

"Hi . . . uh . . . could I speak to Carly Beth?" I choked out.

A silence. Then: "Who is this?" Mr Caldwell sounded confused.

"It's me," I answered. "Is Carly Beth there?"

"Is this one of her teachers?" he demanded.

"No. It's Steve. I—"

"I'm sorry, sir. I can't hear you very well. Can you speak up? Why did you wish to speak to my daughter? Perhaps I can help you?"

"No . . . I—"

I heard Mr Caldwell speak softly to someone else at his house. "It's an old man, asking for Carly Beth. I can barely hear him. He won't say who he is."

He came back on the phone. "Are you one of her teachers, sir? Where do you know my daughter from?"

"She's my friend," I croaked.

I heard him turn again to someone else in the room, probably Carly Beth's mum. He muffled the phone with his hand, but I heard what he said: "I think it's a nut. Some kind of crank call."

He returned to me. "Sorry, sir. My daughter can't come to the phone." He hung up.

I sat there listening to the buzz in my spider-filled ear.

Now what? I asked myself.

Now what?

I must have fallen asleep in the desk chair. I don't know how long I slept.

I was awakened by Dad pounding on my bedroom door. "Steve—dinnertime!" he called in.

I sat up with a start. My back ached from sleeping sitting up. I rubbed my wrinkled neck, trying to rub away the stiffness.

"Steve—are you coming down to dinner?" Dad asked.

"I—I'm not very hungry," I croaked. "I'm going to take a nap, Dad. I think I'm getting sick."

"Hey, don't get sick the night before Hallowe'en," he replied. "You don't want to miss out on trick-or-treating."

"I—I'll be okay," I stammered in my hoarse voice. "If I get a good night's sleep, I'll be fine."

Yeah. Right.

I'll be one hundred and fifty. But I'll be fine.

I let out an unhappy sigh.

"We'll bring you up some soup or something later," Dad called in. Then he disappeared downstairs.

I stared at the phone. Should I try Carly Beth again?

No. I decided. She won't believe it's me. She'll hang up the way her father did.

I scratched my ears. I could feel the spiders crackling around in them. I touched the bare spot on top of my head where the skin was ripped apart. The skin was soft and wet. I could feel the patch of hard skull that showed through.

"Ohhhh." Another long sigh.

I've got to think, I told myself. I've got to think of a way out of this.

But I felt so weary, so sleepy.

I pulled myself up and slumped to the bed. A few seconds later, I fell sound asleep.

I awoke to bright sunlight streaming through my bedroom window.

I blinked several times, startled by the bright morning light. Morning. Hallowe'en morning.

It should have been a happy day. An exciting day. But instead. . .

I reached up with both hands and touched the sides of my face.

Smooth!

My cheeks felt smooth. Soft and smooth.

I rubbed my ears. Small ears. *My* ears. No spiders!

I raised both hands to my hair. And touched *my* hair. Not the stringy, old man's hair.

Hesitantly, carefully, I touched the torn spot on top of my head where the skull showed through.

Not there!

"I'm me again!" I cried out loud. I let out a long *whoop* of joy.

No old man's mask. No old man's voice. No old man's body.

It had all been a dream. A horrible nightmare.

Still blinking in the light, I gazed happily around my room.

"I dreamed it all!" I cried.

Going down to that dark shop basement. Pawing through the box of masks. The man in the cape. The mask of the old man. Sneaking it home and trying it on.

The mask sticking to my skin. Refusing to come off.

All a dream!

All a horrifying nightmare that was over now.

I was so happy! This had to be the happiest moment of my life.

I started to jump out of bed. I wanted to leap around my room, to dance for joy.

But then my eyes blinked open. And I woke up for real. . .

. . .I woke up for real.

And knew that I had only *dreamed* that it was all a dream!

I grabbed my face—and felt the craggy wrinkles, the heavy scabs. I rubbed my nose and brushed the green gobs stuck in my nostrils.

I had dreamed that the mask didn't exist.

I had dreamed that I had my own face back. My own voice and body.

All a dream. A wonderful dream.

But now I was really awake—and really in trouble.

I pulled myself up and brushed the stringy, yellow hair out of my eyes. "I have to tell Mum and Dad," I decided. "I can't spend another day like this."

I had slept in my clothes. I staggered to my feet and dragged my old body to the door. I tugged open the door—and saw a note taped on the other side.

Dear Steve,
Hope you're feeling better. Mum and
I had to visit your Aunt Helen this
morning. We left early to beat the
traffic. We'll be home in time to help
you with your tramp costume. Love,
Dad.

My tramp costume?

Not this year. Besides, since I was now at least one hundred and fifty, I was a little old to go trick-or-treating!

Screwing up the note in my hand, I made the long trip down to the kitchen, holding on to the banister, taking one step at a time. I had a sudden craving for a steaming bowl of porridge and a cup of hot milk.

"Oh, no!" I croaked. I was starting to *think* like an old man!

I made myself a breakfast of orange juice and cornflakes. I carried it to the table and sat down to eat. The juice glass felt strange against my fat, brown lips. And it was almost impossible to chew the cornflakes with just one long, crooked tooth.

"What am I going to do?" I moaned out loud.

Then, suddenly, I had an answer.

I decided to go ahead with my plan to terrify the first graders. Why shouldn't I pay back those bratty kids for all the trouble they gave me day after day on the soccer field?

Yes! I decided. When Mum and Dad get home, I'll greet them and show off my old-man costume. They won't know it isn't a costume. They'll think it's really cool.

Then, later, I'll go to the spooky old Carpenter mansion to meet the kids. And I'll scare the first graders out of their masks!

And then what?

Then I'll find Carly Beth. It won't be hard to find her. She's having a Hallowe'en party at her house after trick-or-treating.

I'll find Carly Beth and get her to tell me the secret. I'll get her to show me how to remove this horrible mask.

Then I will be a very happy guy.

Sitting there alone in the kitchen, struggling to choke down my cornflakes, it seemed like a really good plan.

Too bad it didn't work out the way I hoped.

When Mum and Dad returned home that evening, I hobbled downstairs to greet them. They both gasped when they saw my ugly, scabby face.

Mum dropped the bag she was carrying. Her mouth fell open to her knees.

Dad's eyes bulged. He stared at me for a long time. Then he burst out laughing. "Steve—that is the *best* costume!" he exclaimed. "Where did you get that?"

"It's disgusting," Mum said. "Oh. I can't stand that open patch on top of the head. And that horrible hole in your tooth."

Dad walked in a circle around me, admiring my new look.

I had put on the patched, black suit that I wore as my tramp costume. And I had found one of my grandpa's old canes in the wardrobe, which I leaned on now.

"It's great!" Dad declared, squeezing my shoulder.

"I bought the mask at a party shop," I croaked. It was *almost* the truth.

Mum and Dad exchanged glances. "The old man's voice is very good," Mum said. "Have you been practising?"

"Yes. All day," I replied.

"Do you feel better?" Dad asked. "We didn't want to disturb you this morning since you weren't feeling good. Your mum and I had to leave so early..."

"I'm feeling much better," I lied. Actually, my legs were trembling and my whole body was drenched in a cold sweat.

Feeling weak, I leaned harder on the cane.

"Yuck! What's that in your hair?" Mum cried.

"Spiders," I told her. I shuddered. I could feel them crawling over my head and in my ears.

"They're so real-looking," Mum declared, raising a hand to her cheek. She shook her head. "Are you sure you don't want to be a tramp? That mask must be so hot and uncomfortable."

If she only knew how uncomfortable it was!

"Leave him be," Dad scolded her. "He looks great. He's going to terrify everyone on the street tonight."

I hope so, I thought. I glanced at my watch. Time to get going.

"Well, he's terrifying *me*!" Mum exclaimed. She shut her eyes. "I can't stand to look at you,

Steve. Why did you buy something so ... so ugly?"

"I think it's funny," Dad told her. He poked a finger at my long tooth. "Great mask. Is it rubber?"

"Yeah. I guess," I muttered in my quivering, old voice.

Mum made a disgusted face. "Are you trick-or-treating with Chuck?"

I yawned. I suddenly felt sleepy. "I promised my soccer players I'd meet them," I croaked. "Then I'm going over to Carly Beth's house."

"Well, don't stay out too late," Mum said. "And if that heavy mask gets too hot, take it off for a while — okay?"

I wish! I thought bitterly.

"See you later," I said. Leaning on the cane, I began dragging myself to the front door.

Mum and Dad laughed at my funny walk.

I wasn't laughing. I wanted to cry.

Only one thing kept me from breaking down and telling them the truth. Only one thing kept me from telling Mum and Dad that I was trapped inside this horrible mask, that it had turned me into a weak, ancient creature.

Revenge.

I could see the terrified expressions on the faces of my soccer team. And I could hear their howls of horror as they went running for their lives.

That cheered me up and kept me going.

I grabbed the doorknob and struggled to pull open the front door.

"Steve—wait!" Dad cried. "My camera. Wait. I want to take a picture." He disappeared in search of the camera.

"Your trick-or-treat bag!" Mum cried. "You forgot your trick-or-treat bag." She rummaged around in the front cupboard until she found the shopping bag with little pumpkins all over both sides.

I knew I couldn't manage the cane and the shopping bag. But I took it from her anyway. I'll throw the bag away when I get outside, I decided. I didn't plan to trick-or-treat. I knew it would take me half an hour just to walk up someone's driveway!

Dad burst back into the living room. "Say cheese!" he cried, raising his little camera.

I tried to twist my wormy lips into a smile.

Dad flashed the camera once. Then three more times.

Blinded by flashbulb lights, I said goodbye and made my way out the door. The white circles followed me into the night. I nearly fell off the front doorstep.

I grabbed the railing and waited for my heart to stop pounding. Slowly the flashes of light faded from my eyes, and I began to pull myself down the driveway.

It was a clear, cold night. No wind at all. The nearly bare trees stood as still as statues.

I limped on to the pavement and started in the direction of the Carpenter mansion. There was no moon. But the street appeared brighter than usual. Most houses had all of their front lights on to welcome trick-or-treaters.

I stuffed the shopping bag into a rubbish bin at the foot of our neighbours' driveway. Then I continued down the block, my cane tap-tapping on the pavement.

My back began to ache. My old legs trembled. I leaned over the cane, breathing hard.

After half a block, I had to take a rest against a lamppost. Luckily, the Carpenter mansion was on the next block.

As I started on my way, two little girls came hurrying down the pavement, followed by their father. One girl wore colourful butterfly wings. The other wore lots of make-up, a gold crown and a long fancy dress.

"Ooh, he's ugly," the butterfly whispered to her friend as they came near.

"Yuck!" I heard the princess reply. "Look at the green stuff in his nose."

I leaned close to them, opened my lips in a snarl, and rasped, *"Get out of my way!"*

The little girls both let out frightened squeals and took off down the pavement. Their father flashed me an angry stare and hurried after them.

"Heh-heh-heh." An evil cackle escaped my lips.

Seeing their frightened faces gave me new energy. Leaning on my cane, I tap-tapped my way across the street.

A few minutes later, the Carpenter mansion came into view. The huge old house stood dark and empty. Its stone turrets rose up to the purple night sky like castle towers.

Huddled under a streetlamp at the bottom of the weed-choked front garden stood my soccer team. *My Hogs. My first graders.*

My victims.

They were all in costumes. I saw Power Rangers and Ninja Turtles. Mummies and monsters. Two ghosts, a Beauty and a Beast.

But I recognized them anyway. I recognized them because they were shoving each other, grabbing at trick-or-treat bags, shouting and fighting.

I leaned against my cane, watching them from halfway down the block. My heart started to pound. My whole body trembled.

This was it. My big moment.

"Okay, guys." I murmured softly to myself. "It's *show time!*"

I was trembling with excitement as I dragged myself up to them. I stepped into the light, my wormy lips twisted in a frightening sneer.

I stared from one to another, giving them a chance to see my terrifying face. Giving them a chance to see the spiders crawling through my hair. The wormhole in my tooth. The patch of skull poking up through my rutted scalp.

They grew quiet. I could feel their eyes on me. I could sense their instant fear.

I opened my mouth to let out a frightening growl that would send them running for their mummies.

But Marnie Rosen, wearing a white bride's dress and veil, stepped up to me before I could get it out. "Can we help you, sir?" she asked.

"Are you lost?" one of the Power Rangers asked.

"Do you need directions?"

"Can we help you get somewhere?"

No. No!

This wasn't going right. This wasn't going the way I'd planned—the way I'd dreamed!

Marnie took my arm. "Which way were you headed, sir? We'll walk with you. It's kind of a scary night to be walking around a strange neighbourhood."

The others pushed in closer, trying to be helpful.

Trying to be helpful to an old man. An old man they weren't the least bit scared of.

"Nooooo!" I howled in protest. "I'm the ghost of the Carpenter mansion! I've come to pay you back for trespassing on my front garden!"

I tried to shriek—but my voice came out in a weak whisper. I don't think they heard a word I uttered.

I've got to scare them, I told myself. I've *got* to!

I raised both hands together in the air as if I planned to strangle them all.

My cane flew out of my grasp. I lost my balance and tottered over backwards.

"Ohhhh!" I let out a groan as I hit the pavement sitting up.

They all cried out. But not in fear. They cried out because they were worried about me.

Helping hands reached down to pull me to my feet.

"Are you okay? Here's your cane." I recognized Duck Benton's scratchy voice.

341

I heard murmurs of sympathy. "Poor old guy," someone whispered.

"Are you hurt?"

"Can we get you some help?"

No. No. No. No. No.

They weren't terrified. The weren't the tiniest bit afraid.

I sank on to the cane. I suddenly felt so weary. So totally exhausted I could barely keep my head up.

Forget about scaring them, Steve, I told myself. You've got to get to Carly Beth's house before you collapse. You've got to find out from Carly Beth how to get the mask off. How to get your old face — and strength — back.

Marnie was still holding on to my trembling arm. "Where are you trying to go?" she asked, her freckled face filled with concern.

"Uh . . . do you know where Carly Beth Caldwell's house is?" I asked in a weak croak.

"It's on the next block. Across the street. I know her brother," I heard Andrew Foster say.

"We'll take you there," Marnie offered.

She gripped my arm tighter. A mummy stepped up and took my other arm. They began to walk me slowly, gently down the pavement.

I don't believe this! I thought bitterly. They're supposed to be scared out of their costumes! They should be shrieking and crying by now.

But instead, they're *helping* me walk.

I sighed. The sad thing was, I felt so tired and weak, I couldn't have made it to Carly Beth's without their help.

They led me halfway up her driveway. Then I thanked them and told them I could make it the rest of the way.

I watched them scurry away to go trick-or-treating. "I guess Steve isn't going to show up," Duck said.

"He was probably too big a wimp to go out on Hallowe'en night!" Marnie joked.

They all laughed.

Leaning heavily on the cane, I turned towards Carly Beth's house. The lights were all on. But I couldn't see anyone in the windows.

She probably isn't back from trick-or-treating yet, I decided.

I heard chattering voices. Footsteps on the gravel drive.

I wheeled around to see Carly Beth and her friend Sabrina Mason hurrying across the lawn, heading towards the house.

I recognized Carly Beth's duck costume. She wore it every year. Except for last Hallowe'en, when she wore that terrifying mask.

Sabrina was some kind of superhero. She wore silvery tights and a long silvery cape. She had a silvery mask pulled over her face, but I recognized her long, black hair.

"Carly Beth —!" I tried to shout. But her name came out in a choked whisper.

She and Sabrina kept chattering excitedly as they hurried across the lawn.

"Carly Beth —! Please!" I cried.

Halfway to the house, they both turned. They saw me.

Yes!

"Carly Beth —" I cried.

She pulled off her duck mask and took a few steps towards the driveway. She squinted hard at me. "Who are you?"

"It's *me*!" I cried weakly. "I —"

"Are you the man who tried to call me earlier?" she demanded coldly.

"Well . . . yes," I croaked. "You see, I need —"

"Well, leave me alone!" Carly Beth screamed. "Why are you following me? Leave me alone, or I'll get my father!"

"But — but — but —" I sputtered helplessly.

The two girls spun away and began jogging to the house.

Leaving me standing there in the driveway.

Leaving me all alone.

Leaving me *doomed*.

I let out a bitter wail. "Carly Beth—it's me! It's me! Steve!" I cried. "Steve Boswell!"

Did she hear me?

Yes.

She and Sabrina had stepped on to the stone path that led to the front porch. In the square of yellow light from the porch, I saw them both turn around.

"It's Steve! It's Steve!" I repeated, my throat aching from my desperate cries.

Slowly, cautiously, both girls made their way back to me.

"Steve?" Carly Beth stared hard at me, her mouth falling open.

"Is that a mask?" Sabrina demanded, keeping close to Carly Beth.

"Yes, it's a mask," I croaked.

"Yuck. It's disgusting!" Sabrina declared. She pulled off her silver mask to see better. "Are those spiders? Yuck!"

"I need help," I confessed. "This mask—"

"You went to the party shop!" Carly Beth cried. The duck mask fell to the ground. She raised both hands to the sides of her face. "Oh, no! No! Steve, I warned you!"

"Yes. That's where I got it," I said, pointing to my hideous face. "I didn't listen to you. I didn't know."

"Steve, I told you not to go there," Carly Beth said, her expression still tight with horror. Hands still pressed against her cheeks.

"Now the mask won't come off," I wailed. "It's stuck to me. It's part of me. And it's—it's turning me into an old, old man. A feeble old man."

Carly Beth shook her head sadly. She stared at my ugly face, but didn't say a word.

"You've got to help me," I pleaded. "You've got to help me get this mask off."

Carly Beth let out a frightened sigh. "Steve— I don't think I can."

I grabbed her duck feathers and held on. "You've got to help me, Carly Beth," I begged. "Why won't you help me?"

"I *want* to help you," she explained. "But I'm not sure I can."

'But you had a mask from the same shop last Hallowe'en," I protested. "You pulled the mask off. You escaped from it—right?"

"It can't be pulled off," Carly Beth said. "There's no way to pull it off."

Over her shoulder. I saw three kids in costumes at the next house. A woman appeared in the doorway. I saw her dropping sweets into the three trick-or-treat bags.

Some kids are having fun tonight, I thought bitterly.

I am *not* having fun tonight.

I may never have fun again.

"Come into the house," Carly Beth suggested. "It's cold out here. I'll try to explain."

I tried to follow them up the driveway. But my legs wobbled like rubber. Carly Beth and Sabrina practically had to carry me into her house. They dropped me down on the green leather couch in the living room.

On a table across the room, a carved jack-o'-lantern grinned at me. The pumpkin had more teeth than I did!

Carly Beth dropped down on the couch arm. Sabrina sat on the edge of the armchair beside it. She leaned over and sifted through her trick-or-treat bag. How could she think of sweets at a time like this?

I turned to Carly Beth. "How do I get the mask off?" I croaked.

Carly Beth chewed her bottom lip. She raised her eyes to me, her expression grim. "It isn't a mask," she said softly.

"Excuse me?" I cried.

"It isn't a mask," she explained. "It's a real face. A living face. Did you meet the man in the black cape?"

I nodded.

"He's some kind of weird scientist, I think. He made the faces. In his lab."

"He — he *made* them?" I stammered.

Carly Beth nodded solemnly. "They are real, living faces. The man in the cape tried to make them good-looking. But something went wrong. They all came out ugly. As ugly as the one you're wearing."

"But, Carly Beth—" I started.

She raised a hand to hush me. "The caped man calls the faces The Unloved. No one wants them because they turned out so ugly. They are The Unloved. They're alive. And they attach themselves to anyone who comes near enough."

"But how do I get it off?" I cried impatiently. I raised my hands and tugged at my rutted, scabby cheeks. "I can't spend the rest of my life like this. What can I do?"

Carly Beth jumped up and began pacing back and forth in front of Sabrina and me. Sabrina unwrapped a Milky Way and began chewing it, watching Carly Beth pace.

"The same thing happened to me last Hallowe'en," Carly Beth said. "I had chosen a really ugly mask. It was so scary. It attached itself to my head. And then it turned me evil."

"And what did you do?" I cried, leaning forward on my cane.

"I went back to the party shop. I found the man in the cape. He told me there was only one way to get rid of the mask. It could only be done with a symbol of love."

"Huh?" I gaped at her. I didn't understand.

"I had to find a symbol of love," Carly Beth continued. "At first, I didn't know what the man meant. I didn't know what to do. But then I remembered something my mum had made for me."

"What?" I demanded eagerly. "What was it?"

"It was that head," Sabrina chimed in, her mouth bulging with chocolate.

"My mum had sculpted a head of me," Carly Beth said. "It looked just like me. You've seen it. Mum sculpted it because she loves me. It was a symbol of love."

Carly Beth dropped back down beside me. "I placed Mum's sculpted head over The Unloved face. And The Unloved disappeared. The ugly face slipped right off."

"Great!" I cried happily. "Go get it. Hurry!"

"Huh?" Carly Beth stared at me, confused.

"Go get the sculpted head," I begged. "I've got to get this thing off me!"

Carly Beth shook her head. "You don't get it, Steve. You can't use *my* symbol of love. It will only work for me. You have to find *your own* symbol of love."

"But maybe it won't work for Steve's mask," Sabrina interrupted. "Maybe each mask is different."

"Give me a break, Sabrina," I muttered angrily. "It's got to work! Don't you understand? It's *got* to!"

"You have to find your own symbol of love," Carly Beth repeated. "Can you think of one, Steve?"

I stared back at her, thinking hard.

I thought. And thought.

Symbol of love . . . symbol of love. . .

No. I couldn't think of anything. Not a single thing.

And then an idea popped into my mind.

I leaned on the cane and tried to pull myself up from the couch. But my feeble arms gave way, and I fell back into the cushion.

"You've got to help me get home," I told Carly Beth. "I've thought of a symbol of love. It's at my house."

"Okay. Let's go!" she replied.

"But what about the kids coming over here?" Sabrina asked, swallowing a chunk of Milky Way. "What about the party?"

"You stay here and greet them," Carly Beth told her. "If Steve really can find a symbol of love at his house — and if it works — we'll be right back."

"It'll work," I said. "I know it will."

But I had my fingers crossed. Which made it even harder to climb up from the couch.

Carly Beth saw me struggling. She took both my hands and pulled me to my feet. "Yuck! What are those things moving around in your ears?" she cried, making a disgusted face.

"Spiders," I said quietly.

She swallowed hard. "I sure hope you find something that works."

"Me too," I murmured as she guided me to the door.

Carly Beth turned back into the living room. "Don't eat all the chocolate while we're gone," she called to Sabrina.

"It's only my second piece!" Sabrina protested with her mouth full.

We stepped into the darkness. Some kids in costumes were coming up the driveway, all carrying bulging trick-or-treat bags. "Hey, Carly Beth—where are you going?" a girl called.

"I'm doing a good deed!" Carly Beth replied. "See you guys later!" She turned back to me. "I can't believe you didn't listen to me, Steve. You look really disgusting."

"I can't even wipe the green globs out of my nose!" I wailed.

Holding me by the shoulder, she guided me towards my house. We crossed the street on to my block. I heard kids laughing and loud music inside the house on the corner. A Hallowe'en party.

As we passed the house, I stumbled over a moving shadow. Carly Beth caught me before I fell. "What was that?" I cried.

Then I saw it scamper silently across the street. A black cat.

I laughed. What else could I do? I had to laugh.

Go ahead, cat, I thought bitterly. Go ahead and cross my path. I couldn't have any *worse* luck — could I?

My house came into view past a row of tall evergreen shrubs. Through the shrubs, I could see that nearly all the downstairs lights were on.

"Are your parents home?" Carly Beth asked, helping me across the grass.

I nodded. "Yeah. They're home."

"Do they know about the . . . uh. . ."

"No," I replied. "They think it's a costume."

As we stepped on to the front doorstep, I could hear Sparky start to bark inside the house. I pushed open the door, and the little dog let out an excited *yip* and leaped up at me.

His paws landed on my waist and pushed me back hard. I toppled against the wall.

"Down, Sparky! Please! Get down!" I pleaded in my old man's croak.

I knew Sparky was glad to see me. But I was too feeble for his usual greeting.

"Down, boy! Please!"

Carly Beth finally managed to pull the dog off me so that I could stand up. Then she held on to Sparky until I regained my balance.

"Steve — is that you?" I heard Mum call from the living room. "You're back so early!"

Mum stepped into the living room. She had changed into the grey flannel dressing gown she usually relaxes in at night, and she had her blonde hair in curlers.

"Oh, hi, Carly Beth!" she cried in surprise. "I wasn't expecting visitors. I — "

"That's okay, Mum," I croaked. "We're only staying a minute. We came back to get something."

"Don't you love Steve's costume?" Mum asked Carly Beth. "Isn't that the most horrible mask you ever saw?"

"You mean he's wearing a mask?" Carly Beth joked. She and Mum enjoyed a good laugh.

Sparky sniffed my shoes.

"What did you come back here for?" Mum asked me.

"Those black-and-white biscuits," I replied eagerly. "You know. The ones you bought me yesterday."

Those biscuits were a symbol of love.

Mum had told me how she had driven two miles out of her way to buy them for me. She knew they were my favourite biscuits in the whole world. And she had driven out of her way to buy them because she loves me.

So the biscuits were the perfect symbol of love.

I couldn't wait to bite into one. One bite, I

knew—and I'd be able to pull off this horrible mask.

Mum's face twisted in surprise. She narrowed her eyes studying me. "You came back here for those biscuits? Why? What about all your trick-or-treat sweets?"

"Uh . . . well. . ." I stammered. My brain stalled. I couldn't think of a good reason.

"He had a strong craving," Carly Beth chimed in. "He told me he's been thinking about those biscuits all night."

"That's right. I had a craving," I repeated. "Sweets can't compare, Mum. Those biscuits are the best."

"I love them, too," Carly Beth added. "So I came back with Steve. We want to bring them to my Hallowe'en party."

Mum tsk-tsked. "What a shame," she said.

"Huh?" I cried, feeling my heart skip a beat. "What do you mean? What's wrong?"

Mum shook her head. "The biscuits are gone," she replied softly. "The dog found the box this morning and broke into it. I'm sorry, guys. But Sparky ate them all."

Mum's words sent a cold shiver down my back. I let out a weak moan. And stared down at Sparky.

The dog gazed up at me and began wagging his stubby tail. As if he were pleased with himself!

"You've ruined my life, Sparky!" That's what I felt like screaming. "You greedy pig! Couldn't you save me just one biscuit? Now I'm doomed. Doomed to live with this gross, frightening face for ever."

And all because Sparky loved black-and-white biscuits as much as I did.

Still wagging his tail, Sparky ran over to me and brushed his furry, black body against my leg. He wanted to be petted.

Forget it, I thought. No way I'm petting you — you traitor.

I heard Dad calling Mum from the other room. "Have fun, guys," Mum said. She waved to Carly

Beth and me and hurried off to see what Dad wanted.

Have *fun*, guys?

I'm *never* going to have fun again, I realized.

Feeling weak and defeated, I turned to Carly Beth. "Now what do we do?" I whispered.

"Quick—pick up Sparky," she whispered back, motioning to the dog with both hands.

"Huh? Do what? I'm never touching this dog again!" I croaked miserably.

Panting hard, his tongue hanging to the floor, Sparky brushed my ankle again.

"Pick him up!" Carly Beth insisted.

"Why?"

"Sparky is your symbol of love!" Carly Beth declared. "Look at him, Steve. Look how much that dog loves you."

"He loves me so much, he ate all my biscuits!" I wailed.

Carly Beth frowned at me. "Forget about the biscuits. Pick up the dog. Sparky is your symbol of love. Pick him up and hold him against you. And I'll bet the mask will come right off."

"I guess it's worth a try," I said softly. I started to pick up the little black terrier. My back creaked as I bent down. My aching knees cracked.

Please work! I pleaded silent. *Please let this work!*

I reached for Sparky—and he darted through

my hands and ran across the carpet towards the den.

"Sparky—come back! Sparky!" I cried, still bent over, still reaching out both hands.

The dog stopped halfway across the living room and turned back.

"Come back, Sparky!" I called in my old man's quivering voice. "Come back, boy! Come back to Steve!"

His stubby tail started wagging again. He stared at me, head tilted, and didn't move.

"He's playing games with me," I told Carly Beth. "He wants me to chase him."

I got down on my knees and motioned to Sparky with both hands. "Come, boy! Come! I'm too old to chase you! Come, Sparky!"

To my surprise, the dog let out a *yip*, ran back across the room, and jumped into my arms.

"Hug him tight, Steve," Carly Beth urged. "Hug him tight. It's going to work. I know it will!"

The little dog felt so heavy in my weak, aching arms. But I held him against my chest. Held him tight.

Held him as tight as I could.

Held him for a long, long time.

And nothing happened.

After about a minute, the dog got tired of being squeezed. He jumped out of my arms, bounced over the carpet, and disappeared into the living room.

I tugged at the mask with both hands.

But I knew I was wasting my strength. It didn't feel any different. Nothing had changed. The hideous face was still tightly attached to my head.

Carly Beth put a hand gently on my shoulder. "Sorry," she murmured. "I guess each mask is different."

"You mean I need something *else* to get it off," I said, shaking my old, spider-infested head sadly.

Carly Beth nodded. "Yes. Something else. But we don't know what it is."

I uttered a helpless cry. "I'm doomed!" I wailed. "I can't even climb up off my knees!"

Carly Beth slid both of her hands under my

shoulders and lifted me to my feet. I steadied myself, leaning on the cane.

And then I had an idea.

"The man in the cape," I croaked. "He'll know what I can do."

"You're right!" Carly Beth's face brightened. "Yes, you're right, Steve. He helped me last Hallowe'en. If we go back to the party shop, I know he'll help you!"

She started to pull me to the front door. But I held back. "There's just one little problem," I told her.

She turned back to me. "Problem?"

"Yeah," I replied. "I forget to tell you. The party shop is closed. It went out of business."

We walked there anyway. Well, I didn't exactly walk. I limped and hobbled, feeling weaker and more feeble every second. Carly Beth practically had to carry me.

The streets stood empty, glimmering dimly under the rows of streetlamps. Lights were going out in all the houses. It was pretty late. All of the trick-or-treaters had gone home.

Two dogs followed us down the street. Big German shepherds. Maybe they thought we'd share our Hallowe'en sweets with them. Of course, I didn't *have* any Hallowe'en sweets.

"Go away," I snarled at them. "I don't like dogs any more. Dogs are useless!"

To my surprise, they seemed to understand. They turned and went loping across a dark front lawn, disappearing around the side of the house.

A few minutes later, we passed the row of small shops and stepped up in front of the party shop. Dark. Empty.

"Out of business," I murmured.

Carly Beth pounded on the front door. I peered into the blue shadows beyond the dusty front window. Nothing moved. No one in there.

"Open up! We need help!" Carly Beth shouted. She banged on the wooden door with both fists.

Silence inside. No one stirred.

A cold wind swept down the street. I shivered. I tried to bury my ugly head in my shoulders. "Let's go," I mumbled. Defeated.

Doomed.

Carly Beth refused to give up. She pounded the door with both fists.

I turned away from the window — and gazed at the alley beside the shop. "Whoa. Wait," I called to her. "Come over here."

I dragged myself to the alley. Carly Beth followed. She rubbed her knuckles. I guess they were sore from pounding so hard on the door.

I could see from the pavement that the trapdoor was shut. But I led Carly Beth into the alley. We stopped beside the trapdoor.

"It leads into the basement of the party shop,"

I explained. "All the masks and other stuff are down there."

"If we can get down there," Carly Beth whispered, "maybe we can find a way to help you."

"Maybe," I whispered back.

Carly Beth bent down and grabbed the wire handle to the trapdoor. She tugged it up hard.

The door didn't budge.

"I think it's locked," she groaned.

"Try again," I urged. "It sticks. It's very hard to open."

She bent down, grasped the handle in both hands, and pulled again.

This time the door swung up, revealing the concrete stairs that led down to the basement.

"Come on. Hurry, Steve." Carly Beth tugged my arm.

My last chance, I thought. My last chance.

Trembling, I followed her down into the heavy darkness.

We huddled close together as we made our way across the basement floor. Pale light from a streetlamp floated in through the open trapdoor.

Across the room, I heard the steady *drip drip drip* I'd heard before. The large boxes stood just where Chuck and I had left them. Three or four of them were still open.

"Well. Here we are," Carly Beth murmured. Her words sounded hollow, echoing softly against the stone basement walls. Her eyes darted around the room, then stopped on me. "Now what?"

I shrugged. "Search through the boxes, maybe?"

I stepped over to the nearest one and peered inside. "This one has all the masks," I told her. I picked up a monster mask covered in bristly fur.

"Yuck," Carly Beth groaned. "Put it down. We don't need another mask."

I dropped the mask back into the carton. It made a soft *plop* as it landed on the other masks. "I don't know *what* we need," I said. "But maybe we can find something. . ."

"Look at these!" Carly Beth cried. She had pulled open another box. She held up some kind of jumpsuit. It had a long, pointy tail on the back.

"What's that?" I demanded, stepping around two boxes to get to her.

"A costume," she replied. She leaned into the box and pulled out another one. A pair of furry tights covered with leopard spots. "The box is filled with costumes."

"Big deal," I grumbled. "That's not going to help me."

I sighed. "*Nothing* is going to help me."

Carly Beth didn't seem to hear me. She leaned over the edge of the box and pulled out another costume. She held it up in front of her. A shiny black suit. Very fancy. Like a dinner jacket.

As I stared at it, my face began to tingle.

"Put it down," I said glumly. "We need to find — "

"Oh, *yuck!*" Carly Beth cried. "This suit — it's crawling with spiders!"

"Huh?" I gasped. My face tingled harder. I heard a loud buzzing in my ears. The tingle became an itch.

"Hey, I'll bet this is the costume that goes with

your mask!" Carly Beth declared. She carried it over to me. "See? Spiders and more spiders!"

I scratched my itching cheeks. The itch was quickly becoming painful. I scratched harder.

"Get it away from me! It's making me itch!" I cried.

Carly Beth ignored my plea. She held the shiny black suit up in front of me, beneath my itching, burning face.

"See? You have the head — and this is the body that goes with it," she said, holding it against me. Admiring it.

"Put it away!" I shrieked. "My face — it's burning! Ow!"

I slapped frantically at my cheeks. My forehead. My chin.

"Owwwwwww!" I howled. "I feel so weird! What is *happening* to me?"

"It's burning hot!" I shrieked. *"Owwwwww!* What is *happening?"*

I grabbed the sides of my face, trying to soothe away the burning pain.

As I gripped my cheeks, the face began to slide under my hands.

I felt it begin to rise. Up, up.

I pulled my hands away—as the old man's head slid over my own. Lifted off. Floated up.

Cool air greeted my cheeks. I took a deep breath of the cold, fresh air.

The craggy old head hovered above me for a moment. Then it floated towards the shiny black suit in Carly Beth's hand.

The head floated down on to the collar of the suit.

Carly Beth let out a startled cry as the suit's arms thrashed out. The trouser legs kicked. The suit twitched and squirmed as if trying to break free.

Carly Beth let go of it and jumped back.

A smile spread over the ugly old face. The suit legs lowered themselves to the floor. The old man performed a little dance, arms flapping, trouser legs hopping.

And then he turned away from us. The head attached to the suit. The trouser legs bent at the knees, he shuffled towards the steps.

Carly Beth and I both cried out in shock as the old man climbed up to the steps and disappeared out of the trapdoor.

We stood there, eyes bulging, mouths wide open. We stared at the opening at the top of the stairs. Stared in silence. Stared in amazement.

And then we both began to laugh.

We fell on each other, laughing, laughing till tears rolled down our cheeks.

I laughed louder and harder than I have ever laughed. Because I was laughing in *my* voice. Laughing with *my* face. My *real* face.

The old-man face had found its body — and escaped.

And now I was *me* again!

This had to be the best Hallowe'en ever! I had never been so happy in all my life just to have things *normal*.

Carly Beth and I danced down the street as we made our way home. We sang at the top of our lungs. Sang and twirled each other around.

And danced and strutted down the middle of the street.

We were both so happy!

We were half a block from my house —when the creature leaped out from behind a hedge.

It opened its jaws in a broken-toothed roar.

Carly Beth and I grabbed each other and uttered shrill cries of terror.

The creature had bright purple skin that glowed in the light from the streetlamp. Fiery red eyes. A mouth full of broken, rotting teeth. And a fat, brown worm poking out from the middle of its cheek.

"Huh?" I stared at the worm as it bobbed from the creature's skin. Stared at the frightening purple face.

And recognized it.

"Chuck!" I cried.

He let out a hoarse laugh from behind the mask. "I gotcha!" he bellowed. "I got both of you! You should have seen the looks on your faces!"

"Chuck —"

"I've been waiting here. Waiting to surprise you," he rasped. The disgusting worm bobbed up and down in his cheek as he talked.

"You didn't see me grab this mask when I ran out of that shop basement," he growled. "I kept it a secret. I wanted to give you a good scare."

"You scared *me* to death!" Carly Beth admitted, giving him a playful shove. "Now take off the mask and let's go to my house."

"Uh . . . I have a problem," Chuck replied, lowering his voice.

"Problem?"

Chuck nodded. "I'm having a little trouble getting this mask off. Think you guys could help me?"

Goosebumps

R.L. Stine

Reader beware, you're in for a scare!

These terrifying tales will send shivers up your spine:

GOOSEBUMPS

Reader beware – here's THREE TIMES the scare!

Look out for these bumper GOOSEBUMPS editions. With three spine-tingling stories by R.L. Stine in each book, get ready for three times the thrill ... three times the scare ... three times the GOOSEBUMPS!

Reader beware – you choose the scare!

Give Yourself Goosebumps

A scary new series from R.L. Stine – where
you decide what happens!

Choose from over 20 scary endings!

HIPPO GHOST

**Secrets from the past... Danger in the present...
Hippo Ghost brings you the spookiest of tales...**

Castle of Ghosts
Carol Barton
Abbie's *bound* to see some ghosts at the castle where
her aunt works – isn't she?

The Face on the Wall
Carol Barton
Jeremy knows he must solve the mystery of the face on
the wall – however much it frightens him...

Summer Visitors
Carol Barton
Emma thinks she's in for a really boring summer, until she
meets the Carstairs family on the beach. But there's
something very *strange* about her new friends...

Ghostly Music
Richard Brown
Beth loves her piano lessons. So why have they started to
make her *ill*...?

A Patchwork of Ghosts
Angela Bull
Who is the evil-looking ghost tormenting Lizzie, and why
does he want to hurt her...?

The Ghosts who Waited
Dennis Hamley
Everything's changed since Rosy and her family moved
house. Why has everyone suddenly turned against her...?

The Railway Phantoms
Dennis Hamley
Rachel has visions. She dreams of two children in strange,
disintegrating clothes. And it seems as if they are trying
to contact her...

The Haunting of Gull Cottage
Tessa Krailing
Unless Kezzie and James can find what really happened in
Gull Cottage that terrible night many years ago, the
haunting may never stop...

The Hidden Tomb
Jenny Oldfield
Can Kate unlock the mystery of the curse on Middleton
Hall, before it destroys the Mason family...?

The House at the End of Ferry Road
Martin Oliver
The house at the end of Ferry Road has just been built.
So it can't be haunted, can it...?

Beware! This House is Haunted
This House is Haunted Too!
Lance Salway
Jessica doesn't believe in ghosts. So who *is* writing the
strange, spooky messages?

The Children Next Door
Jean Ure
Laura longs to make friends with the children next door.
But they're not quite what they seem...

The Girl in the Blue Tunic
Jean Ure
Who is the strange girl Hannah meets at school – and
why does she seem so alone?